CLUB NOVUS

RANDALL FLOYD COOPER

ISBN: 978-1-7369715-2-9
Cover Design: Monica Dubray

Thank you to my family & friends who've supported me in so many ways. Thank you for reading, listening, and watching all of the works I've been a part of. Special thank you to Kenzie, Natalie, Angie, Nate, Dylan, David, Tim, Milo, Kat, Dustin, and Palace. They've gone above and beyond in supporting my dream, and I don't know if I'd be doing what I'm doing if it wasn't for their encouragement and belief in me.

PROLOGUE

"Eddie, do you have any plans for today?" My mother asked as she cooked a pan of scrambled eggs with toast. The bread was smeared with her famous strawberry jelly, a local delicacy sold at the general store a few miles away. The aroma of sizzling bacon filled the room, making my mouth water in anticipation.

"Well, I'm not sure," I replied, waiting at the kitchen table. "I was going to call Michael at 12:30. He just got back from vacation last night, so I'm sure we'll do something."

"That's right, he was at Disney World," my mother said. "Did he go anywhere else?"

I shook my head. "Nah, just Disney World." Even my best fake smile couldn't deceive my mother; she could always see right through me.

"We'll go on a fun trip someday, I promise," my mother said with a nod.

As I sat at the table and gobbled down my brunch, my mother stared at me, frowning. She hadn't touched her food.

"Eddie, there's something I want to get off my chest." She paused and picked at her fingernails. "I'm sorry we can't take you on any fun trips right now. But I'll do everything I can to make it happen in the future." Her shoulders sagged with the weight of wanting to provide more.

"It's okay, Mom," I reassured her. "I understand. We're poor, and Michael's family is rich."

Whomp!

My mom pounded the table with the bottom of her fist. "You do not talk like that! Do you understand me? You haven't said anything like that to anyone else, have you?"

"No?" I said, earnestly wondering what I said wrong.

"Don't talk to your friends about our finances or their finances. We take good care of you." She paused, and her knee started bouncing underneath the table. "You know, your father and I love you very much."

"Of course. I love you, too, and I love Dad, too. Sorry, I didn't mean anything by it. I swear, I don't talk to my friends about money or anything."

"Good." My mother took a deep breath. "You know, some people in life are born with certain privileges. Sometimes things don't work out the same for everyone, but that's okay. Everything will be all right. Ten years ago, when you were first born, we thought we'd have more for you, but life sometimes throws you complications that you can't prepare for. I didn't know I would become so sick. But it happened."

I felt my throat closing up. It became harder to chew, but I increased my biting speed and swallowed a chunk of my breakfast with a gulp of milk. My eyes burned with tears.

My mom reached her hand across the table, and she placed it on the top of my wrist. "It's okay, Eddie. No need to cry about it."

I wiped away the tears from my eyes. *Perhaps when I'm older, I won't weep as easily. I never see my dad cry,* I thought.

"Is dad working late again tonight?" I asked.

"Yes, which is why he's still sleeping." My mom focused on her plate like it was the end of the conversation.

Even though I burned to know why, I knew not to ask about my father's work. If I did, I'd become horrified. My dad was a detective for our town, and I knew he was working on something that would give me nightmares. This is why my parents kept the newspaper away from any room in the house except for their bedroom.

I remembered the conversation with my dad two weeks earlier.

"Eddie, I'm working on something that will cause me to be late some nights. Don't worry, everything is okay. You're okay too. Tell me immediately if you hear any rumors from your friends about anything, and I'll straighten it all out for you. In the meantime, don't watch the news." My father winked.

At 12:30, I called Michael from the house phone in the living room.

"Hello, who is it?" Michael's mom answered.

"Hi, Mrs. Carter, it's Eddie. Can I talk to Michael?"

"Oh, hello, Eddie! Sure, I'll grab him for you in just a moment."

Michael's mom hummed away as she set down the phone and went to retrieve Michael. I could hear someone enter the kitchen as footsteps got closer to the telephone.

"Hello?"

"Yo, Michael! What's up, dude-er?"

Michael put on a funny, deep voice that he called his mobster impression. "Eddie, my boy, the man of the hour. What's happening, hotshot?"

4

I snickered. "Nothing really. Same old same old. You want to hang out today?"

"You read my mind! Let's make it happen, cap'n. I have to show you something, too! It's really cool, and it'll blow your mind. Want to meet me at Wimpy's?"

"Uh, I'm not sure if I can. I don't think I can really buy any ice cream."

"Don't worry about it; I got you covered. Birthday money, baby. We can live like kings today!"

I chuckled with delight; excitement rose in my chest. "Okay! Sounds good. I'll meet you there at, uh, 1:00?"

"That works for me. I got big plans for us today.

"Whatcha thinking?"

"I can't ruin the surprise! All I can say is that I have a fun day planned, though. Bring your bike too! Do you copy? Over! *Kshhh*."

"Roger Dodger, over, *kshhh*," I said, following it up with a laugh.

"All right, sounds good. I'll see you later, alligator."

"In a while, crocodile," I said.

We both cracked up and hung up the phone at the same time.

"Ma! I'm going to go hang out with Michael. I'm not sure how long I'll be gone for, but we'll be riding bikes."

My mom walked into the living room and gave me the family cell phone. "Call me if you're going to do anything for dinner or if you'll be back home for dinner. No matter what, I want you to give me a call at 5:00 and let me know what you're doing."

"Okay, sounds good!"

I sprinted into the garage, kicked off the stand on my bike, and entered the small suburban paradise of Lockweed, Michigan.

Wimpy's ice cream parlor was at the end of the small strip of downtown Lockweed. It took me a half-hour to get there since the downtown area was 4 miles away from my house.

As soon as I arrived, I saw Michael hanging out by his bike with a small silver box hanging around his neck. He was wearing a t-shirt with an old rendition of Mickey Mouse at the center with a giant smile. Michael had thick-framed black Ray-Bans and a round face with curly hair.

I braked to a complete stop, and that's when Michael pulled up the box to his eye, and a flash came from the center of it.

"What the hell, man!" I yelled, covering my eyes.

"Relax, I just took a picture, that's all. Dude, this is what I wanted to show you. My dad bought me this really cool camera; it's called an SLR. It can take amazing pictures. And it even has a lens that can do this." Michael rotated the lens up and down, growing and retracting. "I really wanted a DSLR, because you know, it's digital, but my dad said he wanted me to practice with this first since it's film, which is kinda lame, but still really cool."

I marveled at it for a moment. The top was labeled "Canon." It was the biggest photo camera I had ever seen.

"Wow, that's so cool."

"I only have 23 pictures left; I thought we could maybe take a bunch of cool photos today."

I shrugged. "Sure, I guess. Anywhere in particular you want to go?"

"Yeah! I thought that maybe we could go..." Michael's lips curled up into a mischievous grin. "Let's go to Melville."

"Melville?" My eyes widened. "The ghost town?"

"Yeah! ...Why the long face?"

"I don't know if I really want to go there. It's kind of creepy."

"Exactly! Which would make it the perfect spot to take really cool photos. C'mon, dude, I'm buying you ice cream. You have to come!"

I rolled my eyes. "Okay, I guess so. I just hate lying to my mom."

"Who said you had to lie to her? Just tell her we went bike riding around and went through Melville. She doesn't need to know that we were taking pictures there."

"I just know she would be upset, even if we were just riding through there."

"It's really not that big of a deal. I've gone before with my older brother."

"Really? You and Jake went?"

"Yeah, just walked around. Let's get some ice cream, though. That will put you at ease."

We went up to the back of the line, where only three people waited in front of us. It was a hot summer day where the humidity made me sweat after being outside for a few minutes. Fortunately, I put on a lot of sunscreen before heading out the door, and I remembered to bring my Detroit Tigers old English "D" ball cap. I ordered a vanilla chocolate frozen custard twist. Michael got the creamsicle twist. We had to finish the ice cream fast before it melted, which was no problem for either of us.

"Now, let's get over to Melville, shall we?" Michael asked with his devilish grin, orange ice cream on the edge of his lip. He wiped it off with the back of his hand.

"All right, all right, let's see what it's all about," I said.

We got on our bikes. Traveling to the end of the downtown strip, Michael led the way. We kept riding. Even when the sidewalk came to an end, we spilled onto the main road and kept traveling south.

"This is it, right here. We go down this path." Michael pointed to the right.

I would have never noticed the opening. It blended in with the rest of the trees on the side of the road. But there was an arched tunnel to our right through some branches.

"How did you know this was here?" I asked.

"Look at the ground, bro." He pointed. Remnants of an old train track blended into the cement below us. "Melville was a little train spot back in the day. My brother knows more about the history than I do, but basically, it got shut down and became totally useless, which is why Melville doesn't really exist anymore."

Michael rode his bike through the tunnel of branches, and I followed behind. "Ow!" A few twigs scratched my body as I made it through the other side. We kept riding our bikes through the rough terrain. Sweat poured down my sides, but we kept trucking along. The trees provided much-needed shade and coolness, but that didn't last long. We made it through the tunnel of trees and came across an abandoned train depot with three small buildings next to it. The structures had no windows, the bricks were chipped, and the walls inside were crumbling.

We pulled up our bikes to a two-story brick building. There was a sun-faded sign with chipped paint hanging on one rusted screw: WINSTONS.

Michael parked his bike and stood in front of the building. "Wow. I know I said I've seen it before, but it still looks so cool. Don't you think?"

I gazed at the dilapidated building but didn't see the same appeal. It made me sad to think that the building had a purpose in the past. But it no longer fulfilled anything except for occupying space in the middle of the woods. I imagined all the people who came and went when the train was active.

"Here, Eddie, stand in front of the building. Let me take your picture. It'll look awesome!" Michael put the camera up to his face, but I didn't have the same enthusiasm. I swung my leg off my bike, approached the building, and smiled in front of the camera.

Michael pressed a button, and then I heard a snap.

"No flash that time?" I asked.

"I'm not actually supposed to have the flash on for outside photos." Michael snickered. "Hey, come over here. I want to show you how to take photos so you can take a few pictures of me."

"Uh, sure. Don't you just press the button, and that's it?"

"It's actually a little more involved than that."

I walked over to Michael, and he showed me how to operate the camera. I found the shutter speed, iris, and f-stop to be confusing, but Michael explained everything and adjusted all of the settings for me.

7

"I guess all you gotta do is press the button. But I just wanted to show you all of the other things in case you were interested."

"Yeah, it's really cool. You just want your picture in front of the building?"

"Absolutely!" Michael ran in front of the abandoned entrance at the same spot I was in. I held up the camera to my eye and pressed the button.

Snap.

"All right, now that we got the front, let's go inside," Michael said.

I shook my head. "You can't be serious."

"Yeah, come on, man, it's no big deal. What's the matter?"

"I don't know, man. It just doesn't feel right." I grimaced. "Do you really want to go inside?"

"Of course. Unless you can give me a really good reason why we shouldn't go inside, we're doing it," Michael said.

"I'm pretty sure it's trespassing, so it's illegal. If we get caught, we could be in big trouble."

"Yeah, but who's going to find out? There's no one around here. Even if we did get busted, your dad works at the police station. He'd let us off the hook, and you can put the blame all on me if you really want."

"I just don't see the appeal of going in."

"Come on, please! We can take some really cool photos inside. Plus, I'll let you in on a little secret. You're going to lose your mind when I tell you this."

I sighed.

"Jake and I went inside before. It's really not a big deal!"

"Really?"

"Cross my heart and swear on my grandpa's grave; we've done it before. It's easy to sneak in. We'll be in and out."

I hung my head. "Okay fine, you win. I can't believe I'm doing this."

Michael beamed. "It's going to be a blast! I knew you'd come around."

"You better tell me about this little secret of yours." I smirked as I stepped up to Michael.

"Of course, but first, we need to get in the first room here. Just beyond this window since the door is boarded-up." Michael approached a window with no wooden planks covering it. A few wasps floating around made my heart race. Michael swung his leg over the bottom of the window and climbed inside. "Dude, it's so cool in here." I heard Michael snap a few pictures. Every sound echoed.

I clambered over the window sill and joined Michael inside the desolate room. A rat scurried away, and a few bugs stood on the wall perfectly still. The walls were cracked, and some were crumbling. Graffiti, abstract designs, and obscenities were painted on the walls if they weren't already crumbling. Black mold was growing in a few spots.

A flash and a snap came from my left. Michael chortled. "I don't want you to be mad. That picture is going to look really cool. You were looking at the walls as if it was blowing your mind."

"I'm just thinking about all of the past events that unfolded here. Do you think this was a restaurant?"

"My brother told me it was probably a brothel at some point. Do you know what that is?"

I shook my head.

"It's a whorehouse, you know, where people go and do it with each other."

I cringed. "Is that the secret you wanted to share with me?"

"What? Of course not. I just thought it was a cool little fact that my brother told me about."

"Who knows if it's even true, though. What if your older brother is messing with you?"

"Are you calling him a liar?"

"I don't know, maybe." I chuckled. "Seriously, dude, what's this secret you got? It's driving me crazy over here."

"So this is big news, buddy. Brace yourself. I don't know if you can handle this. I should have told you to bring an extra pair of underwear."

"Just spit it out." I rolled my eyes.

"Okay, okay, I'll tell you, but you sure you can handle it?" Michael grinned.

"I don't think I'm ready, so I'm just gonna leave," I said sarcastically, but I turned around.

"Wait, wait! Fine! So, my parents said that next year during my birthday, I could bring a friend to our family trip if I wanted to. So, if that was something you were interested in, you could come with me to Disney World next year!"

I dropped my jaw. "Dude, are you sure?"

"Yeah, of course. Why wouldn't I be?"

"I just don't want you to be messing with me about this 'cuz that would be amazing! I would love to go anywhere you want! I understand if you don't want to go to Disney World again, though."

"Are you kidding me? Of course, I want to go back there again. It would be awesome, especially if you're there with me. There's so much to do and see. Plus, there are millions of people, so there are lines everywhere, but it's the most fun I've ever had. I feel like it's impossible to explore it all in one trip."

"Well, yeah, man, I'm down!" I jumped up in the air. Excitement was coursing through my veins. Suddenly, I didn't mind being inside the abandoned structure."

"Hey, let's go upstairs next. If we can even find the staircase. Jake and I only made it this far, but let's keep going."

I probably would've backed down, but I was too thrilled about the Disney news. "Uh, Yeah, let's give it a shot."

Michael led the way as we tiptoed over the creaky wood floors. Some spots had holes in them but not large enough for us to fall in. We made our way through a hallway and another room with a staircase in the back. It was hot inside the abandoned structure. Tiny shards of glass glimmered from the streaks of sunlight coming in; it made my heart drop. All of the steps on the staircase had broken wood, it was completely uneven, but there seemed to be enough stability. I put as much weight as I could on the broken-up wooden rail next to me whenever it was there. We made it up to the top of the steps without any issue.

Walking down a hall to our left, we saw a rusted iron ladder at the end leading up outside. A heavenly light shined down on it.

"Oh, dude, check it out. We can get on top of the roof!" Michael yelled as we creaked our way to the end of the hall. Standing next to the ladder and looking up through the hole, I saw the sky and puffy white clouds. Michael tried jerking the ladder, but it was intact and sturdy.

"I'm gonna try going up." Michael put his hands on the rungs and took each step one by one. The ladder held still as Michael made it to the top.

"Wow! It's such an amazing view up here, Eddie. You got to come up here and check this out!"

"Okay, I'll be there in just a moment," I yelled. As I climbed up the ladder, I heard something drop and land on the wooden floor downstairs. It was faint, but enough to make my skin tingle.

Maybe we really shouldn't be here right now, I thought.

I hurried my climb up the ladder until I made it through the opening. It was bright and hot on the roof. It took a moment for my eyes to adjust, but I saw Michael standing tall and proud, staring at the empty street, lost in a trance.

"You okay, Michael?" I asked.

"Yeah, man, I'm just taking it all in. This view is awesome. Did you have any trouble getting up?"

I chuckled. "If I did, you would have heard me scream."

I thought that would make Michael laugh, too, but he was still gazing out at the street.

"Good, I'm glad you got here okay. Now, I want you to take a picture of me with the street and the other buildings as the background. I think it will look really cool." Michael handed me the camera. "The settings are good. You just have to take a picture."

"Sounds easy enough." I put the camera back up to my eye and rotated the lens enough to get Michael in focus.

Snap.

"I think it looks good, man. By the way, when I was walking up the ladder, I heard something drop on, like, the first floor," I said.

"Do you know what it was?"

"No, that's why I'm telling you. It kinda freaked me out."

"Oh, I don't think it's anything to worry about. I'm sure things are falling, breaking, and leaking all the time. I mean, did you see those crumbling walls? Perhaps another section fell over. Don't let it creep you out. We've been fine this whole time, and we're on the freakin' roof."

"Whatever you say." I handed the camera back to Michael.

"You know what we should do? This camera has a setting where you can set a timer, so if you want, set this on top of a rock or something, set, like, a 30-second timer, and then we can take a picture together."

"If you want to do that, that's fine by me, but it's your camera, so you should set it up."

"With pleasure! Now, just move to the front of the roof."

I watched my footing with every step since there were pitfalls to the left and right in a few spots. For the most part, the top felt sturdy enough.

Gulp.

I made it to the front edge. I had a better view of the ghost town, and I could see further out into the distance of trees but nothing else besides that. Michael was right; the sight was captivating. I stood there, letting the cool breeze rejuvenate my sweaty skin.

"Just stay right there... Lemme just adjust the focus a little... Stay still..."

"In case you haven't noticed, I haven't moved an inch." I smirked.

"Okay, but you just did by talking! Shut up and stay still." Michael snickered. Michael had to balance the camera on top of a rock, but he was successful. "Okay, I have it all set up. Are you ready?"

"I've been ready the moment you started setting up."

"Perfect!" Michael sprinted towards me and put his arm around my shoulders, and I felt his hand rest on the top of my head. I assumed he was giving me bunny ears. He probably thought he was discreet, but I didn't care.

The camera stared at us for a moment before snapping all by itself.

"Hooray! We're done. That was actually pretty easy." Michael jogged to the camera on his tiptoes and put it around his neck.

"Okay, we had our photoshoot. Can we leave now?" I asked.

"Just give me one more second," he said as he took a few pictures of the surroundings of the structure. "All right, we can leave now." Michael shook his head. "I swear, man, you're a little bit of a chicken."

"What makes you say that?"

"Because you're in such a hurry to leave. To be honest, I would be down to stay here a little longer. It's just so amazing. Are you really not that interested?"

"It kind of gives me the creeps. Plus, it's illegal. Just knowing we're not allowed to be here freaks me out, too."

"You're such a goody-two-shoes." Michael cracked up.

"Whatever, man. It's not like your dad works for the police department here. I'm going to go back to my bike. If you want to stay here and take more pictures, be my guest. I'd rather wait by the front at this point."

"No, no, that's okay. We can get going now. I might check out one of the other buildings if you're down to wait for a moment."

"That's all you, man. Go for it."

Both of us climbed down the ladder and trod our way to the top of the staircase.

A chilling groan of someone in pain came from the opposite side of the hall. It echoed all the way to our ears from one of the other rooms.

Michael spun around and stared at me with wide eyes. The hairs on the back of my neck stood up. Both of us froze in place.

"Did you just hear that?" Michael mouthed to me.

I nodded. "What should we do?" I mouthed back.

We heard something shuffle and crinkle like a plastic tarp, followed up by a grizzly throat-clear and the sound of someone stomping.

"Run!" Michael shouted as we flew down the staircase and sprinted through the rest of the structure as if we were on fire.

Hopping over the window, we made it back outside. Michael hopped on his bike and pedaled in the opposite direction.

"Where are you going, dude?" I yelled as I got on my bike.

"It's closer if I take this route to get back to my house! Go home, or come with me! We need to get the hell out of here!"

A tall shadowy figure emerged from the building. I was too scared to look at the person in the eye.

Goosebumps covered my body. Adrenaline powered my legs to pump the pedals at a speed I didn't know I could. I shot down the trail going back through the tunnel of trees. When I felt like I was far enough ahead of anything chasing me, I took a quick glance behind.

There was no one following me.

I pedaled all the way back home, periodically looking behind to see if anyone was there, but I never spotted anyone. I saw a couple of people going out for a walk, but they were coming from the opposite direction. *What happened with Michael,* I wondered. *He's probably doing just fine. We had a good head start on whoever was in that building.*

When I made it back to my house, my mom saw me as soon as I walked into the living room. She was sitting on the couch, knitting a blanket.

"Well, you're home early," my mom said.

"Really? I've been gone for a few hours. Or at least that's what it felt like." I couldn't stop fidgeting with a hangnail.

"How'd it go? What did you two do?"

"We just went and got ice cream. And then we just rode our bikes around the town." Hopefully, that would be the end of the questioning. I wondered if she could tell that I was trembling.

"Sounds like a pleasant afternoon."

"Oh, you know what else happened? Something exciting! Michael said that his parents might take me to Disney World next year! They said that they're willing to let Michael bring a friend for his next birthday trip." I was about to bounce off the walls.

"Wow, you're right. That does sound exciting," my mom said smiling.

"Would it be okay if I joined Michael and his family for that?"

"Absolutely. Just don't plan on the trip happening just yet. You never know what might come up."

"Yeah, I understand. I think it'll happen for sure, though. Michael's family goes on a vacation every year."

"Okay," she laughed dryly. "We'll see. I'd still like to take you and Dad there someday too."

"That would be amazing! I'd be down to go four times in one year!"

My mom stopped knitting for a moment. "Maybe we could make it happen two years from now."

"I can be patient!" I grinned.

My mom nodded, and I ran up to my bedroom and turned on my GameCube, and entered a virtual world of delight for a few hours.

I was hoping I would get a call from Michael, but it never happened. Even after my mom and I finished eating dinner, there was still no word from him.

Maybe he's just waiting for me to call him, I thought. *I'll give him a ring later.*

I read a book in my bedroom for a while, but I kept thinking about Michael. It wasn't until 8:00 p.m. rolled around that I really felt uncomfortable. *That's it, I'm going to give him a call.* Just as I stood up out of my chair, the phone jingled from the living room.

"I'll get it!" I yelled as I jogged down the stairs. When I got to the living room, the ringing stopped.

My mother was already standing with the phone held up to her ear. Her brow was scrunched, and her mouth fell ajar.

"No, I'm afraid he never came over," my mom said.

"What's the matter?" I whispered.

She held up her finger at me, listening carefully to every word coming from the other end. "Yes, as a matter of fact, he's right here. I'll give him the phone."

"Who is it?" I whispered.

She covered up the mouthpiece with her hand. "It's Michael's mom. Apparently, Michael didn't come home earlier. She's wondering when and where was the last time you saw him."

My heart thumped in my neck. It felt like a nightmare, but it was all too real. I took a deep breath and held the phone up to my ear. My mother stood over me, analyzing my face.

"Hello?" I uttered into the mouthpiece.

"Hi, Eddie. I'm glad you're okay. I'm just a little frazzled at the moment. I'm sorry if I don't sound very coherent, but I'm wondering if you, by chance, know where Michael is?" She sniffled. Even though it was through the receiver, I could hear her lips quivering. "Michael didn't warn me about staying out late. The last time I talked to him was this afternoon when he said he would get ice cream with you and ride bikes.

Can you tell me everything that happened on your bike ride? What time did you leave to go back to your house?"

"We got done with our bike ride around 4:00 p.m. That's around the time I got home. We split up, and that was the last time I saw Michael."

There was a pause on the other end of the phone. For a moment, I thought Michael's mom had hung up, or the signal dropped.

"Hopefully, he's just riding his bike around still. Can you tell me where exactly the last time you saw him was? Do you remember the street name?"

The pressure was mounting on my brain to a point where I thought I was going to scream. I wanted the call to end. I wanted Michael to walk through the house door and greet his mom. I didn't want to have to reveal what we did. If he was okay, I'd just be getting him in trouble when he got home. What would Michael want me to do? What would my parents want me to do?

"Uh. Well, I, uh... I'll just tell you everything that happened today." My eyes brimmed with tears, and my voice thickened. "So we got ice cream, and Michael paid for it." I sniffled. "Then he had this camera and said he really wanted to take pictures, and so he told me to follow him because he knew of a spot where we could take cool photos. So we traveled to the other side of town and went to Melville, where they have a few abandoned buildings. You know, where the old ghost town is? I didn't wanna go, but he said he and Jake would go there, and it wasn't a big deal." Tears poured down my cheeks, and my mother gasped.

"Edward Vincent Wright..." my mom muttered.

"Yes, what happened next?" Michael's mom asked.

"We went inside this old abandoned building because Michael really wanted to. We took some photos while we were inside, but I told him I didn't really want to. I didn't want to make him mad, so we took the pictures, and then we heard something stepping towards us. That's when we ran out of the building, got on our bikes, and went our separate ways. He said the route to his house would be faster if he went the other way, but I went in through the way we came in since that's all I knew. I'm really, really, really sorry. But that was the last time I saw him, and that's all the information I have. I know, I know, looking back on everything, I shouldn't have let him go alone. But I thought it would be safer or faster if he went his own way. It all happened so fast. I'm so sorry, Mrs. Carter."

My stomach felt like it was getting a nail hammered through it.

"Oh my God, oh my God, oh my God," Michael's mother repeated on the other line.

Then she let out an ear-piercing scream. You could hear her voice through my entire living room from the phone. I felt like she was no longer listening. Not that I said anything else, but even if I did, she wouldn't be able to comprehend another word.

My mother gazed at me wide-eyed and shook her head; a small tear trickled down her cheek. She uttered, "Give me the phone."

I handed it back to her, and she said, "Mary. I know it's not easy, but I need you to take a deep breath. This is what we're going to do next. I'm going to call my husband at the station, and we're going to look into this immediately. Michael's going to be okay. We need to put positive thoughts out there. Michael is going to be okay. We're going to find him. He's a young boy who probably forgot to call home. Maybe he got lost on his way riding his bike, we don't know for sure, but he's going to be okay. We're going to get him home as soon as possible. Just stay home, I'll call my husband, and then I'll call you back, and we can go from there."

They exchanged goodbyes, and my mother hung up the phone.

"I'm really sorry, Mom. I'm really sorry I didn't tell you about it earlier! Michael didn't want me to tell anyone that we went there, and he was really excited about it, and I just felt really pressured, and I didn't really know what else to do!"

"Eddie, it's fine. There's nothing we can do except call Dad at work and get a few police cars on the road to look for him. You shouldn't have gone to the ghost town; you should've just come back home. But there's nothing we can do about that now. There's no sense in hollering at you about it. We need to focus on Michael, and we'll do everything we can to make sure he's fine. Do you understand?"

I nodded.

My mother called the police station immediately, and she told me to go to the other room.

"Let me talk to my husband. This is Wilma. Thank you."

I sat on the top of the steps, listening as carefully as I could. My head pressed against the wooden rail.

"Roy," my mom continued, "something happened to Michael. Yes, Eddie's friend. He never came home this evening." My mother told him all about what I had done and where I had gone. I wish she didn't, but there wasn't another way. My dad had to know if we were going to have any luck at saving Michael.

That night, police cars drove through all the streets of Lockweed, Michigan. My mother and I went to Michael's house and stayed with his mom for the evening. I wanted to join the search, too, on my bike, but my mom wouldn't let that happen. Michael's father drove his car alongside the police cars all night long.

The next morning, Michael was still missing.

16

He was never found at all.

They only discovered his SLR camera on the ground in the thick woods around Melville.

I

6 months ago from the present day...

Flying down the empty freeway at 75 miles an hour, John blew past a sign: SPEED LIMIT 55. It was just John and Barry inside the latest Dodge RAM pickup truck.

"You don't give a damn about getting a ticket, do you?" Barry asked John from the passenger seat, following it up with a chuckle. Barry had a buzz cut and a beard with a similar length. Both of them were in their mid-twenties, but Barry was 5'8, seven inches shorter than John.

John had a thicker beard but a pudgier face. "You said you wanted to make it to Peter's at a decent hour. We got a late start. I don't know what to tell you. To get there fast, we gotta go fast."

"Relax, man, I feel like we could go 60 miles an hour and be good. I've heard Indiana cops are dicks, and they pull you over if they see different license plates. And in case you can't tell, no one is around. We are in the straight-up boonies. We stick out like a sore thumb in your giant ass pickup truck going faster than the speed of sound."

John didn't want to respond. He felt like Barry was a pestering bug flying around him that he wanted to smash. "Let's give Peter another call."

"Dude, I already tried calling him four times in a row. He'll see that he has missed calls, and he'll get back to us."

"Call him again."

"You do it if you're so concerned."

"Can't you see I'm driving?"

Barry snorted. "Actually, it's probably best for my safety if I call him. We don't want you distracted while you're completely disregarding the posted speed limit." Barry pulled out his phone and called Peter's number, and put the phone on speaker, turning down the pop-country music playing over the radio.

Four rings went by before there was an answer.

"Heyyy, I'm really sorry I missed all your calls. Today has been crazy. You guys have no idea," Peter said.

"A text would have been nice! How crazy could it have been? I guarantee you've had your phone in your hand, you asshole," Barry said.

"Thanks, Barry. Look, I'm really sorry, but a family emergency came up. How far away are you guys?"

"Considering we just got into Indiana, we got about another four hours according to the GPS," John said.

"Ah, I'm really sorry, and I know you're traveling far-ish, but I seriously can't meet up with you guys or get you into my building by the time you get here. In fact, I don't know if I'll be able to hang out tonight at all."

"Damn, man, are you serious?" Barry asked.

"Yeah, so I don't know if you just want to turn back around and go back to Ohio, or if you want to maybe try finding a place in Chicago, you can do that, too. Or, I thought of another idea you guys might like."

"You can't even go back to your place and let us go in?" Barry asked.

"Hey, if I could, I would have offered that immediately. I'll tell you guys more about what's happening when I see you. It's a lot to go over, but basically, my cousin is in the hospital. As you know, he was going to hang out with us, but since I'm his only family member within two hundred miles, I need to be with him. You know, make sure he's okay, and tell the doctors what's up with his medical history because right now, he physically can't talk."

"Holy shit. I'm really sorry to hear that, man," John said.

"But you can't even step away, meet up with us and just literally hand us a key? Or what if we met up with you there?" Barry pressed.

"Dude, I really can't believe you're asking me this right now," Peter said.

"Oh, come on, I took tomorrow off of work. This was supposed to be a three-day weekend of pure, unadulterated partying. I understand if your cousin is in the hospital or whatever, but at least let John and I hang out at your place, and you can swing by whenever."

There was a pause on the other side of the line. "Uh, I can probably get to you guys tomorrow afternoon, but I'm going to stay in the hospital for now. I know it's shitty. Believe me, I was really excited for this weekend, but now I'm in a weird headspace. If you guys could find a cheap roadside motel or something, come back here tomorrow, and we'll figure something out. But tonight, I cannot leave the hospital."

"All right, yeah, I understand. We'll figure something out. Talk to you later, Peter," Barry said.

19

"Hope your cousin feels better," John said.

"Thanks, guys. I'll for sure see you tomorrow if you come out. I think my cousin will be all good by then. Saturday, though, we'll for sure watch the Ohio State game. I have a reservation and everything still. I'm really sorry about all this, but you guys don't have to buy any drinks this whole weekend. I got you," Peter said, and he ended the call.

Barry pressed his hands against his eyes and sighed. "What are we going to do, man?"

"I thought maybe it's just best if we turn back around and plan for another weekend. I know it sucks that we called off work tomorrow, and we both really want to watch the game at an Ohio State bar, but maybe it's best if we try to do another weekend."

"What? Are you insane? I wasn't talking about that. I was more so wondering where the hell are we going to stay from here to Chicago? I don't want to stay at a roadside motel. I bet if I do some research, we can find a decent hotel, maybe a cool town to watch the Thursday night football game."

John rolled his eyes. "I don't know, man. Do you really want to go through all this?"

"Yes! Of course! Peter said he would be good to meet up with us tomorrow. You and I can at least go out clubbing on Friday night if he can't. Then on Saturday, we can hang out with his friends and get shitfaced while we watch the game. That sounds amazing."

John thought about it for a moment.

"I'm not getting any younger over here, Johnny boy. What's it going to be?"

"Okay, I'm down, but look up a place for us to stay now and figure it out as soon as you can."

"All right, I'll try."

John contemplated." If you could, find a cool place with maybe a little downtown area and a sports bar. Have a few beers, watch the Thursday night game, go back to our hotel or B&B, whatever you find, and we'll call it a night. That sounds awesome."

"Yeah, that sounds all right to me. I'm also going to look up what might be a good place to meet singles in our area." Barry smirked at John.

"You can't be serious. Let's just have a chill night. We're about to rage all weekend. Might as well take this chance to conserve some of our energy."

"I don't even know who you are anymore. I'm down to feel like death tomorrow if we can salvage a good time here."

"But where? There's nothing around us. I'm not trying to have a hangover all day while I drive to Chicago tomorrow."

"You say this now, but once we start getting some beers in you, and some ladies start talking to us. You'll change your mind." Barry snickered. He focused on his phone and searched for the nearest sports bar. "Hell, I'd be down to go to a strip club too if we find one."

"No. We're not doing that. I'm not trying to spend a ton of money while we're in transit."

"I'll pay your cover and your drinks. How about that?"

"Sure, I'd go then," John lied. He just wanted to get Barry to stop talking. And he knew if he said no, Barry would keep pestering.

The car was silent for five minutes as Barry kept scrolling and typing on his phone.

"Well? Any update?" John asked.

"Yeah, I think I found a place. Oh boy, have I found a place!" Barry cracked up.

"When you calm down, tell me the name."

Barry settled his laughter down and exhaled with delight. "Dude, this place is called Big Henry's. It's a sports bar with really great neon out front. Looks like they're mostly a Purdue, Indiana, and Notre Dame bar."

"Of course they are. We're in Indiana. Kinda weird they don't just pick one."

"Yeah, I don't know, that's kinda dumb. Commit to one team or don't." Barry shrugged. "But hey, I think this is perfect, let's go to this townie bar. Big Henry's." Berry snickered. "I bet it's going to be a big party at Big Henry's. They'll have the Colts game going on, so it should be fun."

"Works for me," John said. They rerouted their directions to Wilton, Indiana, to Big Henry's sports bar. Only an hour away. "Do they have a hotel nearby?"

"Yeah, they got a little inn. This downtown looks pretty nice, a cool little old area. Like an old train town." Barry turned up the country music and texted some other friends.

John kept driving until they arrived at Wilton around 8p.m. They approached a building with a faded sign and looked like it had been there since the '90s. Big Henry's. Blue font, a white background, a quarterback throwing a football, and a player with a basketball on both sides. There were neon signs of the Notre Dame logo, the Indiana University logo, and the Purdue logo in the front windows. A few people stood outside smoking cigarettes. The sun had already set, but it was a warm winter night. John and Barry went inside and grinned. The whole bar had a massive string of multicolored holiday lights on the wall. The bar had a shelf near the ceiling, decorated with football helmets, footballs, and basketballs. Everyone wore a blue and white shirt. All of them were Colts fans.

"It's like a cult in here," John said.

"More like a... COLT. Get it? Cult, Colt? They're Colts fans... Nevermind. Bad pun," Barry said. "I'm just relieved I'm wearing a blue shirt."

The entire bar at the front was filled; clumps of people circled together. Near the back, there was an open table in the corner.

"Looks like we got here just at the right time. I can't believe how crowded it is. It's 20 minutes until kickoff," John said.

Barry and John took a seat and stared at the single-paged double-sided menu. Barry set down the menu after looking at it for ten seconds. "All right, I'm going to get a burger and fries and a Miller Lite."

"That sounds good to me. I wish they had some IPAs here, though," John said.

"Dude, come on, do you see where you're at? They don't serve craft beer here."

"I know, it's annoying. It's the 2020's. Figure it out." John chuckled.

"I think it's awesome. This place has decided not to evolve."

A server stepped up to their table. "Are you two ready to order?"

Barry's eyes lit up at the sight of her. "Oh, yeah, we're ready to order. But first I want to introduce myself because I'm about to ask you something. My name is Barry, and I'd love to get one date with you, please?" Barry was smooth in his delivery, and he followed it up immediately with a laugh. "I'm joking, but you are beautiful."

"Uh, thanks," the server said as she laughed and blushed. "But can I actually take a real order for you?"

"We'll both get two Miller Lites and burgers and fries," Barry said as he knocked on the table once.

The server smiled at Barry the whole time. Amused. "Sounds good. Making it easy for me. I'm Kim if you need anything else." She walked away.

Barry turned around to check her out.

"Dude! What the hell is wrong with you?" John said. "I don't want to have these people spit in our food. You're a wild animal."

"Oh, come on, I'm just having some fun. She thought it was funny and she smiled. Harmless flirtation from a good-looking guy. I'm not some random creep."

John shook his head and exhaled. "Do you hear yourself sometimes? That's exactly what you are, a random creep. You're gonna get us in trouble, I swear. What if her boyfriend is at another table nearby or something? Did you ever think about that? Of course you didn't, because you don't think. At least take some time and case the joint a little. You're over here going for the throat and also ruining my reputation."

"Relax, we'll be fine." Barry held up his hand and focused on the massive TV set across the bar.

Kim returned to the table with two large pint glasses filled with golden liquid. The aroma of light beer made Barry's mouth water.

"The burgers and fries will be right out," Kim said.

"Is it mandatory for the whole staff to wear Colts shirts for game nights?" Barry asked as his eyes softened. He was all smiles.

Kim's lip curled up. "Yeah, but I'm also a fan, so I don't mind wearing it. I don't see you guys wearing any gear."

"We're actually not from around here. We're from Cincinnati."

"Oh, welcome to Wilton. I'm sure you'll enjoy your stay."

"Is this a common vacation spot or something?"

Kim shrugged. "It's a nice little town with a decent amount to do. We get a fair amount of out-of-towners. Mostly during the summertime when they can walk around the downtown area without freezing."

"No kidding? We were actually on our way to Chicago but had a change of plans. This looked like the nearest sports bar, and it sounded like a good time."

"You guys came to the right place." Kim smiled. "I'll be right back with your food in just a second." She turned and bounced away to other tables, making her rounds.

Barry gazed at her as she left. "Hey, dude, did you notice her tattoo under her t-shirt on the left arm?"

John looked unamused. "No, I didn't have a very good angle."

"I couldn't really tell what it was, but it looked wicked. You know I dig girls with tats, man. I think I'm in love."

"God, I can't take you anywhere, I swear." John laughed, but he was irritated. John knew that Barry wouldn't change his demeanor no matter what he said.

The football game started, the audio of the room switched from classic rock to the game. Every patron focused on the nearest TV, but they continued their conversations.

Kim approached their table with two baskets, each with a burger and a pile of fries. She delivered the food and set ketchup and mustard bottles at the center of the table. "Everything look okay?"

"All that's missing is your number," Barry said.

Kim laughed it off but stood in front of their table. "Sorry, don't think I can do that while I'm on the clock."

"Oh, but perhaps afterward?" Barry raised an eyebrow.

Kim shrugged. "Maybe. Just holler at me if you need anything."

"I actually do have a question. I noticed you have a tattoo on your left arm? I was wondering what it was? It looks beautiful."

Kim's lips curved all the way up. She rolled up her sleeve, displaying her tattoo. A woman's head was attached to a demonic bird with large talons and broad bat-like wings.

"Whoa, what is that?" Barry asked.

"It's a harpy."

"I have no idea what that is."

"It's just a Greek mythology creature."

"What's the meaning behind it?"

"Just thought it looked cool. I always wanted a tattoo, and it seemed to fit me. I plan on getting a whole sleeve someday."

"That's awesome. I love it. I actually have a tattoo of my own." Barry rolled up his hoodie sleeve, and on his right shoulder, he had a scarlet block "O" with a gray buckeye in the corner. "Johnny and I went to *The* Ohio State University."

"Wow, so you guys didn't even grow up around here?"

"Nope. Just traveling through, but we plan on staying the night here."

Kim's eyes widened. "Oh, no kidding? Are you planning on staying at the inn just down the street?" Kim pointed with her thumb.

"We haven't made reservations yet, but yeah, we probably will." Barry nodded.

John glared at Barry but bit his tongue.

"So, neither of you have any plans after this?" Kim asked.

"Just going to watch the game here and drink a few beers," Barry said.

"You guys should really check out the rest of Wilton. Are you familiar with any of the other places here?"

John and Barry both shook their heads.

Kim smirked. "Cool, cool. Well, this will probably come as a surprise to you, but Wilton has a great nightlife scene. Both of you seem really cool, and I'd love to show you around. And if you'd want, you could probably crash at my place. I have a loft downtown."

Barry grinned. "That would be amazing, Kim. We'd really appreciate that, thank you."

"Of course, I'll be back around, but I have other tables to get to." Kim walked away, beaming.

As soon as she left, Barry cracked up. "Dude, this place is unbelievable. The women must never meet guys that are worth a damn around here. That was way too easy."

"Way to go," John said. Barry couldn't tell if John was being sarcastic or serious. Either way, Barry didn't care.

"I just wonder what kind of nightlife is here in Wilton, you know? It seems like such a joke," Barry said.

"Driving in, it looked like there were a few businesses or bars up the road. Seems pretty cool for a small town," John said.

Barry and John ate their burgers, drank their sweet, crisp Miller Lites, and doused their fries with ketchup. Both of them were highly satisfied with their experience at Big Henry's. They waited around, watching the rest of the Thursday Night Football game, and they left once Kim finished her shift.

The three of them joined together at the front of Big Henry's.

"Let's check out the downtown strip," Kim said.

Kim led the way, and Barry talked her ear off while John walked a few feet behind them.

It was one of John and Barry's last tangible memories before everything became a blur.

They lost track of time.

The sun rose up from the horizon, and the only sign left of John and Barry was their car parked in Big Henry's lot full of their belongings. The car was towed by the owner at 4 p.m. and no one came to claim it.

I I

One year ago...

Mitchell and Carol Boykins drove their Chevy hybrid at the posted speed limit on the empty Indiana highway. It was the middle of June, and the grass was a vibrant green, along with clumps of trees they saw in the distance. Nothing was around except for flatlands.

Mitchell was a tall, scrawny guy with a stylish haircut, big plastic frame glasses, and he always wore a button-up shirt that fit him a little tight. His jeans had a similar tightness.

"It's so crazy to me that you've never been to a big city," Carol said from the passenger seat. Carol was a year younger than Mitchell. She wore a bright blue floral dress purchased from a vintage shop the week before. Her hair was long, but she had bangs that neatly covered her forehead. The large plastic frame glasses looked similar to Mitchell's, but hers had a vintage cat-eye shape.

"Hey hey hey, I've been to Arlington, Chesapeake, and Virginia Beach." Mitchell smirked.

"Our state doesn't count," Carol said.

"Well, we went to Honolulu for our honeymoon. That's a pretty large city."

"I mean, you've never been to New York or Chicago."

"I don't know if it counts for you either. You went to New York when you were like 10 years old. You barely remember it."

"That's not entirely true. I remember how amazing it felt taking the Staten Island ferry and seeing the whole city in front of you. And then the excitement of the subways and all the lights in Times Square, I'll never forget those moments. Now that I'm thinking about it, I wish we were able to go there."

"No matter what, I'm excited about Chicago. At least we have friends there we can visit."

"Don't get me wrong, I'm ecstatic for Chicago, but I do want to take you to New York someday."

"Yeah, I'm all for that." Mitchell looked at Carol and smiled before focusing his attention on the road. His stomach grumbled like an irritated old man. "So, do you have any thoughts on where you'd want to go to dinner? I was thinking something fast. Chipotle or Qdoba both sound good to me."

Carol winced. "Yeah, those places are fine and all, and I like them, but I'm in a mood."

Mitchell exhaled, but the corner of his lip curled up. "Uh-huh, and what's your mood?"

"I want something that's a diner in an airstream. You know what I'm talking about? Those trailers that look like they're made of stainless steel, and they're a diner with all sorts of kitschy collectibles and a 1950s theme?"

"I can picture it clearly," Mitchell said with a hint of annoyance.

"I want to go to a place like that. That would be so fun, and it would be even better if it was in some small little town with a unique charm only found in less populated Americana. You know what I mean?"

"Yeah, but who knows when's the next time we might find a restaurant like that. We could be on the road for hours until we find something exactly like your description. Can we just settle for a diner nearby?"

"You must be pretty hungry, huh?" Carol stared at Mitchell from over her glasses.

"Did you not hear my stomach growling just a moment ago?"

"I'm just curious! That's all. What's the max amount of time you're willing to wait?"

Mitchell's head bobbed from side to side as he thought about it. "No longer than 30 minutes. I've been a little hungry for a while now."

"Okay! I'll be quick. I'll settle for a diner, but you bet your ass I'm looking for a stainless steel 1950s nightmare." Carol winked and buried her head in her phone, swiping madly through search results. "Oh my God! I think we hit the jackpot! 20 minutes away, a little town called Wilton, Indiana, has exactly what we need. This place is called Buckwheat's!"

"Can you settle down? You're yelling in my ear," Mitchell said, but laughed about it.

"Look at this place! Look at this place!" Carol held her phone in front of Mitchell's face while driving.

His eyes quickly flicked from the road to the screen. He spotted sections of silver steel, a green neon sign up top with the name of the restaurant, and then a clock above it. Above the clock was another sign, white letters with a red background. "Open 24 hours!"

"That looks like what you want." Mitchell smiled. "Could you put it in the GPS, please?"

"Already on it!" Carol had the phone in hand and adjusted the directions from Chicago to Buckwheat's. They were only 19 minutes away.

As Mitchell continued driving, Carol swiped through all of the photos of the diner and read through the menu. She smiled from ear to ear.

Arriving at the restaurant, they parked in front of the Buckwheat's lot and approached the main entrance. Before walking inside, Carol turned around. The sun was making progress down the horizon. It would be nighttime soon, and the golden landscape of Wilton captured Carol's breath.

A cute, small city with buildings made of brick, some painted with pastel colors, and a river running through the edge of the town. There appeared to be a train depot structure all the way at the other end of the main street, still in excellent condition. Exploring the curious town piqued Carol's interest, capturing her imagination and running wild with it.

"Carol, are we going inside?" Mitchell asked as he held open the door to Buckwheat's. An air-conditioned breeze came through the open entrance and hit the back of Carol's neck.

"Yeah, I'm ready. Sorry about that, this little town is so beautiful." Carol giggled to herself as the two of them walked inside. She was immediately impressed with the theme of Buckwheat's.

A long counter with stools made of shiny steel with a red cushioned cap. The floor had a checkerboard pattern, and there was a fake jukebox at the end of the restaurant, glowing with a rainbow of colors. Pictures of the 1950s festooned the walls, Elvis Presley, Marilyn Monroe, automobiles, vintage Coke, and gasoline signs. Buckwheat's smelled of a variety of other foods. Carol could see the cooks in the back taking tickets and preparing meals.

"Wow, this place is so perfect," Carol whispered to Mitchell. "Where do you want to sit? Part of me wants to sit at the bar and get the full experience, but those booths are enticing. Perhaps the host will determine our fate."

A server in a black t-shirt with Buckwheat's written on the front approached them and smiled. "Sit wherever you'd like!"

"Well? Did you make up your mind?" Mitchell asked Carol playfully.

"Yeah, follow me." Carol walked to the restaurant's end and slid into the back booth. "There, that way we can stare out the window and see this cute little downtown, but also I have the view of the entire restaurant to take it all in." Carol beamed. "Sorry, I guess you don't have a view of the restaurant unless you want to sit on my side?"

"That's okay. As long as I'm sitting across from you, I have the best and most beautiful view of the whole place." Mitchell's lips curled up as he sat across from Carol.

Carol grinned. "You're too sweet, you know that?"

The same server came to their table and dropped off two menus. "Breakfast is served 24 hours, just so you know. Nothing on the menu is off-limits. By the way, I adore your glasses."

Carol adjusted her frames. "Thank you so much! It totally fits the whole aesthetic here."

"I know, how perfect. I haven't seen you before. Are you two from around here?"

"No, we're just passing by, but we might stick around and check out some of the other places. This is a wonderful little town you have here."

"Yeah, it's got everything you could want. That's why I never left."

"Any places you would recommend going to?"

"I mean, how much time do you have? There's enough to do to take up an entire night until the late morning."

Carol laughed. "Well, we're not in a hurry, but I can't imagine us staying out all night."

"Not only that, I can't imagine there's that much to do. It looks like such a small town," Mitchell said as he stared out the window. Analyzing what all could be done in a tiny downtown strip, he couldn't think of anything that would hook him in for an entire night into the morning.

"There are some great bars, but there's also a really great nightclub too," the server said.

"What's it called?" Carol asked.

"It's one of my favorite places to go. It's called Club Novus, but it's a bit of a secret. You can't find it online or any reviews on it."

"That's pretty weird."

"Yeah, but I think they want it to feel like a rave. Like how there's no official place, but they have parties in random abandoned buildings."

"Oh, so it's an underground thing? But it's always at the same building here?"

"Yeah, they have it at the same building, but it's an official business, so you won't be busted for trespassing."

"This is all very fascinating."

"But if the club idea isn't your scene, there's another great bar called The Painted Goose, which I highly recommend."

"I can't imagine we'd be staying here very late. We'll probably hit the road after dinner," Mitchell butted in.

"There's a great ice cream place too in the park along the river. So even if you want to get a dessert after you eat here and explore a little bit, that's a popular spot."

"Thank you so much for all of the ideas," Carol said.

"Sorry, I'm probably talking your ear off. My manager tells me I do that sometimes, but a lot of locals come here, so it's not every day you get someone from...?"

"Virginia," Carol said.

"Wow, quite a ways away from home. Well, thank you for coming into our little diner here. I'll let you two look at the menu, and I'll be right back." The server left their table.

"The Midwestern charm is a real thing. The people here are just lovely," Carol said.

Mitchell was nose deep in the menu, analyzing every item, weighing options in his head. "Uh-huh," he replied, unsure of what he responded to.

"What do you think, shall we stick around for ice cream?"

"Uh, I don't know. I think I want to get back on the road after this. We were making pretty good time, and I wanted something quick for dinner, and this will probably take us a lot longer."

"Yeah, but there's no hurry to Chicago. It's not like we have any plans the moment we get there. We've got plenty of time to kill."

Mitchell sighed. "Yeah, I guess you're right. We'd just be sitting around at the Airbnb."

"And did you see the map? There's still a huge traffic jam in the Chicago area."

"Yeah, yeah, you're not wrong." Mitchell nodded. "Let's see how we feel after we eat. I'd be down to walk around, I think, maybe not ice cream, but we'll see, I guess."

"Ah, the server is already coming back our way, and I haven't even thought of what I wanted." Carol scanned the menu. "Okay, I got it now!"

The server came and jotted down their orders. "I'll put that right in for you."

"Oh, wait! I want to ask before I forget. What's the tattoo on your arm?"

The server rolled up her sleeve, showcasing a brooding three-headed dog with a slight scowl. "It's Cerberus."

"Wow, that's a beautiful tattoo. I've been thinking about getting one forever, but I'm just not sure what I'd get. I think I'd like something artsy or cool like that. Maybe even something simple like a vinyl record."

"Oh! I should mention to you one other thing," the server said. "If you like vinyl records, which it seems like you do, you should really check out The Painted Goose bar. They do this thing where you can pay to play a vinyl record of your choosing. It's really neat and one of my other favorite places to go. I think it's worth stopping in for a beer since you're just passing by."

"Wow, I love that name, Painted Goose. Thank you for the suggestion."

"And that place you can actually look up online." The server laughed. "I'll put your order in. Let me know if you need anything else."

Carol pulled out her phone and went through as many photos as she could find of The Painted Goose. Interior brick, a mural of a painted goose, and a wall of vinyl records made her eyes light up like fireworks. She was impressed by the high ratings, an average of 4.8 stars out of 5. All of the top ratings seemed to say the same thing, so she sorted by the lowest ratings to see who could have possibly said something negative. Some complained about the service being too slow, that the place was too hipster, or that it cost too much to get their favorite record played, but there was one that stood out to Carol.

"I hate to leave a bad review because I enjoyed the atmosphere of the bar, but something was off about the place. When I went outside for a smoke, some guy was watching me beyond the fence of the bar. It was really creepy. From that experience alone, I don't think I'll ever come back to The Painted Goose."

Carol's skin tingled as she read the blurb, but she revisited the top reviews and could feel excitement build in her chest. She knew the tricky part was going to be convincing Mitchell.

"So I looked up reviews of The Painted Goose, and I saw photos, and I really really want to check it out. I also want to check out the park, but I understand if you think we don't have time for both. But a quick walk around the park and one beer at The Painted Goose is all I'm asking."

Mitchell laughed to himself. "You know what, we're on vacation, we don't have anywhere we need to be at any specific time today, why don't we do both?"

Carol and Mitchell had their meal delivered after waiting only 10 minutes. Mitchell had ordered a cheese omelet, and Carol had a veggie pita wrap. They paid in cash, gave a 25% tip, and left the restaurant. Since the sun hovered just about the horizon, they went to the park first. It was a vast open space with a small wooden dock, tall trees, a few picnic tables, and a wide sidewalk along the river. A long line stretched out from a tiny shack selling soft-serve ice cream. Both Carol and Mitchell were glad they stopped. They thought about grabbing ice cream, but instead, they went to The Painted Goose.

31

As dusk came, the one beer turned into more beers. They became friends with other people at the bar.

They lost track of time, and eventually, they lost track of everything.

The night descended into a blur.

The following morning, Carol and Mitchell were nowhere to be found. Their car was left abandoned in the Buckwheat's parking lot.

2 years ago…

Ray Smith and Cole Muir were driving down the road inside a Jeep Compass with a Tennessee license plate. Ray was 29, wearing wire-framed glasses and a full, thick auburn beard. Cole had a thin but neatly styled mustache and was 28. Both of them had been friends since high school.

"My gas light just came on," Ray said.

"Damn, I don't see a gas station anywhere near here. I feel like it's been a while since I last saw one," Cole said.

"Could you check to see where the nearest place is? I'd even be down to stop somewhere to grab some food or maybe a beer."

"Tryin' to start drinkin' already?" Cole smirked.

"Just one beer. It's been a long week, and I've been craving one since the beginnin' of the day, to be honest." Ray snickered. "Sometimes, all you can do is just laugh at everythin' goin' on. I can't believe my dad is practically in a nursin' home already."

"Yeah, man, it really sucks, but at least your mom and sister are there to look after him. They even told you to focus on our weekend, and I agree. We've wanted to do this trip for a little while. We're gonna have a blast. It's our first time in Chicago, and Ronnie will make it a legendary weekend. And if you wanna stop off to get some gas and grab a beer somewhere, I'm all in. You want to drink more than one beer and need me to drive? Let's do it. Whatever you need. I know things have been tough lately, but we can focus on the good and just take a break from everythin'.'"

Ray stared ahead at the road and nodded. "Thanks, I appreciate that." Without wanting to think about it more, Ray said, "Could you find the nearest gas station? Look it up on your phone or somethin'?"

"Of course." Cole pulled out his phone and searched nearby for a gas station. "It looks like there's a cool town called Wilton not too far from us. The gas is pretty cheap, and we can probably hit up a bar. Looks like there's a little downtown area."

"Let's check it out," Ray said.

Driving into Wilton, they stopped off at a gas station. Four pumps stood available, no one was in the lot, but there was a car parked next to the mart inside.

Ray went to the first pump, and it was out of order. He grumbled to himself as he moved his car to the next pump. It looked active, but he had to pay cash inside.

"Good thing I went to the ATM before this trip," Ray said.

"Dude, you always have to travel with cash going on vacation. Goin' into crowded bars, you need to get out of there ASAP. You get the bill, and you can slap down the right amount of cash, tip included, and you're outta there in no time," Cole said.

"I'm gonna be right back." Ray went inside the mart and paid the gentleman at the cash register.

"Could I also get a pack of Marlboro reds, please?" Ray asked.

The man behind the register pulled out a pack of cigarettes and placed it on the counter. "Could I see your ID?"

"Makin' me feel young again." Ray laughed. He wondered if the cashier noticed his beard at all or the slight wrinkles on his forehead. Whatever the matter, Ray took it as a compliment.

The man stared at the ID for a few seconds longer than Ray expected.

"Traveling from Tennessee, eh? Visiting family?"

"No, all my family is back in Tennessee. I'm just travelin' through, and we needed some gas."

"You should stop by somewhere in town and grab a bite to eat. Everyone that's ever visited Wilton has loved it. We're sort of a hidden gem."

Ray smiled. "Yeah, I believe it. I probably will stop by a bar or somethin'."

"You can't go wrong with any of the places here."

"Thanks. Any recommendations?"

"Big Henry's, The Painted Goose, or if you're hungry for a bite to eat, Buckwheat's is a nice diner."

"I appreciate that, thanks. Have a good one, sir."

The cashier smiled and nodded.

Walking back outside, Ray took a moment to admire the view of downtown Wilton and the river at the edge. Within walking distance, Ray saw the smooth silver diner: Buckwheat's. He thought about getting a burger, but the idea of drinking a potent craft beer was too enticing. While Ray filled up his gas tank, Cole turned around.

"Hey, man, I found a pretty cool bar nearby. Apparently, they have a ton of craft beer. You in?"

"Hell yeah," Ray said, followed by a short laugh of excitement.

"Dude, I think you're gonna love this place. Apparently, we have to do public parking, but it's a short walk."

"Fine by me. I'd like to stretch my legs out anyway. What's the name of the bar?" Ray repeated the three recommendations from the attendant in his head.

"It's called The Painted Goose."

"Say no more." Ray grinned.

After the tank filled up, Ray returned to the driver's seat, and both of them navigated to the nearest parking lot.

They parked at the edge of the park next to the river. The only thing separating them from the water was a neatly manicured grass field and a wooden railing. Stepping outside the car, they marveled at the water sitting below the sunset sky before moving towards The Painted Goose.

"Wow, this little town has more than I expected," Cole said.

"Yeah, it's beautiful. The friendliest guy was workin' the register back at the gas station too."

Cole led the way to The Painted Goose. They approached a brick building with a painted sign above the entrance. Walking inside, the place was crowded, but there were two empty spots at the corner of the bar. On the right side was a painted mural of a goose with paisley and psychedelic design. Ray and Cole stared at everything in awe. They sat down at the bar and looked at the wall of vinyl records.

Music from The Beatles, Pink Floyd, The Clash, Grateful Dead, Nirvana, David Bowie, Radiohead, Arcade Fire, Joni Mitchell, St. Vincent, and Miles Davis were just some of the ones on display. The record playing through the speakers was Johnny Cash performing at the Folsom Prison.

A bartender wearing a plaid button-up and slightly baggy jeans with a white towel sticking out of his back pocket approached Cole and Ray. "What can I get you guys to drink?"

"What's the strongest beer you got?" Ray asked and smirked.

"The Dragon's Milk."

"I'll take that."

"And surprise me with your favorite wheat ale on tap," Cole said.

"Sure thing, can I see your guys' IDs real quick?"

"Absolutely." Ray showed his ID, and so did Cole; the bartender nodded. "I'll have those right up for you. Since you guys aren't from here, we do this thing where you can play vinyl records of your choosing for $15 for the whole bar to hear. At the moment, we have a queue of two other albums, but depending on how long you're staying, you might want to pick a record. I tell everyone, in case they're interested."

"Yeah, thanks. I'd actually like to play the Nirvana Unplugged album." Ray handed him $15.

"Excellent choice. I'll add it to the queue."

Cole stared at Ray with wide eyes.

"Why are you lookin' at me like that?" Ray asked.

"How long are we gonna stay here, man? I thought we just said we were going to do one beer?"

"Really? Back at the car, you told me you were down for whatever. If I wanted more, you said you'd be down to drive."

"I mean, it's fine, dude, I really don't mind. But back when we were talking in the car, you made it sound like we were only gonna have one drink."

"Sorry, I definitely felt that at the time, but this place is just way too cool to only have one beer and leave. Not only that, look at some of the women here. They're insanely beautiful."

Cole noticed that when they stepped inside, but Cole scanned the bar again and confirmed Ray's observation. The women at the establishment were indeed beautiful. Not wanting to be a creep, he kept to himself, and so did Ray.

"All right, man. We're on vacation. I'm down to follow your lead. Anything to help you bounce back."

"It's not me who needs to bounce back. I just need everything else in my life to bounce back." Ray said and chuckled.

Cole was relieved that Ray could see some humor during his rough period.

"I'll be a lot better if you think you can be a wingman and get me a girl's phone number from here," Ray said.

"If you wanna buy my drinks for the entire weekend, I might consider it," Cole said, and both of them shared a laugh.

The bartender dropped off their drinks. Cole and Ray sat and talked, and then they ordered another round. Cole still had a decent amount of his beer left, but Ray had a small tulip glass which he finished in no time. They received their second beer and then walked towards the pool table. There was already a game going on, but both of them didn't mind waiting until they finished up. While they stood at a tall table beside the pool game, both of them surveyed the bar.

"Wow, I don't know what's going on but this woman sittin' at the bar by herself in the black dress is hypnotically beautiful," Cole said.

"Not so fast, bro. I think she's with a guy," Ray said.

A man walking around the bar in a slim suit and intense blue eyes sat next to the woman Cole was checking out.

36

"Ah, it wasn't meant to be," Cole said. He gave one last glance at the woman and then at the guy in the suit. Cole's blood ran cold.

The man took a sip of a short cocktail glass while glaring at Cole.

Cole turned around and focused on the pool game in front of them. "Holy hell, did you see that guy?"

Ray casually turned around as well. "Yeah, he's still starin' at us."

"No, man, he was givin' me a stink eye for checking out his girlfriend."

"Don't worry about it; we can take him. He's a scrawny, squirrely fella."

"Yeah, but what if he's a psycho and has a knife or a gun on him?"

"Okay, it's not gonna get that crazy. Relax."

"You never know, dude. People are crazy. He might kill a man for her honor."

"All right, I tell ya what. If I turn around and he's still starin' at you, he's a murderer." Ray smirked and glanced over his shoulder. His lips curved down. "Shit, man, he's a murderer."

"You're joking!" Cole whispered. Panic rose in his chest.

"I wish I was. Take a peek yourself."

"Goddammit. He's probably one of those overprotective guys who snaps at everyone. I barely even glanced at her!"

Ray rolled his eyes. "Just take a glimpse behind me. Check out the wall of albums; you'll be able to see him."

Cole turned around and focused on the wall of records, but he glanced at the man in the suit, and he was still staring at Cole.

Cole spun back around. "Dammit. I just made eye contact with him again. Dude, I'm starting to think, after this beer, we need to get outta here."

"Come on, dude. It'll be okay. We at least have to stick around to listen to the vinyl I picked. I don't want that $15 to go to waste."

"I'll pay you $15 just so we can get the hell outta here."

"Just so you guys know, we're done playing for the night in case you wanted to get in next," one of the guys at the pool table said. He handed the pool cues to Ray and Cole.

"It's okay, man, just don't let your eyes wander and focus on the game. We haven't done anything wrong. There are plenty of people around too; he's not going to try anything crazy," Ray said.

Cole took a deep breath and nodded. Ray collected the pool balls into the triangular frame and set them near the end of the table.

"I'll let you break first," Ray said.

"Thanks." Cole lined up his shot and aimed the pool cue as if it was a precise surgery. Before he hit the white ball, he saw the man in the suit approaching him with a devilish grin.

Cole dropped the pool cue and backed away from the table.

"What's the matter, dude? Did you just see a ghost?" Ray said. He turned around, and the man in the suit had arrived.

"Gentlemen, how are we this fine evening?" The man in the suit had a raspy, jittery quality to his voice.

"Pretty good, man. How are you?" Ray said. "That's a nice suit you got there."

"Thank you." His face lit up. "I always want to dress to impress. You never know who you are going to meet and where you're going to meet them. And you also never know when you might have to strike up a deal."

"Lots of good deals can be made in bar bathrooms." Ray joked.

The man in the suit chuckled, and Cole smiled.

"Now, look, gentlemen. I don't have a deal to strike up with you, but I do believe it's important to make good first impressions, and I believe we may have gotten off on the wrong foot. I like to introduce myself. My name is Mickey."

"Hey Mickey, I'm Ray. This is my friend, Cole."

"It's a sincere pleasure to meet both of you." Mickey bowed his head and smiled. "All right, now that we have introductions out of the way, you're probably wondering why I came over here. Well, I was sitting with my friend here and noticed you were checking her out."

"I'm really sorry about that," Cole said, cutting off Mickey from talking.

Mickey snickered. "I really don't mind. I was trying to see if I knew you two from somewhere. This is one of my favorite bars in town, and I feel like I usually see the same familiar faces, you know, since this is a bit of a local watering hole. Although it does feature some guests from time to time, ya know, with its wall of records attraction. Anyway, I just wanted to give you a warm welcome to Wilton, Indiana, and also mention something else to you."

Ray and Cole exchanged a glance but nodded at Mickey.

"The friend I'm with, she's beautiful, yeah? Same with some of the other women here, you agree?"

"Sure," Ray said.

"Let me fill you in on a little secret. They're just waiting until the doors open up for a club nearby, and then they'll all be heading over. Would you two be interested in going? I help manage the place, and I'd be able to get you in no problem."

Ray and Cole looked at each other with a slight smirk.

"Maybe. We were actually gonna be heading out soon after my album played," Ray said.

"I understand. But this club is one of the best ones I've ever been to, and I've been to places in New York and LA. This place here is a hidden gem. It's whispered about through the east coast and west coast. It's unlike anything you've ever experienced."

"What's it doing here in the middle of nowhere?" Cole asked and chuckled.

"That, my friends, is a good question for the owner."

"But you can get us in, and we could be hanging out with all of these beautiful women here?" Ray asked.

"Absolutely. We'll all be going over there soon. This place is like a little pre-party before the real party begins. And I know these ladies rather well and believe me, they love meeting people from out of town. There's a lot to talk about. And with your southern accent, they'll go absolutely wild."

"What time will everyone be heading over there?"

"This place will clear out 10 minutes before 9:00 p.m. That way, everyone will have enough time to walk over there for the doors to open."

Ray looked at Cole and back at Mickey. "I'll tell ya what, if everyone leaves this place at the time you said, we'll check it out. We'll stop in and have a drink."

"Trust me, this place is a favorite amongst everyone. You're not going to want to leave after just one drink."

"We'll check it out for just one drink," Ray said and smiled.

"You're welcome to stay longer if you'd like. But watch, at 8:50, maybe even a few minutes before, people are going to leave to go to the club. You just walk out these doors, head left, and keep walking until you see the old train depot building. And you can't miss the neon blue sign either: Club Novus." Mickey winked at both of them and walked away from the pool table.

"What the hell was that all about?" Ray said.

"Your guess is as good as mine. That guy was weird. I have no idea what to think," Cole said.

"I'm serious though, if he's right about all the women leaving, I want to at least check it out. See where the night takes us, have a little pre-adventure before we go to Chicago."

"Hey, man, as long as you're smilin' and happy, that's all I care about."

Cole and Ray continued playing their game of pool, and after they finished, they put the pool cues against the wall.

"All right, my vinyl is going to play next. We got about 10 minutes to burn, wanna rip a dart out back?" Ray said.

39

"Absolutely," Cole said.

They went to the back of the bar and down a narrow hallway leading to a patio. Outside, there was a backyard and a fence around it. It was hot and muggy. Only one other person was outside smoking. Cole and Ray lit up a cigarette and stared at the vast field in front of them.

"Are we really about to go to this club?" Cole asked.

Ray shrugged. "I mean, I've never really gone to a legitimate club. Unless you count some of the bars in Nashville, but that doesn't really feel like a city club, you know what I mean? We may as well check it out and see what it's like. It'll be a story to take back home with us."

"All right, man, I trust your judgment."

Both of them continued smoking their cigarettes and looked out at the vast field in front of them. The other person outside finished smoking their cigarette and walked into the bar. Ray and Cole were the only ones left.

Cole looked more to the left and jumped. There was a bearded man behind the chain-link fence. It was hard to see his face with little light, but his face had some grime on it, and his beard and hair looked unwashed and disheveled.

"You two should go back home immediately," the stranger said with a deep gravelly voice.

"Is that guy talkin' to us?" Cole asked.

"Go. Back. Home. Leave this town while you still can."

"Let's go back inside. I'm basically done with this cig anyway." Ray put out his cigarette, and Cole did the same. They went back inside the bar.

"What do you think that guy was goin' on about?" Cole asked.

"I don't know. He was probably a homeless guy who's got mental health issues. I tried to tune him out as best as I could."

"He said to go back home. Like, back to Tennessee?" Cole said and chuckled at the absurdity.

"You're overthinking it. It was creepy, though, seein' that guy appear outta nowhere." Ray felt a chill run up his spine.

They went back inside the bar, and each ordered another beer. Ray's record came on, Kurt Cobain's rugged voice came through the speakers, and they played another game of pool. As the album came to an end, it was a few minutes before 8:50. Ray watched the time on his phone, and as soon as it struck 8:50, he looked up. People at the bar left in droves.

"Wow, that Mickey guy was right. There's still a decent crowd here, but there's plenty of open space now," Ray said.

Cole finished his beer. "All right, man, let's see what Club Novus is all about then, huh."

They brought their empty glasses to the bar and exited through the main doors. They looked to the left, down the stretch of road, a bridge going over the river and to the old train depot. A three-story brick building with a bright blue neon sign above the entrance.

CLUB NOVUS.

They approached the bouncer and were let inside. The last thing either of them remembered was getting through the main door.

The rest of the night blurred together like a fuzzy convoluted dream.

Ray's car was still in the public parking lot the following morning. It stayed there until it got towed over the weekend, and no one ever came to claim it.

1

Present Day...

I walked into the Wilton, Indiana police station, a quiet lobby with wood paneling that was probably last updated in the eighties. It reminded me of the station from Lockweed my father worked at.

Waiting in the lobby, a police officer walked by and scrunched his brow at me. He stared at the desk in the lobby and noticed no one was around.

"Hey, have you been helped at all?" he asked.

"Hi. I actually have a meeting with Sheriff Vernon, but I haven't seen anyone around yet," I said.

The officer waved me in. "C'mon back, I'll take you to her."

We strolled through a narrow hall and arrived at a door with a fogged glass window. He knocked, and a woman yelled, "Come on in!"

The officer opened the door for me, and I smiled at him as I passed him by.

"Thank you, Moe. Where the hell is Willie?" Sheriff Vernon said.

Moe shrugged.

"Whatever. Thanks for bringing the suit in." Sheriff Vernon gave me a smirk as Moe closed the door. "Mr. Wright, it's a pleasure to meet you. I just wish it were under better circumstances," she said.

I shook her hand. "Please. Call me Eddie. A pleasure to meet you as well, Ms. Vernon."

"Call me Martha." She beamed, and I sat down in the chair across from her desk.

I could tell that Martha was probably in her early forties based on her slight wrinkles. She had blonde hair running below her chin in a bob with a beige hat. She was tall and athletic, too.

"I want to thank you for coming in to help with this madness. The second I saw that these missing folks were from out of state, I knew I had to call in you fed fucks."

I chuckled. "You know, my dad was a detective in my small hometown. Never could I have imagined him swearing like that."

Martha seemed embarrassed. "Sorry, I just like to have a sense of humor about things. I understand it's not always welcome. But when you're dealing with bizarre murders, you have to do something to keep you sane. I guess dropping f-bombs and cracking jokes is therapeutic for me."

I nodded. "It's all right. I find it amusing."

"Glad you think so. You know this is the first time I've ever requested help from the FBI for something. It feels weird."

"There's nothing wrong with that at all. It's good you reached out. There's a lot to this case, and I want it to be as collaborative of an effort as possible."

"Great, because dealing with six people from three different states is..." Martha sighed. "Too much. So what do you have so far?"

I pulled open my laptop and started from the top of my notes. "John Allen and his friend Barry Howard were both 25. They were fraternity brothers for Sigma Nu, and both died from extreme blood loss. A tiny puncture was found in the ulnar and radial arteries. This suggests bizarre blood draining from the victims, which is believed to be the cause of death. Both of the punctures appeared to be from a hypodermic needle. John and Barry were from Ohio and studied at Ohio State. Both of them worked in finance but for two different companies in Cincinnati. They traveled west to Chicago six months ago to visit a fraternity friend named Peter. They never made it to Chicago. Neither of them seemed to have ever made any enemies, none that would have warranted a strange death as the one they suffered. There are more notes on them, but none that are very relevant to the other deaths.

"We take a look at Mitchell and Carol Boykins. Two victims from Virginia. Mitchell was 27, and Carol was 26. They married directly after college after graduating from UVA. Coincidentally they were traveling to Chicago as well. Planning for a fun weekend of visiting friends and touring the city. They never made it, and they also had the same puncture marks as the previous victims.

"And then the last two. Barry Smith and Cole Muir. 28 and 29. Childhood friends that grew up in Western Tennessee. They never went to Chicago, but they took a trip almost two years ago. They wanted to visit a buddy of theirs who lived in the city. He claims that they never arrived. Which makes a lot of sense because they were found on the edges of Wilton, Indiana. Dead on a farm. I can't think of a motive for their friend to kill them unless they lost a sports bet." I didn't like saying that joke but I knew it would make Martha grin, and she did.

"See? You have to laugh sometimes. Atta boy, Eddie. I thought you feds might all just be personality-less drones, but you seem like a personable guy."

"It's actually an important part of being in the FBI. Gotta be able to communicate. But did you notice where all of the people were traveling to?"

"Wow, so all of them were going to Chicago. Tell me something I don't know. C'mon, g-man."

"The highway, Indiana 9, is a good way to get to Chicago if you're avoiding tolls. I imagine they stopped in town for an early dinner or late lunch. Perhaps something caught their eye that made them stick around in town. Any insight on where young people would want to hang out?"

Martha rubbed her chin. "You've done your research on the town, I'm assuming, yes?"

"I have."

"Where do you think the kids hang out?"

"If I had to take a guess, I'd say it's Club Novus."

Martha nodded. "You're both right and wrong. People from outside the town, I think, go in and work there. It's invite-only, though, to get in. How they determine it, I have no idea. And I've questioned the bouncer that works there, and he told me he didn't see any of those victims that night. Then I finally got ahold of the owner, his name is Percy. He showed me around his club as a show of good faith, I guess. He told me I could comb through all I wanted. Sure enough, I did some checking with some guys here. Percy understood the protocols and procedures but couldn't find a damn thing that could be incriminating against him or his club."

"It's invite-only to get in there on a regular night?"

Martha nodded.

"So do you think John Allen and the rest of them could've gotten an invite if they were only in town for a brief period?"

"To be honest, I'm not sure. The club-goers, I think, are mostly from out of town. Friends of Percy from all over. No idea how invites get handed out around here, though."

"What about some of the other places? I'd like to perhaps check out other establishments in the meantime that people hang around at."

"Well, let's see..." Martha rubbed her chin. "There's Big Henry's, a bar where a lot of people like to go to catch whatever game is on. But also a popular spot for the Colts games and Pacers games. If you don't show up at least an hour early for Colts games, you probably won't get a spot. That's the place to watch football during the season. Same with Saturdays. They give a lot of love to Notre Dame football, but you can usually watch the Purdue or Hoosier games too. Hell, they have all three school logos made into a neon sign."

"Hmm. John Allen and Barry Howard were both college football fanatics. Do you know if they stopped off at Big Henry's?"

"They probably did, but no one can remember. The bartender can't, the servers can't, nor Clyde."

"Who's Clyde?"

Martha sighed. "Just the guy who's up there getting drunk every day. Retired. Stays as far away from his family as he possibly can."

"Ah. Did you talk to anyone else who may have been there?"

Martha shook her head. "I went in there one night to chat with some people who frequent the bar about the night when John and Barry went missing, but no one had any idea who I was talking about. But it had also been a while. Just like any establishment in a city off the highway, sometimes you just get random travelers passing by. There are so many of them, you forget what they look like, especially if you're going back a year."

"I see. Well, I guess I should start with Big Henry's. Unless there's another spot where the younger crowds like to hang out?"

"So like I said, sometimes they go to Big Henry's, and the other place that's popular with the bohemian crowd is The Painted Goose. I've also talked to the pub owner, Vivian Shelton, but she doesn't have any memory of those six patrons."

"Do both of these places serve food?"

"Yes, sir."

"I wonder if any of the victims went there for early lunch or early dinner. It would certainly make sense."

"Did you see the diner coming in from the highway? It looks like a stainless steel trailer with a green neon sign that says 'Buckwheat's' on the front with a clock?"

"Yes, I did notice it."

"It would make sense if they went there to eat, too. But again, I talked with the restaurant manager and the servers. Couldn't get any information out of them regarding the victims. But perhaps you're aware of special federal questions that I don't have access to that might lead to more." Martha's lips folded up into a smarmy v-shape.

I couldn't help but chuckle. "I'd still like to pay these places a visit. There's a lot of ground to cover here. I appreciate all of the work you've already done. I'm just going to try to blend in as if I'm just a traveler passing by who's taken a liking to this small town."

Martha pursed her brow. "Are you suggesting that you're going undercover?"

"Not exactly if someone asks me who I am or what I'm doing here. I'll just say I'm with the FBI. I will tell the truth. I'm hoping to gain the trust of some people here, and perhaps that leads to clues while investigating buildings in question. If I'm honest, I believe something happened here. Another bizarre note I've yet to mention is that we have no cell phone data on any of them. After talking with the phone company, it's like their phones were taken away and thrown in an incinerator as soon as they got here. The only thing that suggests something happened in one of the establishments in town is that their cars were all left fully packed and towed away. Which would suggest that they made it further than Buckwheat's'."

"I see. Well, if there's anything I can help you with, I'm happy to offer my services to you."

"Thank you. I'm also wondering where I should stay? I saw a beautiful three-story inn up the road from the downtown strip. Might I be able to stay there for an extended period? It seems like a charming place."

"Oh, yes, Laura and Christopher's. You'd be correct. It is a charming place. I think we could set you up with a room for however long you need."

"That would be wonderful. I'd like to settle for a bit before I go out tonight and see where the evening takes me." I stuffed my laptop back into my bag and stood up. "There's one other thing I wanted to ask you. Did you tell many people that an FBI special agent was coming to town?"

"Only my fellow officers, but I don't think they've said a word to anyone."

"Good, I just wanted to keep a low profile. I want to see where the night takes me as if I'm just an ordinary citizen."

"Where are you going to go?"

"First, I'm going to go to the inn, but once I get everything all unpacked, I'm going to go to Big Henry's first, I think."

"Let me go with you to Laura and Christopher's inn. I think if you told the front desk worker, Regina, that you were an FBI agent that was going to be staying for a while, I think she would pass out." Martha cracked up.

"Lead the way," I said, and we left her office into the tiny police station parking lot.

2

Martha and I stepped into our respective cars. I borrowed a black 2016 model Ford fusion. I didn't want anything too new because I felt it would only draw more attention to me. Even then, the cars I saw were mostly late-2000s models. Following Martha to the three-story brick building of the inn, I stepped onto the wide porch, and Martha opened the door for me.

Inside, the lobby had dark hardwood floors with a massive burgundy rug at the center. To the left was a long counter with a young woman working behind it.

Martha approached the front desk and said, "Regina, are your parents around?"

Regina shook her head.

"That's quite all right; perhaps you can help me with my friend here. He's a colleague that works for the FBI," Martha said.

Regina's eyes widened.

"It's okay. It's not a big deal. He's just doing some investigating into the bodies that were found here. You should meet him; he's a great guy. But I have to ask you for a favor. Please don't tell anyone you saw an FBI agent today. He doesn't really want people to know he's here, do you understand?"

Regina nodded.

"Regina, meet my friend, special agent Wright."

I shook her hand, and I said, "Please, you can just call me Eddie or Edward. Whichever you prefer."

"Nice to meet you, Eddie."

"So our friend Eddie here needs to stay for an extended period. He's wondering if you offer any monthly rates."

"We do, actually, but I'll talk to my parents about it, and they'll handle all of the finances for it. There are a few rooms available. Do you have any preferences, Eddie?"

"Put me on the top floor if that's possible. Especially one that might have a view of the downtown strip," I said with a smile.

"Absolutely. Just give me one moment." Regina turned around and stepped into an office door with a glass window where I could see her reach into a drawer and pull out a skeleton key with a wooden tag on it. Entering the lobby, she handed it to me. "Room 304. Top floor with a little view of the downtown. Best view, in my opinion."

"Wonderful, thank you so much, Regina."

"Please come to the front desk if you ever need anything. If I'm not here, my older sister Elizabeth will probably be working here. Or one of my parents."

"Marvelous. I look forward to meeting them."

I walked back out to my car, and Martha helped bring in my bags to my room. We went inside an elevator made of golden bronze with dark red carpeting on the elevator floor. With a sudden thought, I reached into my backpack and pulled out an ultraviolet light. Holding it up to the bottom of the elevator, I was hoping to see a stain of some kind, but there was nothing that would have suggested blood spatter.

Never mind.

"See anything?" Martha asked.

I shook my head.

Martha exhaled a single laugh through her nostrils and said, "You're really chomping at the bit to start investigating this, huh?"

"Something like that."

We arrived at the third floor, the elevator doors parted, and we walked through the small hallway. My steps seemed to echo, it felt like there weren't any other tenants in the other rooms, but I couldn't say for sure. If I had to guess, though, I was the only one on the third floor.

I unlocked the door to my room and stepped inside. As it swung open, I plopped my handbags on the ground to the left and right and slid off my backpack. Martha put my suitcases off to the side and wandered through the space. I had a queen size bed with dark blue comforters and sheets. A desk underneath the window and a tall standing lamp in the corner with a cushioned chair. It was a cozy room that felt more like a studio apartment than a hotel room. Although there was no stove or giant refrigerator, there was a mini-fridge in the corner.

"Well, thank you for helping me move in. I can take it all from here."

"Good luck tonight going to Big Henry's. Call or text me the moment you need any help of any kind. I like the idea of you going in without any attention around you, but I'm worried you might end up like the other six."

"Thank you. I'll be careful and reach out this second something seems off."

"Pleasure meeting you again, Eddie. Meet me tomorrow and let me know how it goes." Martha shook my hand and left the room. Her footsteps faded down the hall. I barely heard the elevator ding as it opened up its doors.

Unpacking my belongings, I carefully slid out a picture frame from my bag with more delicate items. I unwrapped the bubble covering and placed the frame on top of the dresser next to the desk. It contained the photo of Michael giving me bunny ears on top of the abandoned building in Melville.

Whenever I gazed at the photo for longer than a few seconds, my mind started to drift, and I would think about everything that transpired and led up to where I am today.

Oh Michael, oh Michael.

His camera was found. The photos were developed, I owned a copy of every picture he took that day. My dad kept the negatives at the police station.

I remember when the negatives were developed, everyone wondered if there would be another photo taken. Perhaps Michael snapped a picture of the perpetrator.

There was another photo taken.

It was right after we split up, no doubt. Unfortunately, it was nothing more than just a solid black image. There wasn't a sign of another figure or scratch or something bleeding light into the camera's iris. The photo was like looking into a black void.

Michael, I just hope you're doing okay out there. Wherever you are, whatever family adopted you and raised you, I'm sure you had a good life with this new family, and I just hope we can catch up again.

I never let myself think of negative thoughts in regards to Michael. He was never found, so he may still be living in a different part of the country.

No. He is living. He is on the opposite side, the West Coast, or hell, Alaska. Maybe he even got Canadian citizenship. Whatever the matter, Michael is prospering through life and enjoying all of its pleasures and blessings.

I looked away from the photo and continued unpacking, making myself at home. Once I finished up, I sat at the desk by the window and stared out at the small strip of town. It reminded me exactly like Lockweed, Michigan. A stretch of downtown buildings that had been there for almost a hundred years, with cute storefronts and locally-owned restaurants. The resemblance made me shudder.

The closest place to my left was Big Henry's, about a half-mile away. It was a rectangular box-like building that was only one floor. It didn't match the two or three-story brick buildings on the rest of the strip. It looked like it was built as an afterthought, perhaps a few decades after the town had already been in existence.

Across the street was the stainless steel trailer of a restaurant that reminded me of a vintage airstream. It was closer to me on the right.

It was 9:00 p.m. on Friday when I decided to go out to Big Henry's.

I didn't get in my car. It was an easy walk. Perhaps that was a bad idea, but I had my gun in my holster hidden by my flannel.

When I strolled towards the bar, I kept envisioning my expectations for the night.

The plan was to blend in like a fly on the wall. Or a chameleon adapting to their surroundings.

There were three large windows at the front of Big Henry's, a neon sign on each window. One of them had the Notre Dame logo, the N intersecting with the D lit up with green neon. The other was a vibrant blue Indianapolis Colts logo. The other was a Miller Lite logo, a combination of white, gold, and blue.

The front door was made of thick wood and heavier than I thought it would be. There was no host to greet me at the front. I felt like I had to choose a spot as soon as possible. There was a section at the end of the bar that was free. Three open seats, I took the one at the end, giving myself a two-chair gap with the person next to me. The pub was crowded, all of the tables were filled, and most of the bar had someone sitting, looking up at the massive flat screen. Paying attention to nothing else around them. A Cincinnati Reds game played on most TVs, peppered throughout the walls between framed Indiana sports memorabilia.

I took my seat, and a bartender approached me, setting a napkin and a glass of water on top of it. The bartender was a younger guy, no older than his early 30s.

"Hey, need a minute, or do you know what you're drinking?"

I smiled at him for a moment. "Could I get a non-alcoholic beer in a glass?"

"I'm happy to do that for you. What kind would you like?"

"I'll take the non-alcoholic Budweiser."

"Coming right up." The bartender spun around and opened up a fridge at the bottom, pulling out my drink. As he poured at an angle to get to the perfect layer of foam at the top, I surveyed the rest of the bar and thought about what food I should order.

A hamburger seemed to be what most of the patrons were eating. I might as well do the same.

Most of the customers were in their 30s. There was a group of six people who were probably in their 20s, howling with laughter. An old man with gray fuzz and a sweat-stained Colts hat three seats away from me spun around to glare at the young people cracking up. Some of them slapped on the table and shrieked with laughter. I tried to listen to their conversation, but they were all laughing so hard I couldn't begin to figure out what was so humorous. The old man grumbled expletives and fixed his attention back on the game.

"Those brats shou' be at The Painted Goose. 'The hell are they doin' here?" The old man said, but he didn't say it to anyone in particular. He was talking aloud, aiming his voice without direction.

"Excuse me, but what's at The Painted Goose?" I asked.

The old man glared at me. "Was I fuckin' talkin' to you?"

"Easy there, Clyde. I will kick you out if you talk to any guests like that again," the bartender said as he delivered my drink. "Don't worry about Clyde. He's just a bit rough around the edges sometimes."

"Sorry 'bout that," Clyde said to me and sighed. He took a drink of his massive 32 oz glass of beer which was almost gone. "I'm jus' tryin' t' watch the game. Tha's all. But no, we got dem' asses from The Painted Goose comin' up in here laughing about God knows what."

The bartender stood in front of me, but he scowled at Clyde the entire time. The bartender shook his head and faced me. "Did you want anything to eat? We'll be closing the grill in about an hour."

"A burger with a side of fries would be great. Thank you."

"I'll put that in for you." The bartender turned around and wrote down my order, and typed on the digital display behind the bar. I noticed there was a woman who must have been in her 30s delivering food orders to people. For the most part, the bar was relaxed. No one was in a rush; the patrons were enjoying the game. A couple sat on the opposite end staring at the screen. Three burly guys sat next to each other, watching the game. Two girls sat a few seats away from them, and then there was Clyde and me.

Not that I cared about the baseball game, I felt pressured to watch it to blend in a little more. But since the place wasn't bustling with people, the bartender came up to me and said, "I don't think I've seen you around here before. New in town?"

"Yes, I'm actually taking a bit of a vacation."

"Ah. So, where are you from?"

"Michigan. And you?"

"Born and raised here. My uncle owns the place."

I smiled. "So he must be Big Henry then?"

"The very same." The bartender chuckled. "Michigan is a beautiful state. Where are you from in Michigan?"

"Lockweed."

"Ah, I can't say I'm very familiar."

"I'm not familiar with Wilton."

"Just traveling through town then?"

"Not quite. I'll be staying here for a little while."

"Oh, well, welcome then. People don't know this place very well, but it's a bit of a diamond in the rough, I think. I mean, I've lived here my whole life and never felt the need to move. I'm kind of surprised you're staying."

"Why is that?"

"I feel like most people somehow find it on their GPS while traveling to either Indianapolis or Chicago or perhaps going the other way and going to Cincinnati or something. This seems like a popular stop for out of towners. People who want to grab a bite to eat or even others taking a day trip from around the area. How long do you think you'll be staying?"

"Not sure, probably however long my work takes."

"What's your work?"

I smirked, worried that my response might cause a dramatic reaction. I never knew how someone would respond whenever I told them what my career was.

"I actually work for the FBI."

The bartender's brow arched, and his jaw dropped. "Really? You might be the most interesting customer I've ever had then. I'm not in any trouble, am I?"

"Not at all." I lowered my voice and waved for him to come closer. He leaned his head in, and I said, "Just trying to get some information on the bodies that were found." The bartender pulled his head back and had a frown. I picked my voice back up to an average level and continued, "I'll be staying here for a little while, I imagine. So I thought I would see one of the more popular places in town on a Friday night."

"Wow. I feel like you're messing with me."

I reached into my interior flannel pocket and pulled out my FBI identification card.

"I guess you're not. Holy shit, I can't believe I'm talking to an FBI agent. So do you just ask everyone you meet if they know any information about what happened?"

"Only if the opportunity presents itself. And since we've become well acquainted, do you happen to know anything about the six disappearances?"

The bartender shook his head. "I wish I could help you."

"No worries. I'm just here blending in with the crowd, seeing if I can detect any cracks anywhere. You know?"

The bartender nodded. Then the server came up to my side and delivered my plate while saying, "Here's your burger and fries. Enjoy!"

"Thank you," I said as the server left. I turned my attention back to the bartender. "Anyway, my name is Edward. Nice to meet you...?"

"Joshua. Nice to meet you, too."

We shook hands before I grabbed ketchup and mustard and drizzled it over my burger. I took a chomp. Cooked to perfection.

"Well, if you need anything else, Edward, I'll be around."

"Thanks, Joshua."

I sat at the bar, surveying everyone around me. Nothing seemed too out of the ordinary. All of the young people who were dying with laughter earlier left their table. Some of the other people departed as well. The bar was still the same crowd from when I came in. I ordered a second non-alcoholic beer and continued people watching, occasionally looking up at the Cincinnati Reds game, which was almost over.

Since nothing exciting was happening, I decided to pay my tab and walk around town. *Perhaps I might see something.*

I wandered further into the downtown area. All of the shops were closed. I saw a clothing store, a tailor, a shoe cobbler, a coffee shop, a pharmacy, sandwich shop, a general store, a bank, and a barbershop. They were all closed and had no lights on. There was also a city hall building and a firehouse a block away with an old Victorian house. The only illumination came from the pale moon above and the amber glow from the ornate lamp posts, black pillars attracting many moths. There was a wooden bridge off the main road that went over a small river. The water didn't rush, but it casually flowed from left to right, a calming white noise. Before the bridge, there was a field with a paved parking lot. There were seven cars sitting still, but the lot could probably fit thirty spots.

Someone was smoking in one of the cars. They were completely obscured in the shadows, but I could see a human figure holding a cigarette as they leaned up against a 2013 Silverado truck. They were about 30 yards away, and it seemed like they were staring at me. I must have been staring at them for a good 20 seconds. Both of us were frozen.

Something in my gut told me this wasn't right. Something was off. I'm not sure who that was or why they were there, but they were locking eyes with me. Perhaps it was the disappearances that were gnawing at my subconscious. I tried to reason with my body that everything was okay, but nevertheless, I shivered.

The figure finished their cigarette and tossed it on the ground, but they hadn't shifted their focus yet.

How long will this staring contest go on for?

I was the first to look left and noticed the two-story brick structure broken off from the downtown string of buildings. It had a beautifully painted mural that read, "The Painted Goose." It was painted with puffy lettering, and at the end was a goose with a paisley pattern with a rainbow of colors. The building was up-lit by white LED lights.

Four people stood outside in a circle in front of the building, having a cigarette. They were talking, but too far away for me to hear. Occasionally they laughed.

I returned my focus to the shadowy figure leaning up against the back of a truck, but they were gone. Part of me thought I shouldn't have let them out of my sight. But I felt like I may have dodged a bullet. Perhaps our staring contest would have only made things worse.

Further down the main road, I saw a glowing blue sign that must have been Club Novus. They had their own parking lot packed with cars, but no one was outside, not even to have a smoke. I couldn't tell what the sign said, but I knew it had to be the nightclub.

My eyes focused back on the parking lot, and I wondered about investigating the shadowy figure that was staring at me. Although, it felt like it would be looking for trouble. *Perhaps it would be best if I just went back to my room for the rest of the night.*

Strolling through the empty and sleeping downtown strip, I could see Big Henry's, which only had a few cars in their parking lot. But I stopped for a moment.

I heard footsteps echoing to a stop from behind.

I spun around, and the shadowy figure that was leaning up against the truck's bed was standing in the middle of the downtown strip. As soon as we made eye contact, he went down an alley.

Now I had a reason to investigate.

I sent Martha a text message: I'm walking around the town by myself at night, and I think someone is following me.

I thought she might call me right away or reply back in a second, so I waited, but my curiosity got the better of me. Backtracking again, I came up to the mouth of the alley, but I stopped myself.

I should really investigate, after all, what if this is the killer?

But what if I'm being lured into a trap?

If I do go in, and if anything happens to me, they're going to send the cavalry. Surely the criminals would know that.

Or would they? No one really knows I'm here right now. They have no idea that an FBI agent is in their town.

What if this person had taken Michael?

I stepped forward into the dark alley. Only one old amber light flickered eight feet above my head. The odor of sour garbage lingered in the air. With each tiptoe, the echo bounced between the two buildings.

"Hello? Is anyone in here?" I asked.

I stood still with my ears perked.

"You shouldn't have come here," a smooth broadcast-like voice replied. I couldn't tell where it was coming from exactly, but it came further in the alley.

"Just so you're aware, I'm a federal agent. I am armed. I'm only investigating the disappearances that happened here."

I was desperate to hear any response. Hopefully, they would be able to offer some help, but I didn't see that happening.

"I'm going to walk to the end of the alley and back. I would really like to speak with you if I could. You're not in any trouble, at least that I'm aware of." I crept through the alley to the very back, constantly searching for some clue where this person could be. I had a sneaking suspicion he was watching me, wherever he was. Reaching the end of the alley, it was just a field with no cars or people around. Going back through the passage, I didn't see anything out of the ordinary.

Damn.

But the trip wasn't a total loss. I at least had a story to share with Martha when I met with her the next day.

"I didn't mean any trouble. Sorry if I ruined your evening. Have a good night," I said as I walked out. My exit was slow, in case I heard a reply, but there was nothing.

}

Going back to the inn down the street, I walked into the lobby and heard the receptionist say, "Stop, someone's here."

When I fully opened the door, I expected to see someone else in the lobby, but there was no one. Only the receptionist at the desk.

She smiled at me and waved. "Good evening, sir. How are you?" the receptionist asked. She looked a lot like Regina, except she was taller and just a little bit older.

"I'm good. Thank you. How are you? Is everything all right?"

"Of course. Do you need help with anything?"

"No, I already have a room. Sorry, you weren't in the middle of a call or anything, were you? I don't mean to take up your time."

"No, not at all." Her eyes were wide, and she had a broad smile. I got the sense that she was hiding something from me. "What's your name, if you don't mind me asking?"

"Edward Wright. Are you sure I'm not interrupting anything? I could have sworn I heard someone talking when I walked in."

"Nope. It's just me." She let out a laugh. "So wait, are you the special guest?"

"What do you mean by that?" I took a step closer to the counter.

"Regina, my younger sister who was working here earlier today, told me that there was someone from the FBI staying with us, and I think she said it was Edward."

I smiled. "Yes, that would be me."

"Oh my God! I feel so cool right now talking to an FBI agent. This is so wild. What's it like? I bet you have some crazy stories, huh?"

I chuckled. "Nothing too crazy. It's probably a lot more boring than you'd expect. It's not all that glamorous and action-packed like the TV shows or movies make it out to be."

"I also half expected you to have no personality and talk like a robot, but you seem pretty personable."

Her smile was infectious. I couldn't help my lips from curling up. "The FBI likes people who can communicate, I guess. So what's your name? Do you usually work evenings?"

She nodded. "I do. My name is Elizabeth."

"I bet you see some interesting characters that come in during the night shift?" I said.

"This is actually a recent change for me. *Blech.* I used to do the day shift, which I much prefer, but since I'm older and have more experience, my parents wanted me to work nights now. Which is dumb because my mom or dad used to do it but now, since Regina is old enough to work here and is no longer in school, I have to be here. But, no, I don't really see too many people, to be honest."

"That must be nice then, a relaxing shift free of any stress?"

Elizabeth took a deep inhale and let out a sigh. "Yeah, that part is nice, but it's tough when all of your friends want to hang out while you're at work."

"Where do you and your friends like to hang out?"

"Why? You wanna bust them for something?"

I smirked. "No, I'm just curious."

"I'm teasin' ya anyway. We mostly go to The Painted Goose. But sometimes we go out of town whenever we don't want to see everyone we know, ya know? It's a small town, and people can be annoying sometimes."

"Yeah, I understand the desire to explore other areas." I dreaded the idea of having to comb through other small-town nightlife scenes to see if the victims may have gone somewhere else after all. *But then, their cars were all left here.*

Elizabeth tilted her head. "Do you actually have any interest in going to bars? Or is it all part of the investigation? Aren't the FBI supposed to be super straight-laced and void of any fun?"

I laughed. "I can still go out and have a life outside of this. And yes, I do enjoy frequenting bars. But it's part of the investigation and also immersing myself in the environment. And then, deep down, I actually enjoy sitting in a dive bar, alone with my thoughts."

Elizabeth nodded. "How old are you? It always seems like the FBI is such an adult job. Like I'd guess you were 45, but based on how you're dressed and lack of wrinkles, I'd say you were twenty-five."

I laughed again. "I'm actually thirty. But you say that the place to go is The Painted Goose?"

"I think so. There's also Big Henry's if you're into being miserable."

"I actually just came from there."

"Horrible, wasn't it?"

"It wasn't so bad."

"You didn't stay until close. Couldn't have been that much fun."

"The Painted Goose is that much better, huh?"

"Of course. It's the only tolerable place around, if I'm being honest."

"Have you ever been to Club Novus?"

Elizabeth pursed her brow. "No. Even if I did get an invite, I probably wouldn't go. The idea of a nightclub in this town is stupid. Besides, dance clubs blow."

"You never got an invite? But you live here? Shouldn't you be allowed to come and go as you please?"

"Yeah, I don't know. They're very selective about who they let in. It's bizarre. Am I salty about it? Maybe. And maybe that's why I hate the idea of nightclubs. But my friend got an invite once, I think, but she never went."

"So local people can get invites?"

Elizabeth shrugged. "I don't know, man. I think it's just my friend group."

"What's your friend's name that got an invite?"

"Annabelle. You're not going to talk to her or anything, are you?"

"Uh, I don't know. Should I?"

"I just ask because I think she would freak out if an FBI agent talked to her. Also, she hates cops."

"But I'm not really a cop."

Elizabeth narrowed her eyes at me. "Yeah, but you really are, though. I guess you're just a fancy cop."

I snickered. "Fair. Well, if you don't mind asking her how she got an invite, I'd really appreciate that."

"Trying to go nightclubbing?"

"I suppose."

"I'll ask her for you. I'll see what she says."

"Thanks. I really do appreciate that. I have one more question, and then I'll let you get back to it. But, what would happen, do you think, if I tried to go into Club Novus right now? Would they turn me away?"

"Yes, they would say something. 'This is for club members only.' And then the big buff bouncer dude wouldn't let you in."

"I see. Well, thank you for all the information you've given me. Have a good night, Elizabeth. It was a pleasure chatting with you."

"Anytime, Edward. Sleep tight." She waved as I went up to the elevator, pressed the button, and stepped inside.

As soon as the door closed, I could've sworn I heard Elizabeth angrily whisper, "Shut up!" to someone or something.

It made my skin tingle.

I should've asked her about the man who followed me.

Perhaps it was best I didn't. I checked my phone and saw that I had a message from Martha: *I think I know who that is. He's harmless. Just an odd bird. I'll tell you about him tomorrow. Don't worry. Call it an early night.*

Huh, strange, I thought. I slid my phone back in my pocket and went into my room. As I got ready for bed, I checked the window and looked out onto the town. I couldn't believe how colorful it was at nighttime. There was a mix of neon from Big Henry's, Buckwheat's, and even Club Novus in the back and the orange glow from all the street lamps. There was hardly any activity. One car drove south through the strip. A couple of people walked into their vehicles at Big Henry's. Buckwheat's also had a few cars in their lot. I imagined they'd have a little bit of a bar rush soon once the watering holes stopped serving. I decided to stay up and watch to see what would happen when places closed. Once the lights switched off, a few people got in their cars at Big Henry's and drove outside the town. I saw a handful of people from The Painted Goose walk to Buckwheat's.

While nothing appeared out of the ordinary, there was one thing I found strange. Looking out the window with my binoculars, not a single car left the lot at Club Novus. It was still packed after two a.m.

I waited another half hour before going to bed to see if there was any movement. There was none. The lot was still full.

I lay down on my bed, and it took me a while to fall asleep. I kept thinking about the man who followed me, and what if he came into the lobby and caused trouble? What if someone broke into my room?

Eventually, I would fall asleep after tossing and turning for a couple of hours. The bed, though, was quite comfortable.

As I lay there sleeping, I woke up at one point to the sound of footsteps and two people giggling. My heart rattled as I sat up in my bed and listened carefully. The footsteps and laughter grew louder. If I had to guess, there were two people. One male and one female based on the tones. Goosebumps popped up all over my body as I heard them stop and fumble with their belongings. Someone shoved a key into a lock, and I thought it was my door, but it was the door across the hallway. I jumped out of bed and ran up to the peephole, but I was too late. The couple had already gone inside their room.

I took a deep breath, trying to get my heart rate to settle back down.

No need to be frightened, Eddie. Other people are staying in the room across from you. That's perfectly normal. Now it's time to crawl back into bed.

I trudged back to the mattress and plopped back down. Surprisingly, I fell asleep rather quickly.

As I was lying in bed, I felt a drop of a slimy liquid on my forehead. I wiped off the goo and opened my eyes, instantly becoming paralyzed.

A woman's head with entirely white eyes floated above me and grinned. With a close look at her curly hair, I noticed it was scaly and shifting around in place. There were a couple of slithers and hisses that came from her hair. Her mouth was cracked open as saliva kept oozing down on my head. I tried to run and scream, but I had no control of my body.

A serpent-like tongue dangled out of her mouth and fell down like a spider sliding down a web. The tongue went in my mouth and wrapped around my own tongue, gripping it like a snake. The pain was so sharp I screamed and woke up.

My heart was racing. I was in the middle of a cold sweat.

Did I really just yell?

I was sitting up in my bed, and I took a deep breath. It was early morning. The sun had just come in through the window, rising from the east with a gentle glow. Scanning my room, there was nothing out of the ordinary. Everything was quiet. I got off the mattress and looked out the window to see a thin layer of fog hover over the ground on the street of Wilton, Indiana. The sun gave the world a blue and orange coating. I opened up my window and listened to a few birds chirping merrily. I got lost in the moment, gazing out into the town. Nothing unusual was happening. Just as quiet and empty as it was late last night. The Club Novus parking lot was also empty. Strange.

It's not like me to remember my dreams or have such a vivid one. I can't remember the last time I had a nightmare.

I could have sat by the window and stared out onto the town for the rest of the morning, but I knew it would be best to start my day. I messaged Martha to meet me at Buckwheat's diner whenever she was ready.

4

When I went downstairs into the lobby, I saw a man behind the reception counter I had not met. He was tall, handsome, and had some muscle to him. It wouldn't surprise me if he played football in high school as a quarterback.

"Good morning," he greeted me with a warm smile.

"Good morning." I nodded. The whole lobby had the aroma of an upscale cafe. Combining the magical scent of baked goods and coffee. I was entranced by it. "Excuse me, but do you serve coffee here?"

The man smirked and pointed at the two black coffee carafes to his right. There was a plate of chocolate chip cookies next to it. "Please, help yourself."

I laughed. "You know what, I really shouldn't. I'm supposed to go to Buckwheat's, and I was just going to drink their coffee there."

"But I think you would be making a mistake. We are known for some of the best coffee in town. We use our lobby as a little bit of a coffee shop with chairs and couches. Guests drink for free, though."

"I suppose I'll have a cup." I smiled and walked over to the carafe and poured myself a cup in a burgundy mug. "Thank you very much."

"Please, help yourself to a cookie. I baked them myself."

"Don't mind if I do." I grabbed a cookie and took a bite. I couldn't believe how soft and warm it was. The chocolate was still gooey, and the mixture of salt and butter seemed perfect. "Wow. This is amazing."

"Thank you. I'm glad you like them. How was your stay with us last night?"

"It was okay."

The receptionist scrunched his brow and frowned.

"No, I mean that the bed and everything was great. I just had a nightmare last night. That's all."

"I'm sorry to hear about that. My name is Christopher, by the way. I own the inn with my wife, Laura."

"I'm Edward. I'm planning on staying here for a little while if that's okay? I didn't have a chance to talk with you or Laura, but I did talk with Regina and Elizabeth."

"Yes, that's completely fine. They told us about meeting you. We're glad to have you here, and you can stay as long as you need."

"I appreciate that, Christopher. Hey, I have a question for you. Do you know much about the other business owners here in town? Do all of you know each other for the most part?"

"Why sure, I know the majority of the people pretty well. We all want our businesses to succeed. There's no real competition because everyone seems to be unique in their own way, so they have their special base for the most part. But yeah, I rub shoulders with most of them."

I nodded and took a sip of the coffee. The taste was so good I almost forgot my follow-up question. It was rich, smooth, and full of flavor, like drinking a cup of dark chocolate. "Wow. This coffee is outer-worldly. Thank you."

"Glad you're enjoying it."

"So when you say that you know most of the business owners, who would you say you're not very familiar with?"

Christopher rubbed his chin. "It's a pretty small town. So even if you don't own a business, you probably know a decent amount of the people to begin with if you live here. But I'd say the owner of The Painted Goose is pretty reserved. I don't know too much about her. Same with the owner of the nightclub up the road. Don't know too much about him either."

"If you saw each other walking on the street, would you say hello?"

"Probably not, no."

"Do you know their names?"

"The owner of the nightclub? No. I don't know him. But I think Vivian runs The Painted Goose. Gosh, I can't remember her last name. I don't know. I never really go in there. I'm not much of a drinker. Plus, my daughter goes and hangs out in there sometimes. I don't want to go to one of her favorite places, you know what I mean?"

"You're talking about Elizabeth?"

"Yes."

I took another drink of coffee. I wanted nothing more than to sit down in the cozy lobby near the fireplace and enjoy the rest of it along with the cookie. It would be nice to read the news as well. Even though I'd do that for my own personal enjoyment, it might be helpful to read the local news.

"Is there a local newspaper I can read?" I asked.

"Do you want a physical paper, or would you rather read it on your phone?" Christopher said.

"I have options?"

Christopher nodded.

"I'll take the website, I guess."

Christopher smiled. "The Wilton Observer."

"Thank you, I'm going to sit down over here, enjoy the rest of this amazing coffee and cookie, and read some of the latest happenings in the town."

"Sounds good. I'm here if you need anything."

I walked to the couches and chairs and sat in the cushioned seat up against the window. There was a little table for me to put the coffee and cookie on. Pulling out my phone, I went to the Wilton Observer website and scrolled through some of the articles.

The main headline made me scrunch my brow. I clicked on the article immediately.

"Blood Donations Stolen from Saint Mary's Hospital." With a thumbnail of an empty hospital hallway.

It's hard to imagine the bizarre scenario. You're told to go to the blood bank and get out a bag that would help save someone's life, and there's nothing in there. You go back and tell your supervisor that the blood is gone, that it's empty. The supervisor doesn't believe you and goes to the exact same place you just looked. They're just as dumbfounded.

That's what happened last night at St. Mary's hospital. They've reported a large amount of blood has gone missing.

No one seems to have any indication of where it may have gone off to. Misplacement is possible, but they've been searching through the facility all night without any clues. Fortunately, there's another blood supply, but the area where most of it is stored was completely empty.

The situation is currently under investigation by local authorities.

I went back to the main homepage of the Wilton Observer and scrolled through the rest of the articles. Everything else was tame and confined. Information on the local elections, an article about the local barbershop grooming pets as a limited trial run as they expand their family business into new territory. There was also information about the after-school programs the library was offering in the autumn.

I read through the other articles as I finished enjoying my cup of coffee. In the back of my head, I fantasized about being another member of the Wilton community. It reminded me of my own hometown so much that, in a way, I felt like I was back home. It was a much different change of pace compared to working out of the FBI offices in

Chicago. After I finished drinking my cup of coffee and polished off the cookie, I brought my mug up to the counter to a tray that read "used mugs."

"Thank you for the coffee and cookie again," I said.

"Thank you. It's a pleasure meeting you, Edward."

"Likewise." I waved and exited the inn and walked across the street down a few blocks until I arrived in front of Buckwheat's stainless steel diner palace. Stepping inside, a counter with red spinning stools divided the kitchen and staff from the rest of the restaurant. There were a dozen rows of maroon booths and then a large circular maroon booth in the corner. There were only four other people in the restaurant as it was still early in the morning.

A server walked up to me. She must've been in her forties with her hair in a ponytail. "Sit wherever you'd like, hun," she greeted me with a smile.

I walked to the left side corner up to the booth against the window and sat down.

"Will it just be you for today?" she asked.

"No, I'm expecting another person to join me. So I'll take two place settings," I said.

"You got it." The waitress walked away, and I looked out the window. I checked my phone for any messages, and I received a text from Martha telling me that she was on her way.

"Can I get you anything to drink while you wait for your friend?" the server asked me.

"Yeah, I'll just have a coffee. Thank you."

The server nodded and stepped away. I pulled out my phone again to read some more from the Wilton Observer, but the bell jingled from the restaurant's front door, and it was Martha dressed in her khaki uniform. She scanned the restaurant from right to left, and she smiled as soon as her eyes landed on me.

"How are we doing today, g-man?" Martha asked as she slid inside the booth to join me.

"I had one of the best cups of coffee I've ever had at the inn. And the cookie was amazing, too," I said.

Martha smirked. "Yes, that Christopher knows how to bake a cookie. That's for sure. The coffee here is pretty good, too. I can't remember what it's like at the inn, but I remember it being good."

The server came back and delivered my mug of coffee. "Good morning, Sheriff Martha! What can I get you?"

"Good morning, Daisy. I'll just have a cup of coffee for now. Thank you."

Daisy walked away.

"So, I'm dying to know, who was that shadowy figure that was following me last night?" I asked.

"Wow, we're diving straight into it already. You're not going to ask me about how my morning has been so far?"

The corner of my lip curled up. "How was your morning, Martha?"

"I have two dogs, right? For whatever reason, when one starts barking, the other starts barking like crazy. And unfortunately, the one dog I have is getting a little older. Sometimes I think he sees something out of the corner of his eye and just starts going bonkers. Even though nothing is there. So, anyway, Jupiter started going haywire, and then Saturn joined in, and it was just a bunch of barking that, of course, woke me up. But this sort of thing doesn't happen often. It's always at night time that Jupiter thinks he sees something that isn't there, and then I have to settle down. But that early in the morning? No, thank you. Rough way to start the day, I tell ya."

"Jupiter and Saturn? What kind of dogs are they?"

"Pekingese. Both of them."

"Were you going for a planetary theme or a Roman mythology theme?"

"That's what they were named when I got them from the shelter. I'm not the most creative type, so I just went with the name. My daughter works at a dog shelter, and she thought they were the most adorable dogs she had ever seen. You know those breeds don't come around shelters very often, and they were so nice, and my daughter wanted to take care of 'em, but she has her hands full of dogs at home, so she gave them to me."

"They sound adorable. I'd love to see some pictures."

"I can show you pictures later. You want to know about the person who was following you around last night. Tell me everything that happened, and I think it'll add up and sound familiar."

I explained every detail with the shadowy figure that followed me. While talking, Martha had her coffee delivered, and I took a sip of mine. It was much better than I expected. Like a brew from an independent coffee house, and not to the typical flat, stale diner coffee I was used to.

When I finished, Martha leaned a little closer towards me and lowered her voice. "So, there's this gentleman named Charles Green who lives in the area. I've received a few calls before to look into a situation where he was always the culprit. I don't know why, but he likes to mess with people. He likes to follow them around and then scare them a little bit. He's a strange bird, that's for sure, but he's never hurt anyone.

"Charles just does exactly what he did to you last night to other people. It doesn't really happen as much as it used to, but he still does it to an out-of-towner from time to time. Usually, everyone in the neighborhood already knows him, so they just tell him to get lost.

"Who knows, if you're walking around town at night again and you think he's following you, just say, 'Hey, Charles, I want to talk to you for a second.' Once he knows that you know his name, it's like you just disarmed him. He'll apologize and go home. Which is why he doesn't really do it anymore. Everyone knows him."

"That is a little strange. Does he go to therapy, or has he received any help?"

"Not that I'm aware of. Then again, his family didn't really have a lot of money growing up, so I don't think they ever went to a doctor or a therapist for him. Although when I talk to the folks that went to high school with Charles, they all say that Charles was a little weird, but he was harmless and actually a nice fella to his classmates. His parents both tragically passed away, though, during his high school years. He's an only child too, so it's gotta be depressing that his whole family is gone, and he has no one. I think Charles wants to be social, but he just doesn't know how to express his loneliness and make friends."

"Wow. I feel bad for the guy. How sure are you that it was him that was following me last night?"

Martha sighed. "I would say 100%, but I don't like to talk in absolutes. So I'm going to say 99%."

"Understand. Don't you think it's a little strange that Charles said to me, that I shouldn't have come?"

Martha shook her head. "He likes to creep people out by saying stuff like that. So if he recognized that you were an out-of-towner, he just wanted to mess with you. But really, I think it's a cry for friendship. He wants to make friends with people but doesn't really know the traditional route to make friends. Does that make sense?"

"Sure. Do you know what year he graduated high school?"

Martha contemplated for a moment. "He's older than me, but not by too much. I think he graduated in 1990 from Wilton High."

"Got it. Also, did you happen to see the report that came out in the Wilton Observer about the missing blood?"

Martha blinked and grinned from ear to ear. "Look at you, reading the Wilton Observer! I have to say I'm pretty impressed with ya, g-man."

"So, did you see that article then?"

Martha shook her head. "I didn't have time to look at the local news yet today. I mean, Christ, my shift doesn't technically start until 9:00. I'm visiting you out of the goodness of my heart; consider yourself lucky." Martha smirked.

"Well, some blood went missing at the Saint Mary's hospital. More details need to come in, but initially, I wonder if there is any relation between the deaths and missing blood. I'm beginning to think that someone has an obsession."

"They're making human black pudding or something?" Martha asked in a hushed voice.

I shrugged. "It's all speculation at this point."

"No, but don't you guys notice patterns with obsessions? Like if someone hurts animals as a kid, they're likely to become a serial killer, right? Don't you have something if you suspect someone is a blood collector? Why would they just collect blood and not like body parts?"

"Again, it's all speculation. Any guess you have is as good a guess as mine."

"Yeah, but what are you thinking, Eddie? You must have an opinion or thought on why?"

I drew in a deep breath. "Honestly, I don't know. If I had to guess, I'm thinking someone might be doing a bizarre experiment, or they're running some underground medical practice, and they need as much as possible to serve... Whoever it is they're serving."

"So you don't think it's a vampire?" Martha's lip curled.

"I guess the thought crossed my mind, but I don't entertain the supernatural. Perhaps it could be someone pretending to be a vampire. That's certainly plausible. But I want to focus on the information and evidence. I'm curious about what happened at the hospital, and I think I'll inquire further about what's happening over there. Do you have any contacts at St. Mary's?"

"That's just where any emergencies go. I can't say I know any of the security staff. Sorry."

"That's all right. I think I can just make a few phone calls over there and perhaps get a meeting with someone."

The server came up to our table and asked, "Do you know what ya want? I can give you a few more minutes if you need."

"Edward, are you a pancakes guy?"

"I'm partial to waffles, but I do enjoy pancakes."

"Terrific. You should get the waffles or pancakes here. They're to die for."

"Well, I guess that settles my order. I'll just do plain waffles." I smiled at the server, and she wrote down my order in her little notebook. Then Martha ordered an omelet, and the server bounced away to another table.

"So, is that your plan for the day? Look into the hospital now?"

"I'll definitely place a phone call. But my plan was to go into some of the shops around town and go to the library."

"What's in the library?"

"Yearbooks."

"High school yearbooks?"

"Exactly."

Only five minutes after putting in our order, the food came out to our table. Martha and I enjoyed our breakfast, and she was right; something about the waffle really impressed me. It was rich in flavor and did not need butter. Maple syrup was the perfect complement to the soft spongy waffle.

5

After we finished breakfast, Martha said she was going to the police station, and she was going to be there the rest of the day if I needed her. She offered to accompany me to the library, but I told her that wasn't necessary. I also let her know that I would be going to The Painted Goose to see what that bar was like later.

The library was a block away from the main downtown strip with all the businesses. It was Saturday morning, and some people were walking around, which I found jarring after becoming so accustomed to seeing the street empty most of the time at night. The walk was pleasant, as the summer weather wasn't as humid as it usually was, and the breeze was refreshing coming from the river.

The library was a three-story mansion that was built in the early 1900s or late 1800s. I admired the Victorian aesthetic with the turret on the upper right corner. In a way, it looked like a red brick castle, with a massive porch and a gazebo attached to it. There was a large sign out front that read: Wilton Public Library.

I walked inside the building and to my immediate left was a counter with a young man working behind a computer monitor. Straight ahead, there was a staircase and an elevator next to it. I approached the desk before exploring or doing anything else.

"Hello, how are you?" I greeted the worker with a polite smile.

"Hey, I'm good. Can I help you with anything?"

"Yes, I was wondering if the library carried any copies of old Wilton High School yearbooks?"

"How far are you looking back?"

"Let's start with 1986 through 1994, please."

"Sure, I can grab that for you. Do you have a library card?"

Perhaps I should have had Martha come along. "Actually, I don't have a library card, and nor do I live here. I'm actually conducting an investigation." I pulled out my FBI badge and placed it on the counter, the cover was lifted, and he could see my name and identification.

The young man's eyes widened.

"Don't worry, you're not in any trouble. I'm just learning more about the town's history."

"Yeah, sure. Uh. Let me go get my manager real quick. I'm new here, and I'm not sure how to fill out the checkout form without the library card." He spun around and went inside a room behind him. I had a feeling he was relieved to give the situation to someone else.

As I waited, I drifted into the living room, where bookshelves lined the walls and a few tables underneath windows, perfect for studying or reading.

A woman came from the office behind the counter and said, "Can I help you, sir?"

I turned around and smiled. "Hello, my name is Edward Wright. I was wondering if I could take a look at some older high school yearbooks here in the library."

"Yes, my associate told me about everything. May I see your identification card, please?" Her voice was gentle and polite. She wore large wireframe glasses and had a name tag that said Jeanette with a few pins on her lanyard: books, jokes, and equality flags.

I handed her my badge and identification. She clicked a few buttons on her computer's mouse and then stared at the screen and typed out some other information.

"Okay, you're all set to check out whatever you need to." Jeanette smiled at me. "You know, this is the first time we ever had someone from the FBI here."

"Really? That's a good thing."

"We've had other government agencies come through here and check things out. It's rare, but it happens. Do you mind if I ask why you'd like to see the yearbooks? I totally understand if it has to be kept private. I'm just wondering if I might be able to provide more information to you."

"Sure. Did you grow up in Wilton, Indiana?"

She nodded. "Born and raised. It was my dream to always work here. My mom used to volunteer, and then I would spend a lot of my childhood in these rooms. I did go away to University when I was younger. It was the first time I ever moved away. It was fun, but honestly, I missed it being here."

"Where did you go to school?"

"I went to the University of Chicago. I always wanted to experience the big city, and once I did, I knew it wasn't for me. I missed the serenity of Wilton. But to be honest, those people they found on the farms around here really freaked me out."

My smile vanished. "Yeah, that's understandable. I know how much a traumatic event like that can shake up a small town." Usually, I could keep the conversation going, and I wanted to ask her more questions about her life, but I got choked up. An emotional snake wrapped its strong, lengthy body around my throat.

Jeanette could sense the pause and the awkward beats that passed by. "Well, I'll go get the yearbooks for you. 1986 through 1994?"

I nodded. My lip quivered, and my throat grew syrupy, but I managed to say, "Wait, I have one other question for you. What year did you graduate from Wilton High?"

"1994."

"When you were there, do you remember a classmate in your school named Charles Green?"

Jeanette frowned. "Kind of. We did go to school together, but I think he was older. Either two years or three years older than me. I never really knew him, but I knew of him."

"What did you know of him? Anything and everything if you don't mind?"

"Gosh. It's hard to say. You know, we have such a small town here, but I didn't really know him at school. I think he was a quiet kid. Definitely wasn't in the social spotlight ever. The only reason I knew more about him was his parents both died in a car accident when he was just 18. It was big news, but he never wanted to talk to anyone about it. No memorial or event was held that was public. I think he's an only child, and his parents were his only family."

"Do you know much about his current life or situation?"

"I thought he went on to be some sort of engineer and left town. But I can't remember for sure. It was something one of my friends told me. I'm not sure if he ever came back. He could still be living here, and I'd have no idea."

I pursed my brow. "Do you think if you saw him you would recognize him?"

"I don't think so. No. Is he a person of interest with the case you're working on?"

"Hard to say."

"Okay, well, I'll just get you those yearbooks then."

"Actually, can I start with the 1990 yearbook?"

"Of course, Agent Wright, follow me."

Jeanette walked around the desk, and the associate came back out and stood by. Jeanette led the way upstairs, and I followed. We went up a few flights of steps until we were on the top floor. She guided me to the right, a large room with bookshelves lining the walls and the bookshelves creating a maze in the center. We stepped through the maze until we went down an aisle with all of the Wilton High yearbooks from 1930 onward.

There was a double copy of each one.

All of them were there, and we went down until we got to 1990. Jeanette pulled it out and dusted it briefly before handing it to me.

"If you'd like, there's a room on the other side that's perfect for reading. There are circular tables with bookshelves around, but there's a spot next to the window. Do you need anything else, Agent Wright?"

"Is it okay if I make myself at home and just grab the other copies if I need them?"

"Of course. I'll be downstairs if you need anything. Pleasure meeting you."

Jeanette and I shook hands, and then she took me to the other room, and I saw a table in between two bookshelves underneath the window. "This is perfect, thank you."

Jeanette walked away, and I took a seat at the wooden table. Going back in time with the 1990 high school yearbook. The lettering was silver, and the book itself had a soft brown shell cover.

I flipped through the pages, but I could have stared at them for hours on end. Seeing the black and white photos of a day-long past gave me goosebumps.

I wondered where all of those people were in their lives now. I could probably find most of them still living in Wilton, Indiana, living a similar life as their parents did. Then I thought about my own high school experience.

But I didn't want to think about that for too long. I kept my focus on Wilton, Indiana.

I scanned through all the freshman names, hunting for Charles Green. He wasn't in the freshman section, the sophomores, or the juniors, but by the time I had reached the seniors, I found his photo.

In the middle of the row, he was sandwiched between another person with the last name Green and a person with the last name Graham.

Charles Green was scrawny. He had a smile that didn't show any teeth. His eyebrows were bushy, and he had brown eyes with aviator wire frame glasses. It looked like a genuine smile as if he was happy to be at picture day and back at school. He had a little bit of acne, but overall he was a decent-looking kid. It wouldn't surprise me if he was called a nerd, but maybe he wasn't. I guessed he was 17. There were no quotes, nor any other information about him. Just his picture. I wondered how different he was nowadays.

Next I searched through the sports section to see if Charles was involved in anything there.

He wasn't.

And then, I kept my focus on the activities and after-school clubs. I did find Charles Green in the National Honor Society. He was sitting next to someone by the name of Vince Nelson. Both of them were sitting in the back of the risers; the photo was taken inside the gymnasium. They both smiled ear to ear as if Vince may have told Charles a joke. They sat close to each other, closer than the other people around them as if they were friends. The body language certainly suggested they were.

So Charles Green might have a friend. They were both in the National Honor Society; they seemed to be intelligent and motivated.

I searched through the other club photos to see if there were other Charles Green sightings.

Fortunately, I found one in the Quiz Bowl team. Both of them were found standing next to each other with five other students. Below that, there was History Club with Vince and Charles and students from Quiz Bowl. I wondered what they would even do in a History Club but I kept looking.

Then I found the two of them again sitting next to each other for the AV Club, which had ten other students. Two girls and eight guys.

Then I spotted the last photo with Charles Green and Vince Nelson. The two of them sat next to each other for the marching band photo.

Going through the rest of the yearbook, I made it to the end glossary of student names and all of the pages they appeared in.

I was surprised to see one other photo taken with the two of them. It was a page I must have skimmed over earlier in the book. It was a collage of photos taken during random times of the school day or even after school. As if the teacher in charge of the yearbook handed a camera to a student and said, "Take a bunch of photos of kids having fun."

Charles Green and Vince Nelson were sitting next to each other. The caption read: *Charles and Vince finish work early in drafting class to practice their soldering.*

Charles had a confused smile as if he was a little shy about taking a picture. But Vince had a big grin as if he was amused by the camera being in front of him. Charles was holding a soldering iron up to a silicon chip of some kind, and Vince also had the same setup.

I flipped to the glossary again, and I noticed that Vince was listed on another page elsewhere in the book. I went back in the section with the collage of photos and found one last shot with Vince Nelson.

He was standing in the library with a piece of paper in his hand. He was a stocky guy who could probably play football guarding the quarterback well. The caption read: Valedictorian, Vince Nelson, practices his graduation speech in front of the principal.

Returning back to the section of senior photos, I looked at Vince Nelson's. He reminded me of Charles Green's picture. Vince smiled, but he showed his teeth. They were perfect and straight. He had giant wireframe glasses, wearing a white button-up shirt. His head was large, and he had thin eyebrows and short hair.

I closed the yearbook, put it back on the shelf, and went downstairs to the library's main floor.

6

When I arrived at the main floor of the library, Jeanette was waiting at the counter with the other younger guy at the computer.

"Did you find everything you were looking for?" Jeanette asked.

"Yes, I did. I'm curious, do you know anyone by the name of Vince Nelson?"

Jeanette thought about it for a moment. "Yeah, I think the name sounds familiar."

"He was the Valedictorian of Wilton High School in 1990. It appears he was friends with Charles Green based on the context clues."

"Oh, I see. That's probably why I recognize the name."

"But you don't know if he still lives in town or perhaps is part of the community in any way?"

Jeanette shook her head. "No, not that I'm aware of."

"Thank you. You've been very helpful. I think I will stick around here a little bit and just do some research from my tablet. I can connect to the wireless internet here, yes?"

"Yes, of course, here let me give you the password to the staff Wi-Fi." Jeanette handed me a slip with the information.

I pulled out my tablet. "The connection was successful. I feel like a VIP using the staff Wi-Fi. Thank you so much, Jeanette." I walked away to one of the rooms on the first floor to sit by the window. Mountainous clouds were making their way to Wilton; I checked my phone and saw that rain was in the forecast. Just when I thought I couldn't be in a more conducive environment for sleeping, the rain was making its way. Not that I felt tired. With all the caffeine I consumed, I was wide awake. Wired.

I pulled out my tablet and did a simple online search for "Charles Green Wilton, Indiana." There were no results that led me to any articles that would be worthwhile looking through. I then checked an FBI criminal database, and again, there was nothing on a Charles Green from Wilton, Indiana.

I decided to search for Vince Nelson. That yielded more results than I was prepared for. Vince Nelson received a doctorate in molecular biology from Stanford University. As I clicked the Stanford website, it was just a record of names. I had to go back to my query and click a different link with a short bio from a doctorate awarded in 2004. Vince Nelson held a bachelor's degree in biology from MIT. That's about all the information I could find. With a search of Vince Nelson's dissertations, I was able to find one titled "The New Frontier of Genetic Testing," but there wasn't an option to view it. I felt I didn't need to, but it was interesting to me. I couldn't find any other information on Vince Nelson. It wasn't the most uncommon name, so I ran across multiple Vince Nelsons, but none of them had anything to do with the field of biology or a related career. I was hoping to find other information on him, but there was none. *Perhaps Martha might know more.*

I typed up notes I had so far. There was not much, but it was good to keep every detail and name I came in contact with documented.

When I was done in the library, I strolled around downtown Wilton. Getting acclimated with the buildings in the daytime was better than going at night. I checked the alley where I thought I encountered Charles Green. I couldn't find any clues of where he could have hid. There were doors in the alley into the lofts above the businesses. Perhaps he was able to slip away in there. Then when I checked up above, I saw that there were black metal fire escapes that went out to the top of the building. I could imagine him climbing to hide away. It was impossible to see high up at night in that alley.

The next task on my to-do list was to call the hospital with the missing blood for any breakthrough information. I ate a quick lunch at a sandwich shop downtown and went back to the room at the inn. Regina was behind the counter, and she greeted me with a smile.

The elevator took me to the top floor. I walked into the hallway, and the room opposite from mine had a door open. A man walked out and closed it. He seemed troubled. His eyes were screaming with panic, but he feigned a smile at me. High cheekbones, cleft chin, and a five o'clock shadow; this guy was handsome and shorter than me. His stare was intense though, I felt that something was off. He didn't want me in the hallway.

"Uh, hello," he blurted as I walked up to him. He was wearing a black suit with a white button-up shirt underneath. Undoubtedly expensive, and it perfectly fit him. It was hard to gauge how old he was, but if I had to guess, he was in his late 30s.

"Hello," I said. As soon as I spoke, his eyes bulged. He froze in the middle of the hall and forced a laugh.

"You know what, I forgot something in my room." He nervously chuckled, spun around, and went to his door, fumbling with the key before shoving it in the lock.

"At least you didn't forget your keys," I said with a smirk.

"Excuse me?" he asked, sounding defensive.

"At least you didn't forget your keys."

He stopped and snickered. "Oh, yes, very good. Sorry, I'm in a bit of a hurry."

"No need to apologize. I'm not your boss," I said. I was about to arrive at my entrance.

"Right. See you later." He turned the lock and slipped inside. From the hallway, I could hear a woman's voice followed by him saying, "Shhhh!"

For some reason, I had a feeling he was staring at me through his peephole. I ignored it and walked into my room.

I wouldn't be surprised if that was the guy who followed me the night before. There was a possibility that he could be Charles Green, but highly unlikely. The two looked nothing alike.

Even though it was a brief interaction in the hallway, I pulled out my tablet and entered notes about the squirrely fellow in the hallway.

I pulled out my phone and called the hospital with the missing blood.

It took some phone call transfer juggling from when I called the hospital until I got in touch with the local law enforcement.

St Mary's hospital was located in a city just outside of Wilton called Hickory. I was directed to the secretary's office at the Hickory police station.

"What can I do for you today?" the secretary asked.

"Hi, my name is Edward Wright. I work with the FBI and—"

"I'll transfer you to the sheriff's office."

The phone clicked and rang until a deep masculine voice answered with, "Sheriff Albert."

"Hello, Sheriff. My name is Edward Wright. I'm with the FBI."

"Aw hell." He sighed. "I've never had to really deal with you guys, and I never really wanted to. Whatever it is, I can assure you we have a good handle on things."

"I'm sure you do as well. I just wanted to see what information you may have had on the missing blood at St Mary's hospital."

"Why?"

"Well, I'm in the area, and this might be related to a case I'm working on."

"Uh, I'd rather not disclose this over the phone. You could be some rogue reporter for all I know. I'd feel better about telling you all of this in person. How soon could you get to our station?"

I quickly typed in the address for directions on my tablet and saw that it was only a 20-minute drive. "Does a half-hour work for you?"

"Sure. I can do that. I'll fill you in on the details when you get here after you show your accreditation. Sorry for the hurdle. I just want to make sure."

"I understand." I left the room and the inn and hopped in my car. I pulled up the directions on my phone and drove on the lonely two-lane highways. The drive was a little scenic, there were paths with the trees lining the road, but there was also a lot of flat farmland I passed. Which I didn't mind. Part of me appreciated the quiet and calm roads between Wilton and Hickory.

Hickory didn't have much of a downtown. There was the hospital, and then a mile away, the police station, library, and City Hall spaced out with only a few strip malls in between. I went straight to the police department and walked through the doors. I was ten minutes early from what I said over the phone.

The secretary at the front desk was in the middle of finishing a call. She hung up the phone and beckoned for me behind the plexiglass covering.

"Hi, how can I help you today?"

"Yes, I just called not too long ago. My name is Edward Wright. I'm with the FBI."

"Sheriff Albert told me you were coming. May I see your badge, please?"

"Of course." I pulled it out and slipped it underneath the opening of the plexiglass.

The secretary took the badge, scanned it, and punched a few buttons on her keyboard. "You're going to walk to the door to your right and follow me."

I followed the secretary through the hallway. A few police officers were walking around, bouncing between cubicles like a slow pinball. I was taken to an office door in the back that was light blue with a black nameplate with silver letters: ALBERT OWENS. The secretary knocked on the door, and Albert answered. He was tall, slender but athletic and had a beard. His eyes were tired, but they had a silent charm to them.

"You must be Edward?"

"That's true. Nice to meet you, Albert." The two of us shook hands.

Albert closed the door as the secretary left. His office smelled like coffee; everything was neat and organized. His desk was spotless and had a bookshelf with binders and books covering every bit of space. He took a seat behind his desk, and I took a seat in front of him, old chairs with a steel frame and copper-colored cushions, but they were almost brand new. I noticed he had a paperweight on his desk of the Indiana University logo.

"So, are you able to disclose what you're working on here in Hickory?"

"Yes, although I'm primarily working out of Wilton. This is in regards to the six people who went missing, and then we found their bodies."

"You think they're related to this incident? With the stolen blood in the hospital?"

"Well, I think it's peculiar that the six people have gone missing in intervals. I've noticed six-month gaps between disappearances, at least with the last two, that is, if they were being meticulous. And each body was completely drained of blood. If I'm speculating here, perhaps the criminal wants to try something different and avoid murder since they are now in the spotlight. Whatever it is they're doing, they're using blood, It seems like. St. Mary's is the closest hospital to Wilton where a surplus of blood went missing."

"Wouldn't that be a little too obvious if they're taking blood nearby?"

"Well, I don't think they were anticipating getting caught."

"But a smart criminal would have some foresight on how to handle a situation if they were caught. Right?"

I shrugged. "You would think. Anyway, that's why I'm here. I have a feeling that this blood stealing incident might be related."

"So you're not planning on getting in the way or clogging up the investigation?"

"Of course not. I guess my FBI colleagues might have a reputation for making things difficult with local law enforcement. Still, I assure you, I only want to help. If you already have information, great, I would love to read it over."

"Well, we do have a suspect, and I was planning on paying them a visit this afternoon."

"And I would love to tag along for that. As long as that's okay with you? I won't get in your way, but I might ask some questions if that's all right?"

He stared at me, it was an awkward pause.

"Oh, and, go Hoosiers," I said.

Albert chuckled, and the corner of his lip curled up. He stared at the paperweight on his desk and nodded. "Go Hoosiers. Ed, you're all right. You're more than welcome to join me in questioning this suspect."

"May I ask how this suspect came about?"

"A few nurses noticed this man walking out of the blood storage with an unusual amount on a cart."

Even if this had nothing to do with the case, I felt a flame of excitement in my chest. I was getting closer to something.

1

Albert and I left the police station, and we got in his car, which was a large black Chevy Tahoe. I offered to drive, but Albert insisted since he knew his way around.

"So, who's our suspect?" I asked once we made it inside the vehicle.

Albert turned on the car and the engine hummed for a moment before he switched gears. "He's a physician's assistant who works at the hospital. His name is Drew Allen. He lives over on the edge of Hickory. That's all I really know about the guy."

We made our way onto the street and drove along the narrow but smooth road at a steady 45 mph.

"Do you know if he was well-liked by the nurses? Did they have anything to say about him or his personality?"

Albert shook his head. "I don't really know."

We entered a neighborhood with houses evenly spaced out but plenty of trees in the yards. The homes all had a second floor, and all of them had been built recently. Wide driveways, small porches, but big homes. It was quiet, with hardly any traffic in the neighborhood. We came up to a house that blended in with the rest of them. A soulless house of aluminum siding and brick

"All right, this is his address. He's just a few blocks from my place, whaddya know," Albert said as he parked in front of the house.

"It seems like both of you have good taste in neighborhoods."

Albert chuckled with a bit of confusion. "Yeah, I guess so." We got out of the car and walked up to the front door.

Albert rang the doorbell, and I stood next to him staring up at the windows. After a few seconds, I saw a crease in one of the blinds. It was hard to see through it, but I sensed that someone was staring at us through that fold.

We waited for close to a minute before Albert rang the doorbell again. I could hear the faint "ding dong" through the wall, so I knew it was working. I peered back up at the window, but the crease was gone.

There were no cars in the driveway. Part of me wondered if I just imagined the crease in the window. But the longer we waited, the more suspicious I grew with Drew Allen.

"Maybe we could come back later. But I was told he was here during this time. He usually works overnight at the hospital." Albert turned around, but just as he did, the door opened up, and a man was standing with tired eyes and disheveled hair. He was wearing a t-shirt with khaki pants.

"Can I help you, gentlemen?"

"Hello, we're wondering if we could speak with Drew Allen?" Albert asked.

"What's this regarding?"

"We need to speak with Drew privately."

The man took a deep breath and tightened his lips, but he nodded. "My name is Drew."

"Do you mind coming down to the police station, sir?"

"Again, I'd like to know what this is about."

"There is a decent amount of blood missing from the hospital you work at," I said.

"Oh, okay. Well, I don't really know anything about that. Do I really have to come down to the station?"

"I'm afraid you do. Now, I could put handcuffs around you, but I don't think you'd want your neighbors to see that. Or you could just come down to the police station."

Drew sighed. He rubbed his face, and his hands were twitching as they moved back to his side. "Yeah, okay, I'll come with you."

Albert escorted him to the back seat. On our way to the station, we didn't say a word. Drew tapped his fingers on his thigh, and his knees were bouncing. Occasionally he tried taking a deep breath through his mouth. Still, he looked like he was having a hard time finding his regular rhythm.

When we made it to the station, we went inside the conference room with wooden panels and a few windows.

"Can I get you anything, coffee or water?" Albert asked.

"No. That's okay. I just want to get this over with. Why am I here again?"

"A few nurses saw you go into the blood bank at the hospital and push out a cart. Conveniently, the person working the checkout counter wasn't there for a brief moment. There was no sign-out, but someone did take some blood. When we reviewed the security cameras, they apparently had some issues with the image, which was inconclusive. Nevertheless, staff came forward and said they saw you walking around," Albert said.

"I don't think so. I wouldn't do something like that." Drew couldn't look either of us in the eye. His focus was on the table. His grimace and head shake seemed exaggerated, but perhaps that's just how he usually spoke.

"Do you have any idea who might have taken the blood from the bank then? And I just want to remind you, if you tell the truth to us, it makes things a lot easier."

"I don't have a clue." Drew bit the bottom of his lip, and his eyes became glassy. He had a sheen of tears, and his lip trembled. "Dammit. I can't do this. I have no idea why they picked me for this."

Albert was about to say something but touched his shoulder. I wanted to hear Drew finish his train of thought.

"They told me to just deny, deny, deny, but I can't do that. I've never been someone like that. I'm a horrible liar." Drew had tears pouring down his cheeks.

"Drew, it's okay. I think you made a mistake, but if you tell us more information about who you did this for, it will make the path ahead a lot easier," I said.

Drew sniffled and cleared his throat. "That's the thing, I don't even know. I can start from the beginning, but I'm not sure how helpful it will be."

"That's okay, we can try. Take a deep breath and start wherever you think would be best."

Drew took a long inhale and slow exhale. He did this a few times.

"I don't even know how they found me exactly. I think it was a targeted maneuver by them. I was at a coffee shop working on my laptop. It was all personal stuff, nothing that would be associated with the hospital. This coffee shop was outside of town. Browndale, to be exact. So figure about 20 miles outside of Hickory, about a 30-minute drive." Drew drummed his fingers on the table.

"Got it," I said.

"I was inside the coffee shop, but as I was leaving, I noticed a limousine pull up next to me. It was bizarre to see a limousine in the parking lot of a coffee shop in Browndale. No one was around though, I was the last to leave the coffee shop while the workers were still there closing up. It was at night and completely dark out. Someone from the limousine called my name and waved me over. Their window was rolled down. They said my full name, Drew Allen, which I thought was very bizarre, and my gut was telling me not to go, but I did anyway because I thought it may have been someone I knew."

"I think anyone would do the same in your situation." I nodded.

Drew began picking at his nails. "So I approached the limousine, and there was a guy whose face was still tucked in the shadows. I couldn't get a look at him. He said, 'Hello. How are you this evening?' And I responded with fine. He opened the door and told me to 'Please, get in. I need to speak with you about some things in regards to the hospital.'

"I thought it was all weird, but something told me that maybe I had to do something for work on an emergency call or something. I don't know. But my gut told me not to do it. So I said to him, 'I don't think I can come inside your car. I'm not at work right now.'

"And I swear to you, he pulled out a small pistol and aimed at me. I know nothing about guns, so I couldn't tell you the make or model, but he pointed it at me and said, 'I'm sorry to do this, and I really hate to pull this out, but you need to get inside the limo. All I want is just a conversation. I promise you, you will not be harmed.'

"I've never had a gun pulled on me before. I didn't really know how to react, but my heart was speeding, and I went inside his car. He made me hand over my phone as soon as I got in. My adrenaline kicked in, and my fight or flight response was ready, but I knew I couldn't survive if I tried either. Not to mention it's never been in my blood to hurt someone. You know?

"Anyway. I get in the man's limo, and he assures me many times he's not going to hurt me, and he just wants to discuss business. He tells me not to say a word to anyone about this meeting. I agree to everything, and he makes me shake his hand. He told me to call him Logan. Whether or not that was his real name, I have no idea, but that's what he introduced himself as."

I wrote down the name and nodded at Drew.

Drew continued, "Logan said to me, 'Drew, I wanted to talk to you about a business opportunity that I think you would really like to be a part of. I will give you $500,000 in cash if you can do me a huge favor.'

"My voice was gone. I think my nerves got the better of me or something because I couldn't really talk. So I nodded. What else was I supposed to do?

"Then he said to me, 'Drew, all I need you to do is grab a few bags of blood from the hospital bank. It will be the easiest half a million you will ever make. And don't worry, the blood is going to a good cause. A friend of mine runs their own practice, and they need blood for a dire situation. I've asked around to see who would be able to supply me with blood. You're the guy. Everyone says you're very nice and accommodating. Won't you please help out this life that is in danger?'

Drew itched his brow. Remembering the incident shocked him all over again. "I was flabbergasted. I didn't know what else to do, but I agreed. I said, yes, I could do that. So then he told me how it would all go down. I would pick a date and time that would be most conducive for me to sneak inside the blood bank and take as many bags as possible. It didn't matter the blood type, which I thought was strange, so I grabbed as much as I could one evening. I was told to meet him in a part of the hospital with low security, and I left the cart there, and someone came in and took it. But that night, he picked me up in his limo, we ironed out all the details. I never got his phone number, email address, Facebook account, nothing. He also didn't ask me for my address. This was insane to me because later that evening, after the job finished, Logan came up to my doorstep, and he handed me a briefcase of $500,000."

Rubbing his eyes, Drew cleared away the tears that appeared. He took a moment to pause, but muscled through his strained voice. "I couldn't believe it. Logan told me not to tell anyone; otherwise, I'd be risking my life. I told him I would swear to secrecy, and then he said if anyone noticed what happened to the blood that I needed to deny everything. Logan said as long as I denied everything, I would never have to see him again."

Drew put his head down on the table and started sobbing.

"Drew, it's okay. We can keep this between us," I said. "This doesn't have to get out to anyone else."

It took a moment for Drew to regain his composure to talk once again. "No, but that's why I need to go back home and go to work as if nothing ever happened. I think they have eyes on me somehow, somewhere. If I'm not at work mysteriously, I think they might start to suspect something."

"Do you have any idea who else might be involved in this? Did you get a look at the driver when you were going inside the limo? Did you happen to get a license plate? Would you happen to know the year or model potentially?"

Drew shook his head and rubbed his eyes with a little too much pressure. "I'm telling you, I have no idea. It didn't even occur to me to remember any of that information when I met with this Logan guy."

"It's okay. We have a few things we can research in the meantime. What would you like as far as safety goes in the meantime?" I asked.

"Like witness protection or something?" Drew asked.

"If you think it's life or death."

"Honestly, I think if I just went about my normal life as if nothing happened, I don't think they'll have any idea I spoke with either of you today. If you hold me here, I think they'll know, and they'll grow suspicious. I can't say how they're watching me, but they have to be. They knew my name and saw me in the parking lot at the coffee shop. I was targeted."

I nodded. "You have a shift tonight, correct?" I asked.

"I do."

"And you think it's best if we let you continue working and pretend nothing has happened. This conversation, for instance, never happened. Right?"

"I think that would be the best way to go about it. Yes, sir."

I took a deep breath. "From the FBI side of things, I'm okay with that. I think you're right to let things happen as usual, so whoever was involved in this doesn't try to flee. And speaking of fleeing, you cannot go on any trips or travel in the meantime. Because if you go anywhere, it will look awfully suspicious. Do you understand?"

"Yes, yes. Of course. You have my word; I'll stay and just keep working. I'm so sorry for what I did. It's the biggest regret of my life. But I felt like I was in such danger if I didn't obey this man's rules. Even if there wasn't the money offer, I still would have felt pressured to follow Logan's directions."

"Thank you, Drew, for your time today and for telling the truth," I said.

"Do you mind, when you drop me off, can you take me in a non-labeled police car? Just in case there's a set of eyes on my house, I don't want them to know I was with any of you."

"We can have that arranged. Sheriff Albert, I'll take him home in my car. Also, in the meantime, don't touch any of that money."

"Thank you, sir. I promise I will not take anything from there."

"One last thing, Drew. Could you tell me when you met with Logan? The date is the most important, and time would be helpful if you happen to know it."

Drew thought about it for a moment and then pulled out his phone. "Sorry, I have to look at my calendar to remember the exact date I went there. It was definitely on Saturday..." He swiped once on his phone and spotted it. "It was two weeks ago in June. June 22nd, to be exact. As far as the time, I can't remember exactly, but it had to have been around 10 because it was completely dark out."

"Got it. Thank you for all the information."

Leaving the police department, Albert came with me, and we drove Drew back home. The entire car ride was silent. When we dropped Drew off at his house, he said goodbye, and I waited in the driveway until he made it to the door and went inside.

On the drive back to the police station, I couldn't help but replay the conversation with Drew in my head. "I'm curious, Albert, what do you make of Drew's story?"

"I think he's full of shit," Albert said.

"If he is, he sure pulled out one incredible acting performance in that conference room. He had a full-blown meltdown. Do you have any reason for believing that it was an elaborate lie?"

"Yeah, it was over the top, I think. All of Drew's crying and shaking. It was too much. Ya know?"

85

"It seemed pretty genuine. Plus, the man has spent his whole life devoted to medicine. I don't think he'd be so good at acting and have such masterful control of his emotions. It felt honest. I want to know more about this Logan character. I'm thinking of calling the limousine companies in the area. I'd also like to see if the coffee shop has any security footage from that date."

"Is that something you want to tackle then?" Albert had a slight smile. "I'm totally okay with handing this over to you."

"Sure. I have a feeling this might be related to the case I'm working on."

I received a text message from Martha. She asked me if I wanted to have dinner tonight to discuss what I had found or discovered today. I agreed, and she ended up inviting me over to her house for dinner. Driving back to the police station, I dropped Albert off. I still had some time in the day to make a few calls before I would go to Martha's house for dinner.

8

Back at the inn, Regina was working the front desk again. The coffee aromas were gone, and there were no cookies at the counter. *Too bad, I actually had a craving for another one.* I waved hello to Regina and went up to the top floor in the elevator. As I stepped up to my room, I paused by the door of my neighbor's room. I could hear a muffled voice through the walls.

"... I'm sorry, I'm sorry, I really am, but we have to be careful!" It sounded like the man's voice I had seen in the hallway.

I didn't want to press my luck, so I went inside my room and quietly closed the door behind me. Sitting down in the corner chair, I pulled out my tablet. I began researching all of the limousine companies in the area. There was only one, and it was 15 miles northeast of Wilton.

Lennox Limousine.

Going to their website, it was actually a Facebook page. It appeared that they mainly focused on the hearse business, but a party bus and limousine could also be rented.

I pulled out my phone and gave them a call.

"Lennox Limousine," an annoyed man answered the phone.

"Yes, hello, I wanted to ask about seeing the records of your limousine-specific rentals."

"... You wanna rent a limousine?"

"Uh, no, actually, I'd like to look at your records. You keep a list of clients that have come in and rented a limo from you, correct?"

"You want to look at our books? Why would you wanna do that?"

"Well—" I couldn't help but chuckle. "My name is Edward Wright. I'm with the FBI, and I'm investigating a case. I just wanted to see if I could just see some records of people within the past month. That's all."

"Now it makes sense," the guy started laughing. "Uh, I hate to be a bother about it, but do you mind if you come in tomorrow? I've got no reservations this evening, so I'm closing up shop early so I can get home."

"Sure, we can do that. Would 1:00 p.m. work for you tomorrow? And what's your name?"

"The name's Bill. And yes, 1:00 p.m. would work fine for me. I'll see you then, Mr. Ed. Haha. Mr. Ed. Just like the horse, you know what I'm talking about?"

"It's not very often someone says that reference, but yes. I got it. I'll see you tomorrow at 1:00 p.m. Thanks, Bill."

I hung up the phone and typed more notes on my tablet before I had to get ready for Martha's dinner.

I drove over there around 5:00 p.m. Martha lived in a two-story colonial house with lovely rose bushes in the front. Her yard was vast as if it were her own private piece of land without any neighbors around. There was an American flag high on the flagpole in the center.

I rang the doorbell, and Martha answered immediately. She had a beer in her hand, a bottle of Pabst Blue Ribbon.

"There's the g-man. Come on in. I got some burgers cooking for us on the grill." Martha ushered me inside. The house smelled like garlic, butter, and pepper cooking together on a pan to make something delicious. The dinner smelled heavenly. Her house floor was entirely hardwood with a few large throw rugs, and the walls were covered with nature paintings.

Two excited Pekingese dogs sprinted towards me and jumped at my legs.

"This must be Jupiter and Saturn?" I asked.

"The one with the brown spots is Jupiter. The one with all-white fur is Saturn." Martha snickered. "They really seem to like you. Do you have a dog at home?"

I frowned as I petted both dogs. They kept licking my hand. "No, unfortunately, I can't really be a dog owner. I spend too much time away from home. It wouldn't be fair to the dog or any pet for me to be gone for such long chunks of time."

"You don't have a partner to look after them?"

I shook my head. "No. Again, the lifestyle isn't conducive for having a serious relationship yet."

"Well damn, Eddie, what the hell you working with the FBI for?" Martha let out a boisterous laugh.

"I have my reasons." I don't think Martha was expecting me to answer the question so seriously. She arched her brow at me, though after my response.

"Well, settle in, make yourself at home. I can get you a beer if you like?"

"Nah, that's okay."

"Don't want to cut loose?"

"I figure I'll be working later as I go to The Painted Goose to see what that bar is all about. Perhaps I might find out more information, and I need to have a clear conscience if I'm going to go in there and try to take this case as seriously as I can."

"I understand. Sorry if it seemed like I was pressuring you. I just wanted you to have a nice time while you're here at my house. And I don't want to be rude as I'm drinking a PBR here."

"You're totally fine. Have as many as you'd like. I just won't be joining you, unfortunately."

"Will you have a beer with me before you leave, at least?"

"Sure." I smiled.

Martha strolled to the back of her house to a room with a TV and a long couch. Sliding glass doors connecting to the deck illuminated most of the room.

"This is the theater room if you will. I watch all the big games here on Sundays. Occasionally I'll go to Big Henry's, but the at-home experience is wonderful. You can go to the bathroom whenever you want, you don't have to pay too much for a beer, and you can put your feet up whenever you want."

"The room is incredibly cozy," I remarked as Martha led me to the patio where smoke plumed from a steel grill.

"Come on, let's go outside." Martha opened the sliding door to the deck, and we walked outside.

There was a patio chair on the wooden deck, and I sat on it while Martha opened up the smokey grill and flipped a few burgers. While she did that, I told her about everything that happened to me today.

"Wow, you certainly stayed busy," Martha said and grinned at me.

"Do you have any idea what happened with Vince Nelson or anything about his family? As I was looking at the yearbook, I noticed that he was the only friend of Charles Green's. Based on the yearbook evidence, it seemed like they were close."

"Yeah, I remember Vince Nelson. Vaguely though. Only that he was really brilliant and went away to school to somewhere like Princeton, Yale, or something like that."

"He went away to MIT. Any information on his family?"

Martha shook her head. "To be honest, I didn't really know too much about the people who were two years older than me. Just the year above me and the year below me. Those were the only kids I ever interacted with."

"That's fair. So Vince has no record of living here in his adult life then?"

"Not that I'm aware of. I just knew he was a smart kid. That was it."

"Do you think if you saw him all grown up, you would recognize him?"

"I don't think so."

"Understand."

"Burgers are done." Martha opened up a bag of buns and placed the patties on them. Each burger had cheese on it, and in the kitchen, chopped lettuce and tomatoes were ready to go. I added the toppings along with ketchup and mustard. We ate at the dining table near the kitchen.

"That whole hospital mishap seems like a disaster," Martha said in between bites.

"Yeah, I'm hoping the limousine company can give me some information. It'd be great too if the coffee shop had anything. Although I have a growing suspicion about something..."

Martha handed me a napkin and told me I had something on my face. I wiped it off.

"Thank you," I continued, "so the thing is, I think someone targeted Drew to take the blood. Someone working inside the hospital, I'm guessing. I suppose it could be a friend too, but I really think it would be someone at the hospital. Someone who has a way of communicating with another person. 'Who could I prey on to manipulate into getting me a copious amount of blood and have my tracks relatively concealed.' And they pressured Drew."

"Ah, fascinating, g-man. I'm digging the analysis." She took a swig of her beer.

"Do you happen to know any doctors that live here in Wilton? Or anyone in general who would work at the hospital? Anyone that would make that commute?"

Martha rubbed her chin. "The only person I could think of would be this girl my daughter went to school with. I mean, she's not a doctor or a nurse, but I remember they used to be friends. Her name is Victoria, but people close to her call her Vicky. Her mom is a doctor for sure. I'm not sure if she has her own office somewhere, but I think she also might work in the hospital sometimes. That would be the only one that I know for sure. As far as nurses go, I don't really know anyone."

"Anyone who might have more information on other staff that might work at the hospital? Even custodians?"

"I would give the hospital a call or go over there yourself and see if you can look at the cities where all of the workers live. Sorry, Eddie, I don't have much for you."

I shrugged. "No need to apologize. I feel like I've come up with a lot here so far in what little time I've been here."

"And you think everything that's happening is related to the murders?"

"If the murders were someone being slashed or gunned down, I wouldn't. But since the blood was drained from all six of them, I think this is definitely related. Depending on how well the murderer has eyes on the town, they might already know I'm here

-that the FBI is looking into the situation. Or maybe they foresaw it. Whoever is up to this is definitely a sharp thinker. But I have the feeling that they might not be working on their own."

"I'm a little amazed at how you seem to be progressing so fast."

"I guess it's like finding a loose thread. I naturally gravitate towards something and start pulling it until I get as much information as possible. Honestly, if I didn't have Charles Green stalking me last night, I don't think I'd be able to have done much of anything. But perhaps I would. Looking at the article on the Wilton Observer was definitely a huge help."

"Well, bravo. What time are you going to The Painted Goose?"

"As long as I get there around 9:00 p.m., I'll be satisfied."

"That's in about an hour and a half. Feeling ready?" Martha grinned.

"Ready for what? Isn't it just a bar?"

Martha's head teetered side to side. "It's a bit of a bar punks like to go to. Not bad people or delinquents. That's not what I mean by punk. I mean, kids who listen to punk music, have piercings, tattoos, trendy glasses, you know, that sort of environment."

"Have you been there before to have a drink at night?"

"I have. I really like their pool tables there. So if you want to play some billiards, especially if you're good, you'll have a lot of fun. I think the people that play there are pretty solid."

I grinned. "I remember at Quantico in the break area, we had some pool tables. I spent a lot of time playing there."

"Uh-oh. You might even be able to hustle some people there." Martha winked.

"That's not a bad idea."

"Are you kidding? I just told you that bar is full of punks."

"But you just told me that they're all good kids."

"Yeah, but not if you piss them off."

"I don't have to hustle them. I could just play pool with them." I chuckled.

"Okay, good. I just don't want to receive a phone call at midnight that you got your ass kicked."

"I'll be careful. I promise."

Martha and I continued chatting while we ate a slice of pie that she had baked earlier in the day. It was a warm cherry crumble crust, and it was unbelievably rich. Sweet with a bit of tart from the cherry filling. The crumbles just melted in my mouth. After we finished dessert, I got in my car and drove to downtown Wilton and parked near the inn.

9

It was close to 9:30, but I walked to The Painted Goose, which had a small crowd gathering in front. All of them were smoking cigarettes. The pungent tobacco hung in the air as I entered.

No one noticed me, and no one said hello as I went inside.

New Order's "Blue Monday" was playing over the sound system inside the bar. I could see the vinyl propped up above the bar next to a record player. It was filled with people wearing muted-colored outfits, normcore outfits, and others who were dressed like they were at a punk show. Plenty of piercings, black leather jackets, and denim jackets.

It was a younger crowd than Big Henry's. In fact, it wouldn't surprise me if I was the oldest one there but I noticed a group of people at a circular booth in their mid to late 40s.

Red lights attached to metal poles from the ceiling lit the booths. The walls were exposed brick, except there was a myriad of band posters that were original prints from touring acts coming through Indianapolis. Or just artsy band posters of The Clash, The Ramones, Sex Pistols, Nirvana, and the list kept going on and on. Not to mention, the wall of vinyl records was a marvel. There wasn't a single television monitor anywhere in the establishment. I didn't see a seat yourself sign or a, please wait sign.

I took a seat at the high chair at the bar, and a bartender came up to me after a few minutes of waiting. While I waited, I looked at everyone who was sitting at the bar. It was crowded. There were only two other seats empty out of 20 seats total. The gentleman who took my order wore a band t-shirt, I think, some group I had never heard of. He had a lip ring and a neck tattoo of a winged beast of some kind.

"Can I get a non-alcoholic beer, please?" I asked him.

"We got a non-alcoholic craft brew called negative zone. It's got an IPA flavor. Is that what you want?"

"Yes, that would be perfect." I smiled.

The bartender turned around and reached into a fridge below the liquor area and pulled out a 12 ounce can, and cracked it open for me at the bar.

"Enjoy," he said. "That'll be $3."

I gave him a $5 bill and told him to keep the change.

"Thanks, man."

I nodded and continued surveying the tavern. Towards the back I saw two billiards tables. It was on a slightly raised platform that went up two steps. As soon as my beer arrived, I raised my can at the bartender and took a drink.

Bitter but had a nice citrus finish. I couldn't really listen in on any conversations around me. The music was loud, and everyone was talking close to each other. No one else appeared to be on their own like I was. The billiards area piqued my interest, where a group of three people played on a red fabric table.

I approached a guy and a girl, each holding a cue with the multicolored pool balls sprawled in front of them. They had a friend standing off to the side next to a two-top table. She had straightened brown hair with a dark-colored button-up blouse.

"You're done for, Jill," the guy said as he put his cue up to the white ball and nailed it, knocking two striped balls into the pockets. He went around the table to get a better angle of the cue ball, rocketing another shot, falling a hair short of banking another.

"Quinn, you blow." The woman he was playing with was wearing a low-cut t-shirt with skinny jeans. Her hair was black and curly. Quinn wore a plaid button-up, wireframe aviator glasses, and a firm, short beard.

"Scoreboard," Quinn said.

Jill had measured up her shot next, looking like a scientist analyzing a microscope. After a few draws in and out, she committed to the hit, smacked the cue ball to a solid color ball, and sank it in the corner. She went again and took down another.

"I'm running the table now," Jill said as she finished the last few balls with precise aim.

Quinn sighed and said, "Good game."

The other woman leaning against the table took the pool cue from Quinn and asked Jill, "You need a break?"

Jill stepped to their table and took a swig of a Miller High Life. "Gimme one sec."

"Excuse me," I said. "Perhaps we could play two on two?"

"You want to play with us?" Quinn asked.

I nodded. "Yeah, two on two sounds fun, no?"

"I'm all for it," Quinn said as he looked at the two ladies.

They both said, "Sure."

I pulled out my wallet and a few dollar bills.

"Whoa, man, are you trying to make this interesting?" Quinn asked.

"What? Oh. No, sorry, I was just seeing if we had to pay first before we played," I said.

"I think it might be fun to make it interesting. What's your skill level?"

"I'm decent."

"Yeah, but how decent? Like borderline professional decent? Or mediocre?"

I chuckled. "I'm definitely not a professional."

"How's about a hundred bucks, me and you," Quinn said.

"Dude, let's just play two on two. Don't get all weird about this," Jill said.

The other lady rolled her eyes.

"Oh, come on, he just saw me get my ass kicked by you. He probably thinks he can at least beat me," Quinn said.

"I seriously think you have a problem," Jill said.

Quinn stared at me. "Hey, I'm sorry, I haven't introduced myself. My name is Quinn."

"Edward Wright."

Jill and the other lady smirked and snickered to themselves. "What are you, some kind of businessman? Who introduces themselves like that?" Jill said.

As I shook Quinn's hand, Jill grabbed the pool balls and wrangled them inside the triangular frame, and placed the collection near the end of the pool table.

"What do you say? We playing for 100?" Quinn asked.

I grinned as I took a pool cue from the wall. "Sure, that's a good start."

The table was all set, and Quinn said to me, "Guests first." I took aim at the cue ball and got a feel for the stick. Rubbing it up and down the crook of my hand for a moment before rifling off a shot that sank two solid color balls.

"Bloody hell," Quinn sighed.

"Chill, there's still plenty of game left to be played," Jill said.

Quinn and I went back and forth, sinking down well-executed shots, but because of my early lead, I always had at least one ball on him the entire time up until I dropped the eight ball myself.

"Goddammit, good game Eddie Wright." He pulled out a $100 bill from his wallet and slammed it on the table off to the side.

I picked it up and put it in my pocket. I didn't plan on keeping it, though, but I wanted to see Quinn's reaction.

"Let's go again. $200 this time. Let me break first," Quinn said.

"Are you sure you want to do that?" I asked.

"Yeah, come on, let's go." Quinn framed another triangle and prepared the cue ball.

"Quinn, you legit have a problem, dude." Jill chuckled and rubbed her forehead. The other lady watched in shock as if Quinn was a building on fire.

Quinn had furrowed his brow and seemed rushed with every step when he prepared the table.

"We doing this again or not?" he barked.

I nodded.

"All right."

Quinn led the first break, and he sank a single solid color ball. He held a one-ball lead on me the majority of the game. But as we went back and forth, I eclipsed him with only two balls left to sink. I managed to snipe them both.

"Jesus, this guy is lethal," Jill commented and snickered.

Quinn fumed and muttered something to himself that I could only imagine as obscenities. He shoved his hand in his pocket and ripped out his wallet, slamming $200 on the table. I had set my beer down with the others, and he paused, squinting at my beer.

"What the fuck is this? Drinking non-alcoholic beer?" Quinn blurted.

"Ay, mind keeping your voice down?" Jill asked.

"No, no, no. That's really not fair. I'm like three beers deep, and this guy just hustles me while sober the entire time. What are you a fucking cop?"

"Hey, you don't know anything about him. Don't make assumptions. He doesn't want to drink alcohol. Leave him alone about that," the lady came to my defense, and I was grateful for it.

"Come on, Vicky, you have to admit, it's really not cool about what just happened."

"It's not like you're drunk. You can totally play just fine. You lost. Get over it," Jill said.

I pulled out the $100 bill he gave me and put it back on the table with the $200. "It's all right, man. I wasn't planning on taking your money anyway."

"Dude, I don't need your fucking charity. A bet's a bet. I lost. You won, just take the money and take your sober ass elsewhere."

Jill and Vicky were mortified. Jill especially had a flame in her eye like she wanted to sock Quinn with a haymaker.

"You really can't talk to people like that," Jill said.

"I really ought to drain his fuckin' blood."

"What's the matter with you, man?" Vicky put her hand on his shoulder.

Quinn tried to take a deep breath.

"Yeah, fuckin' cool it." Jill's voice seemed to make him even more frustrated.

Quinn gripped my shirt and got in my face. "You played me, you sunnuva' bitch." His voice lowered to a growl.

"Quinn, you really don't want to do this," I said. I didn't have any fear in my voice. I was calm and collected.

"Why? Are you gonna turn into the Incredible fuckin' Hulk or something?"

I thought that was pretty funny of him to say, but I didn't smirk or laugh. I kept a straight face and said, "No. But if you hurt me, you'd likely go to prison. I'm a federal agent. I don't want your money, Quinn. I just wanted to make friends here at the bar. That's all. I'm investigating the murders that happened in Wilton."

Quinn rapidly looked back and forth between my left and right eye. "I think you're full of shit."

"I can show you my badge right now. Just let go of me. It's okay, Quinn. You're not in trouble, and I don't want you to get in trouble. We can just settle down and have a pleasant evening. You seem like a good guy, and we just had a little misunderstanding. I'm sorry I didn't introduce myself sooner." I reached into my flannel and pulled out my FBI badge, and showed it to him.

Quinn's eyes widened, and he let me go. He lowered his voice to a whisper. "Were you spying on us or something?"

"I can assure you, I was not spying. If it came off that way, you have my sincerest apologies, but I was not spying," I said. "And I never had any intention of taking your money. Please, have it back."

Quinn scowled at me; his anger was coming down from a boil to a simmer.

Realization settled in.

Jill leaned in closer, only a foot away. She could have been there the entire time, and I didn't even notice. "All right, Quinn. Let's just settle down here and cut this guy loose. You don't wanna' make any dumb mistakes," Jill said in a soft voice.

Quinn unclenched my shirt and returned his hand back to his side. His expression switched from hostile to lost puppy. "I'm really sorry about that."

"Don't worry about it, Quinn. We can forget this whole thing ever happened."

"Uh, sure. Thanks."

I returned to the table to grab my beer. Quinn, Vicky, and Jill all sat together.

There was something on my mind, and I needed clarification. I cleared my throat and looked at Quinn. "Although, I do have to ask one small question. What did you mean a moment ago when you said you were going to drain my blood? That's not a threat I've heard before."

"He was just being an idiot, okay?" Vicky snapped.

"And that's fine. But I just want some harmless clarification. Is that threat something unique to Wilton?"

"Yeah, it kind of is." Quinn shrugged. "I mean, that's what happened with those bodies that were found. The blood was all drained from them. Right? So it's just been like a joke kind of."

"And that's what I'm investigating. Just out of curiosity, did either of you see those victims when they were in town?"

They all shook their heads.

"Not to be rude, but even if I did know anything, I'm not sure if I would tell the police department," Vicky said. "In fact, I would really appreciate it if you left our table and left us alone."

"Why wouldn't you tell the police here if you had any information about the murders?"

Vicky tightened her lips and crafted a sentence in her head. "Sorry, I'm being hyperbolic. If I did know anything, I would have told Sheriff Martha. Sure. But I just don't like being involved with cops in any sort of way. I don't trust them."

"I understand."

"Do you?" Vicky narrowed her eyes at me.

"Absolutely. I'd be lying if I said there weren't any corrupt police officers."

"And the systems we have in place are fucked. And you allow it to happen."

I frowned and kept my voice calm. "I'm sorry. I understand your frustrations." I lowered my head and thought about what I wanted to say next. "But I just want to help people. Honestly, it's why I joined the FBI. I can only do so much alone, and one of my duties with the bureau is to provide closure to grieving families. And to put a stop to this monster that is killing people who are traveling through. Have you ever had a close friend disappear or go missing?"

Jill and Vicky both shook their heads, but Quinn nodded. "One time, my cousin went missing for like 12 hours. No one had any idea where he was, but he just went on a long walk and got lost. It was over the summer, and I'd hang out with him pretty much every day. But that day, he was going through some shit, I guess, and just went out for a really long walk."

"Was it frightening when you thought he was gone?"

"Hell yeah. I was like ten, and it just freaked me out. Especially my parents and my aunt and uncle. They were hysterical and crying, but it was all good though because he ended up coming back home."

"Trust me, it's the worst when there is no closure." I took a deep breath. I hadn't planned on diving into my own emotional past and being so vulnerable in front of those strangers, but It came out naturally. They were listening to me.

"What happened?" Vicky asked.

"My best friend when I was 10 just went—" My voice was choked out by an emotional grip over my throat. Eyes brimmed until I felt a drop trickle down the corner of my eye. "Excuse me." I wiped away the tears with the back of my hand.

"That's okay. You don't need to explain the rest," Jill said.

"Sorry, I think I need to step outside for a moment." I forced a smile and took my beer, and went to the exit in the back of the bar. I was outside on a pleasant patio. Holiday lights strewn above on wooden posts and a few tables. There were two other people outside smoking cigarettes to my right. Beyond the chain-link fence protecting the perimeter of the lot, there was a vast field of grass between The Painted Goose and a neighborhood full of houses. I leaned up against the wall, away from the smokers. Tears continued to pour down my eyes, like a pitcher overfilling a glass of water.

Please just make this stop. Make this stop.

10

The exit door creaked open, and I could hear footsteps approaching.

"Hey, I'm really sorry about what just happened a moment ago," Vicky said. "And I'm also sorry if I offended you. I feel terrible. I didn't even introduce myself, but my name is Vicky."

I sniffled and looked Vicky in the eye and feigned a smile. "Nice to meet you. It's okay, though. You didn't offend me. Sometimes I just think about a certain memory, and it just triggers this emotional flood, and I lose control for a moment."

Vicky nodded. "You don't have to talk about it or explain if you don't want to."

"There's not much else to say. This doesn't often happen. In fact, it's very rare for a thought to trigger those memories. I can talk about what happened back then normally. Still, sometimes, depending on the situation, I guess, or my mental headspace, it just all comes out. Seemingly out of nowhere."

Vicky gave me soft eyes. I felt she was listening to me with her heart and soul.

"I'm really sorry to hear about that. Must be tough."

"I wasn't able to say it in there, but when I was younger, I lost my best friend. He never came back home. No one knows what—" I sewed my lips shut. A reinforcement of tears came spilling down my cheeks.

"It's okay. You don't have to talk about it anymore. No need to explain yourself. I'm sorry if I seemed rude or calloused earlier. But you understand where I'm coming from, right?"

I cleared my throat and sniffled. "I do," I said with a strained and shaky voice.

"Can I ask you a question? Do you think something happened here at The Painted Goose?"

After taking a few deep breaths, I was able to find an emotional balance. "I'm not sure. It's hard to say because no one really knows where any of the six victims went when they came into town. I like to think that all of them stopped for a bite to eat at Buckwheat's, and maybe they explored the town afterward. They had to have been coming in somewhat late, I imagine. They didn't come in the morning or early afternoon. I'm thinking dinner or something like that."

"So, are you checking out the nightlife spots in Wilton then?"

"I am. Last night I went to Big Henry's."

Vicky snickered quietly to herself.

"What's so funny about that?"

"I just feel like that's such an old man bar. Like sometimes, Quinn, Jill, and Lizzy will ironically go there since we sometimes want to break from this place, but there is no vibe there for the most part. Like I said, it's just old dudes watching sports, drinking cheap beer."

"Lizzy? Is she with you tonight?"

"No, she had to work."

"Anyway, it wouldn't surprise me if at least two of the victims went to Big Henry's. Can't leave any stone unturned."

"Have you been to Club Novus yet?"

"That's the next place on my list."

"Are you going to try to get in as a regular?" Vicky's brow arched.

"Yes, what do you mean by that?"

"Well, it's hard. You have to get invited. It's a private club."

"How do you get invited?"

Vicky shrugged. "I received a card one time. Don't know how it got there. But I was at a table here at The Painted Goose once. Went to the bathroom while my friends were smoking, and then when I came back, I had this blue card underneath my drink."

My eyes widened. "Do you still have this blue card?"

"Yeah, it's somewhere in my bag." Vicky slid her tote bag off her shoulder and rummaged through it.

"Hey, dude, check this out. Is there a guy staring at us?" I overheard the two men smoking a cigarette at the other end of the patio.

I followed where they pointed, and I saw a figure in the shadows beyond the chain-link fence, staring in our direction.

"Sorry, I'm still looking for this. I've got too much in my bag," Vicky said.

"Vicky, does the name Charles Green mean anything to you?" I asked as I analyzed the shadowy figure.

"No, I don't think I know him. Hold on..." Vicky kept searching.

But I forgot what she was trying to find. My attention was fixed on the man watching us from a distance.

"Yeah, that's definitely someone," the other smoker said.

"Dude, what the fuck. This is getting weird, man," the guy said.

I jogged up to the chain-link fence, and as I did, the man started sprinting in the other direction, outside of the faint area of light provided by downtown Wilton.

"Excuse me!" I yelled out. "Charles Green?"

But the man was nowhere to be found. "Vicky, I'll have to catch up with you later." I climbed the chain-link fence and sprinted through the field. I could hear the smokers continue their conversation, completely confused, but I could feel them watching me. As I followed the shadowy figure's path, I ended up on a road that took me through a neighborhood. There was no sign of anyone walking around or running.

"Damn," I muttered. I was standing underneath a glowing orange street lamp in the middle of a quiet neighborhood. Some houses had lights on, but most of them were completely dark. I hung around a little longer, scanning the premises for any sign of movement or any sign of anyone watching me. There was nothing. "Charles Green?" I raised my voice, and it echoed through the suburb. There was no response. Turning back around, I went back to The Painted Goose. By the time I returned, Quinn, Vicky, and Jill were nowhere to be found. I thought it was a little strange, but the chase that led nowhere and the walk back took me about an hour. Plenty of time to decide to go home for the night. I went up to the bar and ordered a Miller's High Life with alcohol.

I only drank one beer as I sat alone at The Painted Goose. It was crowded but not overflowing, but as more time passed by, more people left. I didn't watch the time closely, but the bartender rang a bell at 1:00 a.m. for the last call. A few people still played pool. The bar had seven people, myself included.

We all stayed until the bar closed at 2:00 a.m. The bartender rang a bell and said, "And with that, we're officially closed! Thank you all for coming in."

Most of the people trickled out of the pub, but the bartender stared at me. "Everything all right, sir?"

"Just peachy," I replied monotonically.

"Did you hear my announcement?"

I smiled. "Yes, I did. I just wanted to ask you a quick question."

"What's up?"

"When I was outside earlier in the back patio, I saw a person staring at me. There were two other people at the patio there as well. We all saw him. I have a theory on who it might be, but I wanted to check and see if that was maybe a common occurrence or uncommon occurrence?"

"For someone to stare at people in the back patio?"

"Well, he was outside the fence, you know, way out in the field. No one has ever complained about something like that?"

The bartender shook his head. "Not that I can recall."

"Does the name Charles Green mean anything to you?" I felt like a basketball player throwing up a shot at the last second of the game even though my team was losing by a lot, and it wouldn't matter.

"Can't say it's very familiar to me. Sorry about that."

"That's okay. I guess I have one last question."

"And then will you get out?" He smirked.

"Absolutely. Have you ever been to Club Novus?"

"Nope. I'm always working here."

"Do you have any friends that may have gone?"

"Nope. They always come and visit me here."

"Has anyone ever come in here and given out invitations to people?"

The bartender chuckled. "Man, you said you had one last question and then asked me three more. No, no one has come in here and handed out invitations that I'm aware of. I don't know shit about Club Novus."

"Thank you. That's all." I stood up from the high chair, reached into my wallet, pulled out $20, and set it on the bar. I strolled out through the door and paused for a moment, scanning the main street of Wilton. No one was around, but Club Novus still had its bright blue neon sign, beaconing through the night like a lighthouse.

I got lost in a trance as I gazed at it. I imagined what might happen if I tried to go in there right now. I'd probably approach the front doors, and the bouncer would say, "Sorry, we're closed." Even though the nightclub was screaming my name in the distance, I couldn't go just yet. But it would happen soon. No stone left unturned.

I meandered back to the inn, slowly opened the entrance doors, and held my ear up to the foyer. I couldn't hear anything. I half expected to hear Elizabeth talk to someone, but there was no conversation. Still, I gently opened the door to find Elizabeth behind the counter making out with a guy.

Out of the corner of her eye, Elizabeth saw me and pulled away from him immediately.

"Edward! How are you this fine evening?" The color drained from her face.

"I'm doing okay. Sorry to have interrupted."

"Please don't tell anyone about this. I don't get to see my boyfriend very much. He has to visit me while I'm at work."

"That's fine. I understand. I won't tell a soul about this, I promise."

"Thanks." Elizabeth gave a smile, but her embarrassment turned her lips into a frown. "How was your night at least?"

"It was okay. And don't worry, you don't have to make small talk with me. I'm sorry I interrupted."

"I need to go to the bathroom anyway," her boyfriend said, and he went around the desk and left.

I was about to press the elevator button, but I held off. I actually did want to talk to Elizabeth. "So, my night was okay. I went to The Painted Goose."

"Good bar, right?"

"Yes, it was. I ended up spending a decent chunk of the evening talking to these people I met. Quinn, Jill, and—"

"Vicky? Oh my gosh. Did you just hang out with my friends for the evening?" Elizabeth recovered her smile.

"I suppose I did. Believe me, I had no idea they were friends with you. They called you Lizzy, though, I think."

"They talked about me?"

"Very little. They just said that you were a part of their crew whenever they went out. Although, there was a strange moment where someone was watching us beyond the fenced-in area."

"Whoa, that's spooky."

"Yeah. Do you by chance know Charles Green?"

"I'm afraid I don't, sorry."

"That's okay. I think I know who it was, and I'm on top of it."

"Of course. I wasn't worried at all, although it does sound creepy."

"Indeed. By the way, I assume that Vicky is short for Victoria?"

Elizabeth nodded. "Yep!"

"This might be a long shot, but do you know if her mother is a doctor? Perhaps a doctor at the hospital, St. Mary's?"

"She definitely works at a hospital, and I'm pretty sure it's St. Mary's. But I don't ever really talk to her, so I can't say for sure."

"Wonderful. Thank you for that information. I might want to have a conversation with her mom."

"Why? If you don't mind me asking."

"Something weird happened at the hospital the other night, and I want to dig into it more."

"It might be tough meeting with her. I know she and Vicky have their hands full with Vicky's grandpa."

"What's going on with Vicky's grandpa?"

"Oh, he's not doing so well. Really bad dementia. Keeps leaving the house and wandering around Wilton. Pretty mean too, and apparently, he used to not be like that. Always a very kindhearted man all his life."

I shrugged and sighed. "Plenty to be pissed about these days."

Elizabeth giggled. "I shouldn't laugh. It's a pretty serious situation."

"Right. I shouldn't have made a joke. It's been a rough night. Anyway, if you see Vicky soon, could you let her know that I'm interested in talking with her mom about the hospital, that is if she works at St. Mary's?"

"Yeah, absolutely." Elizabeth whipped out her phone and tapped at her screen with lightning speed. "I just texted her. I'll let you know what she says."

"I appreciate that. Have a good night Elizabeth. Pleasure talking with you." I pressed the button on the elevator and went back to my room.

11

I sat in the corner of my room by the window view of downtown Wilton. I pulled out my tablet and typed a few notes of everything that had happened throughout the day. From what I could see, nothing appeared to be happening on the street, just a few people walking underneath the warm lights. It was quiet. I relaxed my shoulders and reclined in the chair.

There was a part of me that imagined living in Wilton and having a quiet life.

What if I just worked alongside Martha and took over as sheriff when the time came? I could settle down.

Blips of Vicky entered my daydreams.

On the strip of downtown Wilton, I didn't see any other activity to keep my interest, so I got ready for bed and slipped underneath the sheets. But it took me a while to fall asleep, even though it was late.

I wasn't sure how much time had passed, but it felt like I had lay there for at least an hour. Muffled footsteps from the hallway stopped at my neighbor's door. I heard two people giggling before unlocking their door and going inside. I tried to hear more from them, but there was total silence.

The next thing I remembered was walking through a dark corridor with bright blue lights passing me by, like stars stretching at the beginning of warp speed. I wasn't sure what was up ahead, but my spine tingled.

An echoed slither filled my ears.

The lights flew by faster and faster with each step, and from the center of my vision, I saw something that made me freeze. Snakes hissed, and a giant head emerged from the shadows with the curls encased in the dark, but I could see the hair moving. It was Vicky's face, but her eyes were white. She opened her mouth, and a forked tongue floated out and slipped into my mouth. My tongue was gripped by hers and then ripped out.

I shot up in bed. Coated with sweat, head to toe. Even though I had blankets on, I was shivering. Checking the time, it was 6:00 in the morning, and I was wide awake. Another night of only a few hours of sleep. I couldn't keep doing that. More rest was needed. I took a few deep breaths, went to the bathroom, crawled back in bed, and closed my eyes.

Three hours seemed to blink by. When I checked the time, it was 9:30. I could work with six hours of sleep.

I went down to the lobby and was greeted by the heavenly scent of fresh coffee, giving me a pre-caffeinated jolt of excitement. The cookie didn't sound appealing, but I poured myself a cup of coffee. Sitting in the lobby, I pulled out my phone and checked out the Wilton Observer. There was nothing too interesting on the front page that captured my attention. More feel-good stories and town features on local businesses hosting events of some sort. None of it seemed like a loose thread, but I still perused the articles as I finished my coffee.

When I returned my mug up to the counter, I waved to Christopher. "Good morning."

"Agent Wright. How are you?"

"I'm doing all right. I have a busy day ahead of me."

"On a Sunday?"

"I'm afraid so."

"Well, don't work too hard, my friend. Nothing wrong with a day off. Wilton is a good place to relax in."

I smiled. "You're not wrong. Say, Christopher, I have a bit of a random question for you. Does the name Charles Green or Vincent Nelson mean anything to you?"

"I'm afraid I don't recognize either of those names."

"No worries."

Christopher had a slight frown. "Anything to be worried about?"

"No. I just want more information on them. That's all."

"I wish I could help you."

"That's quite all right. Thanks anyway." The coffee at the inn was too good not to have another mug. I sat back in my chair and continued reading about the articles in the Wilton Observer.

The elevator bell dinged, and the doors parted down the center. A hushed conversation with intermittent snickering came from a couple I hadn't seen before. I wondered if they were my new neighbors, but they were tall and model-like. Both the man and woman could have been on the cover of a magazine. The man was wearing a plaid button-up and slim-fitting jeans. The woman wore a cream-colored romper with a golden necklace.

"Good morning," Christopher said to them.

Both of them were all smiles with their perfect teeth. "Good morning," they said in unison.

I watched them as they left the lobby right away. They didn't even stop and have a cookie, nor did they notice the coffee carafe. Part of me wondered if they were models, and if so, what business could they have in Wilton?

I finished my last drink of coffee and exited the lobby. Outside, the sunlight was strong, and the humidity made my clothes stick to me. I noticed the couple had just entered Buckwheat's. My stomach grumbled, so I went straight to Buckwheat's.

As I stepped inside, I could hear the sizzling and frying from the kitchen. The beeping buttons came from the cash register as someone paid their bill. The smell of syrup and bacon lingered in the air, coffee too. I glanced around for an empty table. It was crowded. I found one at the very back, a booth underneath the window. I was right behind the couple from the lobby. *Perfect.*

Before I went to the empty table, I glanced to the right side of the restaurant. There was a man staring at me in a white suit, blue circular glasses, and a bald head. He was sitting by himself at a booth that could only fit two people. I studied him for a second and narrowed my eyes. I couldn't see his pupils or his eye color. His lenses were too opaque. My spine tingled. He was radically out of place compared to my surroundings of solid color, plaid, and plainclothes.

I turned around and went to the booth in the back behind the couple. As soon as I sat down, a server came up to me, blocking my view of the man with blue glasses. She was wearing a black t-shirt that said Buckwheat's on the front with black pants and shoes. It wasn't the same server from yesterday. She was probably mid-20s, dark hair in a ponytail, with warm brown eyes.

"Hello, can I get you something to start with?" she asked.

"I'll just have the western omelet," I said.

"Is that it? No coffee?"

"Water is fine."

I noticed there was a tattoo on her right arm as she jotted down my order. I could only see the bottom of four limbs of some sort.

"Excuse me, I was just curious what your tattoo was?" I pointed.

The server beamed. "Oh yeah, it's Cerberus." She rolled up her sleeve so I could see the whole thing. A three-headed dog on all fours, the expression on each face was stoic, but the brow was slightly furrowed.

"That's a beautiful tattoo. Where did you have it done?"

"I got it done a while ago at work."

"Here?" I asked.

She cracked up. "Yup, the busboy inked me."

"But seriously, where did you get it from?"

"My other job."

"I just thought about maybe getting one someday, and I was curious if you may have had any recommendations."

She shrugged. "It's not really a traditional tattoo place. One of my friends did it, and she's an amazing tattoo artist."

"I agree. She did an amazing job with that one. So where's your other job, if you don't mind me asking?"

"I'm sorry, sir, but I actually do mind," she said politely.

"That's okay, I understand. Forgive me for asking so many questions."

She smiled, but I sensed she was uncomfortable. I frowned; the conversation didn't go as I had hoped. Perhaps I should've told her I was FBI studying a case? Maybe that would have freaked her out even more. As she walked away from my table, I noticed that the man in the white suit was gone.

The table in front of me was giggling about something. I leaned closer to them to listen to their conversation, but it was tough with the constant flow of dialogue from the entire restaurant.

"I still keep smiling about last night. My face hurts from smiling so much," the woman said.

"So you don't think it's too much to go there again?" the man asked.

"We have another invitation. We may as well use it. That place was a blast."

I left my table and approached their booth. "Excuse me, I couldn't help but overhear your conversation. May I ask what place you're talking about?"

Both of them stared at me as if I had just spoken gibberish.

"Oh, uh, I don't know. It's weird because it seems like a private club because they only let people in with an invitation. But yet, if you're in town at night, you've probably noticed the blue neon sign?" the man said.

"Club Novus, yes?"

"Yeah, have you been there before?" the woman asked.

"No, but I'm very interested in going. I'd love to get an invitation. May I ask how you got one?"

"Uh, we got one from the owner. He was just sitting over there, actually." The man faced the corner where the stranger with the blue glasses was sitting. "Huh, I guess I don't see him anymore."

"That was the owner who was in here?"

"That's what he told us, at least." The man shrugged. "He gave us an invitation for tonight."

"But how did you get an invitation in the first place?"

"Oh, I've had a friend who traveled through town and said it was one of the best nightclubs he had ever been to, and he actually had an invitation and gave it to me. He told me he would have used it himself, but he wasn't going to be in the area anytime soon."

"Do you know where your friend got the invitation?"

"I'm afraid I don't. I'm sorry."

"That's okay. What was the nightclub like? I've been dying to go in. I've heard nothing but great things," I said.

"You heard correctly. It's amazing," the man said.

"What makes it different from other nightclubs?"

"It's hazy inside. They're big on the fog. But there's also a lot of neon in the club. People are everywhere, dancing, drinking, just, you know, having a great time."

"But you're forgetting the best part," the woman said. "It's quite risque."

"Risque? How so?"

"The servers and staff are walking around in tight-fitting clothing that shows a lot of skin, but the outfits are tasteful like a real art deco design to them. It's surprising at first, but it adds to the ambiance. We were invited to a private suite with the owner and sat around with his people the whole night."

"Wow, sounds like you had a great time. I'm a little jealous. So you have no invitations or know how I could go about getting one?"

They shook their heads.

"Well, thank you for letting me talk with you two. Please, allow me to pay for your meal. Have a wonderful day." I smiled at both of them, and their faces lit up at my offer.

"Cheers, man," the guy said as I went back to my table and waited for my omelet to come out. When the server came back with my food, I said, "Hey, I'm really sorry about asking all those questions earlier. I didn't mean to make you uncomfortable at all."

"That's okay. I just wanted some privacy."

"I understand. Again, my apologies."

The diced ham, green pepper, and onions filled my nose with delight. My mouth watered. I grabbed my fork and knife, sprinkled on pepper and salt, and dug in. Each bite was omelet perfection.

12

At 12:20, I took my car and drove to Lennox Limousine. It took me 30 minutes to get there, driving on long stretches of road going 55 miles an hour without seeing any cars. Flat farmlands made for a scenic view. Even if it didn't seem like much, I still found it captivating to stare out into a vast open space.

I pulled my car into a parking lot that shared its space with a pharmacy. Lennox Limousine was a pastel yellow building with a brown sign near the top. It had a large garage door, and an office entrance with a window that had an open sign dangling behind the glass. I turned the chrome knob and walked inside; the wood paneled walls and black tiles made me feel like I was in the 1970's. An old gentleman sat behind a counter. He had a gray mustache and wireframe glasses on the edge of his nose.

"Hello. Are you my 1:00 appointment?" His voice was gruff but soft. It was the exact one I heard on the phone.

"Yes, Edward Wright."

"Mr. Ed. Welcome. I'm Mr. Lennox. In case you missed it, my name is on the sign. You wanna look at documents, right?"

"Correct, a log of people who have rented any limousines from you."

"You see this door here?" He pointed to his right with a dry sense of humor. "Come on through, and I'll show you what I got."

I opened the door inside Mr. Lennox's office. He had two desks, plenty of file cabinets, and a few cushioned rolling chairs. Mr. Lennox took a deep breath and stood up, pointing at a binder on the second desk. "Feel free to sit there. Those are all the logs of people who have rented a limousine from me. Knock yourself out."

Mr. Lennox sat in his chair at the counter, gazing at his phone as I sat at the desk and started flipping through the pages inside the binder. I went to the exact date that Drew Allen received his visitor at the coffee shop, but I didn't see any reservations for that day. *Damn.* I saw that there was a name, though from the night before.

"Are people allowed to rent a limousine for more than 24 hours?" I asked.

"Nope. I've never allowed that during all my years of running this business," Mr. Lennox said.

"Good to know. So no one came in then on this date at the end of June?"

"If it's not in the logs, then no, no one came in that day."

"Do you ever sell your limousines by chance?"

"Nope. I only rent them out."

"Do you have any competitors?"

Mr. Lennox chuckled, which I was surprised to hear. He was so deadpan with all of his responses. "You're not going to find another limousine company until you get to Indianapolis. There's no one around for almost 100 miles."

"And it wouldn't make a lot of sense for someone to rent out the limousine elsewhere and then drive to Hickory, right?"

"That would be dumb. They'd go through me if they needed one."

"Do you by chance know if anyone might own their own limousine?"

"Nope. I got 'em all here."

"Well, thank you for all this information."

"No problem. Is that it then?"

"Yeah, I guess I'll get out of your hair. Unless by chance you happen to know a fellow by the name of Drew Allen, Vince Nelson, or Charles Green?" I stood up. Mr. Lennox was deep in thought.

"Charles Green... Chucky?"

"You know him?"

Mr. Lennox smiled. "Yeah, Chucky Green. Hot damn, I haven't thought about him for a while. Good kid."

My heart raced with excitement. I sat down and pulled out my notepad, and clicked the top button on my pen. "What can you tell me about him? Anything and everything."

"Well, I suppose I'll start with how I met the kid. So back in the late '80s, early '90s, I forget exactly when, but it was around that time. Chucky's parents passed away tragically. I remember driving the hearse for his parents because we don't *just* do limousines here; we also supply funeral homes with hearses.

"Anyway, I found out Chucky didn't have godparents nor anyone else in his life. No siblings or cousins. It's kinda crazy to me that there wasn't anyone he could connect with, but the funeral was massive. Of course, his parents had friends, and Chucky had a couple of his schoolmates attend, I think. He was 18 at the time, technically a grown adult but, Mr. Ed, you, and I both know that an 18-year-old still has a lot of growin' and learnin' to do.

"Now, I had someone close to me pass away when I was close to his age. I was about 25. It was my uncle, and my uncle had asked me to work here when I was 18. This is technically my uncle's business he started up, y'know. And the best thing for me was being able to take my mind off his death by working. Even though my uncle and I worked here together, you might think it'd make me emotional, but it didn't. In fact, it was the opposite. You gotta be well composed driving limos and hearses around. It was actually a welcome distraction from the pain I was going through, and I knew I was making my uncle proud.

"But back to Chucky. You're the one that's asking about him. So after the funeral, Chucky was gracious enough to invite me to the wake, he didn't have to, but I obliged. And I asked him during a moment when he was dry-eyed, 'Hey, are you working anywhere or doing anything when you're not in school?' And he shook his head. So I offered him a job to help detail the limos, wash the cars, and wax the cars. He was good at it. Had a solid work ethic and didn't talk too much. Couldn't ask for better help.

"So then I started letting him drive after he got his chauffeur's license, but the other thing that was great about him was his interest in cars. Chucky wanted to get his hands dirty under the hood, y'know. Always tinkering around and fixing things up, he was really talented with it. So much so, I didn't need a mechanic to come down for a while when I had Chucky around. Chucky would do all of my fixes and keep everything well maintained. I was surprised at how fast he learned about it all too. But, he was also a perfect student in school, as if that's any surprise."

"How long did he work here for?" I asked, still taking notes on everything he said.

"Gosh. I think he worked for me for three years? Yeah, that sounds about right. He started straight out of high school. I asked him if he was going to college, and he said he wasn't planning on it yet. Apparently, he still had some things he was sorting out in his head, but I kept encouraging him to go because the kid was bright. I knew if he had a degree, he'd go far in life. The following year he went to a local community college to take care of his gen ed credits, and I feel like I had a lot to do with that. Not to take all of the credit, especially since he put in all the work, but he didn't have anyone in his life encouraging him like me.

"So after his third year with me and his second year at the community college, Charles Green transferred to Purdue and pursued a mechanical engineering degree." Mr. Lennox paused for a moment and smirked. "That's kind of funny to say, 'innit? Pursued Purdue, pursued Purdue."

"Yes, very funny. So Charles went to Purdue?"

"Yeah, he went there, graduated, invited me to his graduation, which was a very proud moment for me. I went with my wife, and it was only people he had there to support him. Then he moved to Detroit and started working for the automotive companies. He was an engineer at GM last I heard. I haven't heard from him since."

"So you don't know if he moved back to the area or not?" I asked.

"If he did, he hasn't paid me a visit, but it wouldn't surprise me. Chucky was never a sentimental person. I mean, sure, he invited my wife and me to his graduation, but it's only because I asked him about it. Had I not, I don't think he would have invited us."

"When his parents passed away, I assumed that he owned the house after them?"

"Yes, Chucky told me he was staying there while working for me, and he drove his mom's car around."

"Do you know if he ever sold the house?"

Mr. Lennox rubbed his chin and scrunched his brow. "I don't think so. I can't remember if he ever did. I feel like I would've heard about it. But, like I said. He wasn't sentimental. Kept to himself, and to be honest, no one has really ever asked about him until today. What's going on with Chucky Green? He hasn't done something wrong, has he?" Mr. Lennox frowned.

"I'm not sure."

"Why are you asking me about him?"

"Do you think he could ever harm another person? Did he ever show any angry outbursts or questionable behavior?"

"Chucky? I don't think he'd ever hurt a fly. I mean, he kept to himself a lot, but there's nothing wrong with not talking to people. Anytime he ever drove a client, they always had good things to say about him. Nice and polite. I've never witnessed an angry outburst. He cried a couple times on the job before, I remember that, but he had just lost both of his parents. What do you expect?"

"Right, of course, I understand. Charles hasn't done anything to warrant an arrest, but Sheriff Martha over at Wilton says he hangs around town and stalks people at night. Apparently, he doesn't do anything, just follows them around. She's had to talk to him before about it."

Mr. Lennox shook his head and sighed. "I can't imagine him doing something like that. But I don't know, it's been a long time since I've seen him. If Chucky was back in town, I assume he'd come visit me to catch up, but I guess it's possible Chucky hasn't contacted me."

"I'm really sorry to inform you like that, but it sounds like he is around."

"That's okay. I just hope I have helped. You don't think any murders or anything happened in my limos, do you? Is that what this is about?"

"No, Mr. Lennox. I just thought someone may have rented a limousine from you who then used it to coerce someone into stealing blood at St. Mary's hospital in Hickory."

Mr. Lennox's eyes widened. "Oh shit."

"But it doesn't appear that anyone rented out a limousine the night that it happened. Nor do any of the dates seem to indicate someone else came in and did it on a different date. Thank you for your help." I packed up my notebook but then pulled it back out after remembering something else. "Oh, I know we talked a lot about Chucky, but do you remember if he had a friend named Vincent Nelson?"

"No, he didn't really talk about friends, and I never saw him hang out with anyone. At least around here. Whatever he did at home, he could have been a popular guy who threw parties every night, and I'd never know."

"Got it. Thank you for everything. I'm going to get out of your hair now," I said.

"Pleasure meeting you, Mr. Ed. Good luck with your case."

Mr. Lennox shook my hand, and I walked out of the office and back into my car.

13

Entering my car was like being inside an overheated sauna. The summer heat baked the interior, and I immediately rolled down the windows and blasted the AC. Sitting in my car, I imagined what it was like for Charles Green to work here in the early '90s after he had just gone through a tragedy. Mr. Lennox made it sound like Charles had recovered well enough. Getting a degree and an engineering job, but knowing what I know about losing someone important in life at a young age, it's never easy to come to terms with it. It's possible to move on, but the pain is always there, buried somewhere like a pitfall in the mind. I felt sorry for Charles, but stalking people at night wasn't good behavior. Shifting gear on the transmission, I drove out of the Lennox Limousine parking lot and returned to Wilton.

Arriving on the downtown strip, I had planned on going straight to the inn. But as I stopped at a red light, I saw a confused old man wearing a white cutoff t-shirt and boxer shorts searching all around, with his mouth open, trying to form a sentence. He wasn't sure what to say or how to say it. His brow was scrunched; he was concerned and afraid. Teenagers and other young folks walked through the strip eating ice cream or drinking beverages from the local coffee shop, but no one stopped to see if the man was okay. They carried on about their business, but some of them stared at him like an animal in a zoo. Fortunately, there was street parking and an open spot close to the old man.

His confusion reminded me of my own grandfather growing up.

Something was horribly wrong.

I pulled in, parked, turned off the car, and jogged up to the old man.

"Excuse me, sir, is everything all right?" I asked him.

His eyes were lost and helpless. "I uh, don't uh." He tightened his lips, trying to figure out what to say.

"It's okay, I can help you. Do you know where home is for you?"

"J-J-Jerry." He pointed at me and smiled.

"Me? Yes, I'm Jerry," I lied.

The old man seemed relieved. "Jerry, I'm uh, lost."

"That's okay. Where are you trying to go?"

"...H-home."

"Do you know what street you live on?"

He thought about it for a moment and shook his head, and frowned.

"That's okay." I put my hand on his shoulder. "Don't worry, we'll get you home." I wanted to ask for his name, but apparently, Jerry would have known it. If I asked, he might seem betrayed or even more confused. "I have a car right here. Let's get you inside, and I'll take you home after I finish an errand."

"Okay. Thank you, Jerry."

His balance was a little shaky with each step. He used my arm as support to walk to my car. I opened the front door and guided him in. It took him a moment to put one foot in, sit down and then put the other foot in, but I assisted patiently along the way. I strapped his seatbelt in, and he smiled. "Th-thank you... Jerry."

"Of course." I shut the door and ran to the other side of the car and hopped in the driver's seat, and cranked up the AC.

We drove out to the police station, and I parked in the lot and called Martha.

"Eddie, what can I do for ya this fine afternoon? Oh! How did last night go, by the way?"

"Oh, hi, Martha, I actually don't have a lot of time to chat and catch up. I'm in a bit of a situation, and I was wondering if you could help?"

"I could certainly try. What's the matter?"

"I think you better come outside to my car. I found an older gentleman walking around downtown Wilton. He seemed pretty lost and wasn't fully dressed either."

"Copy that! I'll be right outside. You're in the parking lot, yeah?"

"Yes."

"See you in a second."

As I waited in the car, Martha came jogging out of the front door of the station. I rolled down my window, and waved.

"What's the scoop?" She asked.

"I found this older gentleman walking around. Does he look familiar to you? He seems to have moderate to severe dementia. Apparently, I look like someone he knew named Jerry, so I was able to gain his trust by getting inside my car," I said.

"Well, this is an easy one. We just received a call saying that their grandfather was missing, and they had no idea where he was. I'm guessing this is him." Martha smiled and took a triumphant breath. "Let's call Ms. Roberts back and let her know we found

—sorry—let her know that you found her grandpa... Most likely. I can't imagine two old men drifting around Wilton."

With all the weird things I had witnessed so far, it wouldn't surprise me if there were two old men wandering around. I got out of the car and opened up the passenger side door. Martha and I helped the old man stand up. He didn't have a lot of strength to get up or sit down, but he could still take a few steps without issue.

We got him inside the station and put him in a chair in the lobby. Martha gave him a uniform to wear and she also placed a phone call to Ms. Roberts, and I could hear Ms. Roberts say, "Oh, thank God! I'll be right there!" from the receiver while on the other side of the room.

Waiting inside the lobby, I checked on the old man to make sure he was okay. "Do you need to go to the bathroom?"

He shook his head. He had a relieved smile on his face, but there was still some uncertainty in his eyes. I'm sure he was confused about his surroundings. Those thoughts made my heart ache.

A few minutes passed by, and a woman came rushing inside the station. I couldn't believe it, I recognized her immediately.

"Vicky? What are you doing here?" I asked. She was on the verge of pulling her hair out. Her heart must have been racing for a while.

"I came to get my grandpa," she said. "It's good to see you again. Sorry we left the other night, I had to go home early because the nurse was having trouble with him, so Quinn and Jill came over instead." Vicky approached her grandpa and sat next to him. "Grandpa, thank God they found you. Are you okay?"

He didn't reply.

"Grandpa, are you okay?"

"Mhmm," her grandfather nodded.

"I didn't find it pressing to know, and I didn't want to confuse him any more than he already was, but what's his first name?" I asked.

"Earl. Earl Roberts."

"Noted."

Vicky sighed and rubbed her forehead. "I can't believe this happened. The nurse who came in to take care of him just had a no-call no-show. I was at work, and my mom was at work, so we couldn't really do anything about it. I had to leave my job early once the nursing company texted me saying that no one was coming in to watch him today. So I ran home, and he's nowhere to be found. Even his walker was gone. Did you find his walker?"

"No, he seemed to be moving around quite all right without one," I said. "I found him stepping along the strip of downtown Wilton. Right on Main Street."

Vicky's eyes widened. "You have got to be kidding me. Oh my God." She had a sheen of tears over her eyes. "This is such a nightmare. I'm so sorry you had to deal with this, but thank you so much for picking him up. You have no idea how much I appreciate it."

"Of course. I'm happy to help. It was easy for me to get him in my car. He thought I was someone named Jerry. Do you know who that is?" I asked.

Vicky dropped her jaw and covered her mouth. "No way. Wow, I can't believe that. He never talks about Jerry, really, but that was his best friend growing up. Unfortunately, he passed away a while ago, but I've seen old photos of him, and yeah, you kind of do look like him." Vicky laughed and smiled. "Well, that has me a little relieved. I was so scared that my grandpa was lost and terrified out in the world, and then I freaked out, thinking the worst had happened. Especially with the six people who have, you know, disappeared."

"Worry no more. Your grandpa is safe and sound."

Vicky's lower lip quivered, and a tear fell down her cheek. She responded with a barely audible, "Thank you." Vicky stood up and gave me a hug.

I hugged her back and felt my heart flutter.

"I'm glad I saw you again, actually," Vicky said as she pulled away from the hug. Reaching into her bag, she pulled out a blue slip. The front had black rectangular lines forming an art deco pattern with the Club Novus logo at its center. "I found my invitation."

I felt like I had just seen the golden ticket. I felt a rise of excitement in my chest. "Do you mind if I have that invitation and use it to get in?"

"Actually, they use a name, and the person it's assigned to can only be admitted, but from what I understand, I can bring a guest. I thought maybe we could go there together tonight if you wanted?"

"Uh, yeah, that would be excellent. That's the last piece of nightlife I've been wondering about. How perfect. So yeah, let's go there tonight. Perhaps we could do dinner beforehand?"

Vicky nodded. "Yeah, my mom will be home around 6:00 to look after my grandpa, and then we can get dinner around then."

"Wonderful."

We exchanged phone numbers, and then I helped Vicky escort her grandpa to her car. I assisted him into the passenger seat, and then he said, "Th-thank you, Jerry. Good to... see you again."

119

That pulled at my own heartstrings. "Good to see you again too, Earl."

As she pulled out of the parking lot, I couldn't help but cry silently to myself.

I had a flashback to a time before Michael's disappearance. It was the same summer, though, before he had gone to Disney World. I was going to stay the night at Michael's house, but since I'd been riding my bike around the neighborhood so much, my mom thought it would be a good idea for me to spend the day with my grandparents.

My grandparents lived a few miles away from me in Lockweed. So I rode my bike one afternoon all the way to their house. My grandma was ecstatic to see me, but my grandpa was having a hard time remembering who I was. It was the first time that ever happened. And it frightened me, not because he forgot my name once, but he had no idea who I was or that my mom ever had a son.

I thought it would be a good idea to let my grandpa have some time to himself. So I went out to the backyard, where my grandparents had a basketball net on top of the garage. I shot the ball around and practiced some moves, and then my grandpa came outside.

"Hey, Eddie, I'm really sorry about earlier," my grandpa said. His voice was softer than usual, and his eyes had a faraway look.

I noticed he had some trouble with his step, and I rushed to his side to try to help.

"Grandpa!"

But I didn't make it in time.

My grandpa fell like a chopped down tree, and he hit the pavement. He moaned in pain, one of the worst sounds I ever heard. A helpless cry of an old man filled with confusion.

My grandma and I helped him up, got him back in the house, and took him to the hospital. He ended up being okay after the fall, but it was still frightening.

14

I got back into my car and drove to the inn. Up in my cozy room, I pulled out my tablet and typed away the notes from the day. It had been more eventful and fruitful than I had anticipated. I was hoping for a big break at Lennox Limousine, but I was satisfied with what little information I pulled.

I listened for any noise coming from the hallway, but it was silent.

Close to 6:00, I received a text from Vicky: *Hey, I thought we could go to Lorenzo's for dinner. Have you been yet?*

I replied with a no. A few minutes later, I received another text.

It's a fantastic Italian restaurant inside an old house, near the strip, right by the library. Meet me there at 6?

Sounds good, I responded.

I'll make us a reservation for Vicky :)

My heart skipped, butterflies flew in loops in my stomach. It had been eons since the last time I felt any sort of romantic feelings for someone. My days of studying criminal justice in college was the last time I had any interest in someone else.

It felt inappropriate to assume it was a date. Still, when I saw the pictures online of Lorenzo's, it looked like the ultimate romantic dinner spot around Wilton. *Perhaps she just wanted to thank me for saving her grandpa.*

It wasn't romantic, I reminded myself. As much as I may have wanted it to be, and Vicky and I were close in age, I couldn't waver my focus from the case. *But didn't I deserve some happiness too?*

When I left the inn, I drove my car to Lorenzo's. I was wearing my black suit, black pants, and white button-up underneath. The thought of wearing my black tie crossed my mind, but I opted for a green paisley pattern. It felt a little less "federal."

I arrived at the restaurant first, a two-story white Victorian home with a corner turret. The porch was massive, as well as the windows. A green neon sign hung next to the front door, "LORENZO'S," in cursive.

Stepping inside, there was a hostess stand, and I could see the rest of the restaurant. Tables with black cloths and forest green cushioned furniture. Fake tea candle lights adorned every table, and there were plenty of plants with green leaves running along the windowsills, and some hung from the ceiling, next to dimly lit lamps. Almost every table was occupied. There was a consistent flow of chatter and clanging from the kitchen, and the whole place smelled like garlic bread and marinara.

"Good evening," the hostess said with a smile. "How many?"

"I'm actually here for a reservation. Under the name Vicky?"

"Right this way!" She grabbed two menus and guided me to a booth in the corner of the restaurant.

I sat on the side facing the rest of the restaurant. I scanned everyone there to see If anyone was watching me, like that strange man in the white suit at Buckwheat's. 5 minutes passed by, and I saw Vicky walk inside. She looked beautiful with her dark curly hair and a fitted kelly green dress. Her lipstick was dark red.

She approached the table and grinned.

"What a perfect spot this is. I'm glad you picked it," I said.

"After living here for many years, you're destined to have a date here at least once," Vicky said.

"You've been on a date here before?" I asked, immediately wishing I had said something else.

"Of course, but it was a while ago. Still, even if you just want to have a nice dinner, this is the place to go. Although it is a little expensive."

"Get whatever you want. It's on me," I said.

Vicky playfully rolled her eyes. "I don't think so. You're the one that saved my grandpa. I really owe you one."

"And by allowing me as your plus one to Club Novus tonight, that redeems any favor I could possibly want, not that I would expect one."

"You did it out of the goodness of your heart. You're a rare breed."

"So feel free to get the finest filet mignon if you'd like." I had checked the menu, and it was the most expensive item.

"I'm actually vegetarian." She smiled wryly.

"Feel free to get the finest vegetable in the house. It's on me." I smirked, and Vicky giggled. "If you don't mind me asking, how's your grandpa doing? We don't have to talk about it if you don't want to, but he and I became friends earlier, and I wanted to know how he's doing."

Vicky's smile disappeared, and I regretted asking the question. "I don't know. He seemed pretty shaken up about leaving the house. Very unresponsive and quiet. But also he has good days and bad days, as in, some days he's attentive and can hold a conversation, other days he's a curmudgeon and resists care from the nurses. Or, he tries to get out of the house. And today was just a combination of a bunch of horrible things. My mom, though, said she'd watch him, so I don't have to worry about going back home super early. Then an evening nurse will come in and put him in bed and take care of him."

"He's lucky to have you and your mom."

"Thanks, though, for asking. I appreciate that a lot."

"Of course, I know how it can be."

"Someone in your family had dementia?"

I nodded. "My grandpa." I took a deep breath, feeling emotionally shaky from earlier. "Is it all right if we change the subject? I'm sorry."

"Of course. Whatever you want to talk about."

"Thanks, I appreciate it." I took a drink of water and quickly thought of something to say. I felt like there had to be a consistent flow of conversation to avoid any awkward pauses. "Let me ask you something. Where would be the closest place to get a tattoo?"

"A tattoo? Thinking about getting some ink?"

"Not quite. I just haven't seen a tattoo parlor around here, but I've seen a few people in town with them."

"Jill has a tattoo. She got hers from someplace closer to Indianapolis. I'm not sure what the name is, though."

"Just curious. Thanks."

"Should I order a bottle of wine? Are you allowed to drink?"

I chuckled.

"What?" Vicky's lips curled up. "That's a serious question. I don't know if you're allowed to booze on a mission. Yesterday you weren't."

"I'm allowed to cut loose on occasion. Yes, we can get a bottle of wine."

The server came up to our table and asked us for our order. I picked the spaghetti, and she chose the eggplant parmesan. Vicky selected a mid-range Sauvignon. The bottle came out, and the server uncorked it in front of us and poured a glass. Vicky let it sit for a moment before taking a drink.

"This is great," Vicky said.

"Enjoy," the server said, pouring myself a glass before leaving the table.

"Even if it wasn't great, I wouldn't care. I'm not a wine snob." Vicky giggled.

"Me either. Cheers." We clinked glasses, and I took a sip. It was dry but potent with grape flavor. "I actually ended up having a beer last night when I went back to The Painted Goose."

"Oh my god! That's right, you went out and chased a guy. What happened with that? I was dying to know. Can I even ask about that?"

"Sure. There is a guy apparently in Wilton that goes around following people at night sometimes. And I think that was him. He followed me the other evening, or at least, that's what Sheriff Martha says."

"Who is he?"

"Charles Green? I keep asking people about him, but not many people know anything. My gut is telling me he's a part of this case somehow. Linked to the murders."

"Whoa." Vicky took a sip of her wine. "It's crazy. I watch a bunch of murder mystery shows that have actually happened and listen to similar podcasts. But it's wild when it's happening in your own town. Quite scary, actually."

"I'm not sure if there is much to be afraid of at the moment. Especially if you live around here, there seems to be a safeguard on people from Wilton. Out of towners? Watch out."

"That means you." She frowned.

I smiled. "I'll be okay. If anyone tried to do anything to me, they'd be foolish."

"You carry a gun? Do you have one right now?"

I nodded.

Vicky's eyes widened. "I never thought I'd be hanging out with police. You're better than the last guy I dated, no doubt." She sighed.

So I guess this is a date? I didn't let myself get too excited. The mission is my focus, the mission is my focus, the mission is my focus.

"What was he like?"

"Well, we dated for about two years. Honestly, way longer than we should have."

"What makes you say that?"

"We just weren't compatible. See, when you grow up in this area, you know everyone. Your neighbors are almost like family. Especially the kids in your grade. I dated a guy two years older than me. I think he just wanted to be with me for my looks or something because we were on opposite sides of the political spectrum. Never saw eye to eye on anything, and, well, I'll just give you an example. He would hang out at Big Henry's, and I would hang out at The Painted Goose. You know what I mean?"

"Sure, sure."

"He was sports-obsessed and just couldn't really hold much of an intellectual conversation. There wasn't an appreciation for the arts. Like, I could see the beauty in a painting or a sunset, but to him, he never cared." Vicky shrugged. "And it sucks too because everyone around here stays in long-term relationships. You might be surprised how many high school sweethearts are still together in this town. It's like we never developed as a city past the 1950s." Vicky chuckled.

"I'm sorry to hear things didn't work out with your boyfriend."

"It's okay, you live, and you learn. Glad I had the experience, I guess. At least I know what to look for in the next relationship."

"And what is something you're looking for in your next relationship?"

Vicky's lip curved up. "I don't know, but I think I'll know it when I see it."

The way her eyes lit up as she looked at me filled my heart with so much joy I thought I was about to faint. I became a little nauseous, but in the best way. I took another drink of wine. The buzz was settling in as my stomach was empty.

"What about you?" Vicky asked. "What have your relationships been like?"

I laughed to myself for a second, and then my lips fell. "They haven't been the best. In fact, I hardly meet other women, really. There was one girl I saw back in college, but..." My lower lip trembled.

"Oh, I'm sorry, I didn't mean to open any wounds."

"It's okay. I'm not sure why I'm getting choked up. I guess my focus was always on my mission, and it feels weird to vocalize that."

"Your mission?"

I found an emotional sweet spot in my head, thanks to the buzz. No tears, just clarity. "Finding Michael, my best friend when I was younger. I think that got in the way a while ago." The words came out, smooth like a hot knife through butter.

"How could that get in the way? Like, how could she not be more understanding of that?"

"I think it may have consumed me more when I was younger. Not as much attention or thought had been given to her or our future. I guess?" I gulped down more wine. "It's hard to say what it was or where I went wrong, but I don't get hung up on it. Again, there's a lot to focus on with my mission. And then there's my primary mission here, in the now. I need to provide closure to the families and stop this monster from ruining more lives." I felt like I was a bit too honest, but Vicky nodded and listened intently to every word.

Fortunately, the conversation lightened up after that. Then our food arrived, and it was all devoured. It was one of my favorite meals I'd ever had, but I'm sure the wine and company had a significant influence on the taste.

Vicky and I were able to smile and laugh in our other conversations. Exchanging humorous stories from high school and college alike. I felt like I had an insight into how the young people perceived Wilton. Although it was a traditionally generic place, the town's charm and its laid-back atmosphere were hard to reject.

We finished up the wine, and although I ate food, I still had a strong buzz, but it was waning.

"You ready to go to Club Novus?" I asked.

"Yeah, even though I don't think it's a place I have any interest in, I can't help but be curious about what it's like inside."

"Why don't you have an interest in it?"

"Are you kidding me? It's a nightclub. I don't go to nightclubs. I went to one in college, and it was loud, annoying, and uncomfortable. Why? Do you like them?"

I shook my head. "I agree with you, they're not my cup of tea, but I have to investigate what it's like in there. Something tells me that there is more to it than meets the eye."

"Let's check it out then."

15

From Lorenzo's, Vicky and I were able to walk to Club Novus. It was only a few blocks down Main Street until we approached the club with its blue neon sign out front. The parking lot was packed, and it was around 9:30 p.m.

A tall and muscular bouncer stood in the front of the door, just below the neon sign with four lines forming each letter.

"May I help you two?" He asked, his voice hoarse and deep.

"Yes, we'd like to come inside," Vicky said.

"I need to see an invitation."

Vicky reached in her bag and pulled out the blue slip, and handed it to him.

"I need to see your ID as well."

Vicky handed over her driver's license. "This is my guest I'm bringing with me too."

"I need to see your ID too, man."

I pulled out my driver's license and handed it to him. He stared at both of them for a moment with a tiny flashlight before returning our IDs back to us. "Enjoy your evening."

The bouncer unclipped the burgundy stanchion guarding the entrance to the three-story brick building.

We approached the dark blue metal doors, and I pulled them open, but they were heavy. It led us into a dark room only lit by a blue light bulb up above. There was no decoration, only another set of doors. I pulled those open, and we were immersed in the club.

Fog covered the entire place. Industrial music blasted through the speakers. People bobbed their heads and swayed in rhythm to the droning, overdriven, instrumental music. The dance floor had squares of light panels shining different colors. It was a rainbow of lights, but every other piece of light was bright blue. To the left was a massive bar, and there were semi-circular booths in the corners.

Nearly every table was occupied and full. Servers walked around holding a tray of shot glasses, but the staff dressed in clothes that showed a lot of skin. Chiseled men showcasing their abs and muscles wore golden outfits barely covering their privates. The women wore similar outfits. I found one thing in particular abnormal; every single server was wearing a sizable facial mask. A golden hawk face with gold spires coming out of the back, like an art deco sun.

"I feel like I'm in a strip club, but there aren't any strippers," I whispered to Vicky.

"This place is a lot different than I expected. I thought they'd be playing top 40 club music or something. Dance, or electronic, but this just sounds like audio distortion with a slow beat to it. And what's with all the masks?"

A woman approached us, wearing tight golden strands that barely covered sensitive regions with a large golden mask. "Would you like table service? We have one booth left."

"Yes, that would be great. Thank you," I said.

The woman nodded and beckoned for us with her index finger.

We followed, and I noticed through the fog people gazed at us from the other booths. My spine tingled.

The hostess sat us at a booth. "What would you two like to drink?"

"Is there a menu?" Vicky asked.

"This must be your first time here. We specialize in cocktails. Would you like a house cocktail?" she asked.

"Sure, but what's in it?"

The woman didn't reply. She looked over at me. "And what would you like?"

"I would also like one of those house cocktails. But I'm curious to know what's in it? Just in case I might have a food allergy to it," I said.

Again, there was no reply, only a stoic stare from behind the mask. She turned to Vicky. "I prefer talking to you more. The house cocktail comes with a specialized vodka, a rare guava berry juice, and a homemade lime soda."

"Great, that sounds delicious. I don't think either of us has an allergy to that," Vicky said, and she looked at me to confirm, and I nodded.

"Great, two cocktails coming up." The server walked away, and I continued watching the people on the dance floor slowly rub themselves on each other with their eyes closed in delight.

"So, what do you think so far?" I asked and chuckled.

"It's foggy." Vicky laughed. "And loud, and debaucherous. You name it, they got it here."

Thinking back on the interaction with the server, I remembered seeing something on her body that didn't register with me. She had a tattoo.

"Did you notice that the server had a tattoo on her upper arm?" I asked.

Vicky giggled. "Yeah. I also noticed that she didn't like you very much."

"Yeah, I'm not sure what that's about. I didn't say anything wrong or to make some offensive gesture, did I?"

"Apparently, you did. But I didn't notice it."

"How strange. Did you get a chance to see what her tattoo was?"

"I think it was a three-headed dog."

"Really?"

"Yeah."

I thought about how the server at Buckwheat's had a tattoo of Cerberus. I remembered her body type was similar to the woman I just saw.

"Do you know any of the servers at Buckwheat's?"

"Not really."

"I could have sworn I saw a waitress with the same tattoo this morning."

Vicky shrugged. "Unfortunately, it's not uncommon for people to have two jobs just so they can stay afloat."

"Yeah, it's unfortunate."

There was a pause before Vicky said, "So, do you like this place at all?"

"No, not really. This wouldn't be a hang-out spot for me. I will say it is interesting, though. Fun to people watch."

The server came back to our table with two pink-colored drinks.

"Just so you're aware, we don't take cards. Cash transactions only," the server said while looking only at Vicky.

Why wouldn't today accept credit cards when most places did?

"So, would you like to start a tab or pay as you go?"

"That's no problem. Pay as we go." I pulled out my wallet, with more than enough twenties to pay for an overpriced cocktail.

"That will be $10 each," the server said.

I pulled out $30 and gave it to the server.

She slowly reached to grab it and tucked it into a band against her hip. Leaning her head close to me, she whispered, "Thank you, sweetheart."

My skin tingled and I smiled in return as she pulled her head away.

The server left.

"You gave her a $10 tip?" Vicky asked.

"What else was I supposed to do?"

"I feel like she may have manipulated you. She admitted she didn't like you, and you just gave her a large tip to try to create a different perception of yourself."

"No, I would have tipped that amount regardless of how she talked to me."

"Is it because of how she's dressed?" Vicky snickered.

I smiled, embarrassed. "No, no, it's not because of how she's dressed. If it was a male server, I would have given him the same amount. Even if they were all wearing three layers of clothes, I'm just happy to be here, and I want to be invited again. There seems to be a lot going on here. I found these two out-of-towners, and they hung out with the owner in a private room and partied with him and his entourage. That's what I want. I want that experience."

"Why, though?"

"Leave no stone unturned. I haven't seen anything weird that wants me to investigate more at all of the other places I've been to. The Painted Goose, maybe, but not quite like this place. There's more here."

"I just think you want to see more of the almost naked people." Vicky cracked up.

I rolled my eyes, but deep down, I did think it was funny. Picking up my glass, I tapped my drink against hers.

"Cheers," we both said at the same time.

I took a drink, an explosion of fruity flavor where I could barely taste the alcohol. Light carbonation as well. Incredibly refreshing.

"Wow, this is really good," Vicky said.

"Delicious."

We both took another drink.

"Ah, excuse me one moment." Vicky reached into her handbag. "I just felt my phone buzz." Her phone screen lit up her face, and she scrunched her brow. "Huh, it says I have a voicemail from my mom, but I never heard my phone buzz. Sorry, but I'm going to check the voicemail if you don't mind."

"Of course not, please, check it out."

Vicky held the phone up to her face and stared off into a corner. She pursed her brow the entire time. Finally, she put the phone down and looked at me. "My grandpa had to be taken to the hospital tonight."

"Oh no, I'm so sorry to hear that. Do you need to leave?"

Vicky nodded. "Look, I'm really sorry to leave so early, it's been a lot of fun tonight, but I have to go."

"I can come with you if you don't want to be alone. At least let me walk you to your car."

"You should stay here and investigate whatever you can. Because I think once you leave, you can't come back in. You don't have the slip anymore, nor me to come back in with you. I'd hate for your investigation to be interrupted by me. Families are relying on you."

I didn't respond. Vicky slid out of the booth and took her bag. "I'll text you with updates, okay?"

"Sounds good. I'll see you soon; have a goodnight. Can I give you a hug before you leave?"

"Sure."

I stood up, and we hugged for a moment. I could smell her lavender-scented perfume. I wished time could freeze as I held her.

"I'll see you soon," Vicky said, and she walked away.

I sat back down into the booth and took a drink of my cocktail. As I watched the dance floor for a few minutes, the server came back up to my table, but instead of standing next to it, she took a seat across from me, where Vicky was sitting.

"Your friend left?" she asked.

"Unfortunately, she had to take care of some personal manners," I said.

"That's a shame."

"Yeah, she's going through a lot right now. I just hope things can start getting better for her soon."

"I hope so too. So you're still here, though?"

"Is that a problem?"

"Of course not. I want you to enjoy yourself while you're here." She took a drink of Vicky's cocktail.

"Are you allowed to drink on the job here?"

"It might be frowned upon, but no one will know."

"How long have you been working here?"

"Long enough."

I didn't know what that meant, but I didn't bother following up. "Do you by chance work at Buckwheat's as well?"

The server fell silent and took another drink from Vicky's cocktail. She slid out of the booth and strolled away.

"I'm sorry, I didn't mean to offend." My voice became quieter as I finished my sentence. She didn't turn around and kept walking.

I focused on the dance floor as well as the booths around me. The people sitting down were having hushed conversations or silently leaning up against each other with a drink in their hand, looking like they were about to fall asleep. The dance floor had servers come up to random people to hold them by the hand and lead them to the back of the building, but it was so foggy I couldn't see where they went. Certainly, it wasn't an exit since there were no bright orange exit signs in sight, except for the main entrance.

I stood up to walk towards the dance floor and—

–I woke up in my bedroom at the inn. It took me a moment to realize where I was.

I'm back at the Wilton inn.

Yes, but how?

How did I end up in my bedroom?

Was I dreaming the entire time?

What just happened?

I checked my phone on the nightstand next to me. It was charging, and it was 4:30 a.m.

Falling back on my pillow, I wondered what had happened.

The last solidified memory I could recall was approaching the dance floor at Club Novus.

But what happened after that? What the hell happened after that?

16

Panic ballooned in my chest.

My heart rattled.

I was on the verge of having an anxiety attack.

Sprinting into the bathroom, I looked at myself. I was in a t-shirt and boxer briefs, my usual bedtime attire. I didn't remember getting in those clothes at any point. There was no memory. My face and body looked completely normal.

Was I having an episode of early onset dementia?

I rushed over to my tablet to see if I had made any notes.

Sure enough, it was updated, but I had no memory of inputting any of the information in there.

I mentioned my date with Vicky, going to the Club Novus, Vicky leaving early, and me hanging around by myself. I spoke with the server that I thought was the same server at Buckwheat's, and then I walked around the rest of the nightclub and went back to the inn.

But I had no memory of how I made it back. I read the last paragraph in my journal entry.

Although Club Novus is strange and unique, I can't help but feel there's more to investigate. Until next time I'm able to gain entry somehow, there's nothing to report that could be seen as incriminating for now.

I hammered away at the keyboard. "Although there is more to investigate. I can't recall anything that happened when I left the nightclub. I was walking towards the dance floor, and that's when everything went blank. I can't remember faces or anyone on the dance floor. Everyone seemed to blur together, but that is for sure the last time I had a conscious memory."

Two loud voices echoed down the hallway paired with steps that wandered from left to right, bouncing against the walls like a pinball. Then I heard high pitched laughter that irritated me like a morning alarm clock.

"Aw shit, hold on one second," a man muttered. I heard him fumbling with his keys. "Goddammit!" he yelled, and then I heard two people collapse to the ground.

"What the hell!" a woman yelled.

Two people cracked up.

I threw on my pants and put my gun in my back pocket. I sprinted out of the door to find the squirrely neighbor with a beautiful woman lying on the ground next to him.

My neighbor scrambled up to his feet. "Oh shit, man! I am really, really, really sorry! I hope I didn't wake you up!"

"I just wanted to see if everything was all right. The two of you are making a bunch of racket, just so you know."

"Hey man, look, I'm really, really, really sorry." He put his hands up and backed away to the corner. He helped the woman from the ground.

"Why do you gotta be so nervous, Mickey? Relax," she said.

"Goddammit. I've told you a million times why," Mickey uttered. He turned his attention back towards me. "Look, can you forget this whole thing ever happened? Please, my wife could never find out about this. I'm just goin' through some stuff y'know? Just please, keep this between us." His face lit up as if he just had a brilliant idea. "I can even give you something! You look like a young guy. I bet you enjoy some nightlife, well, I have some of the best access to nightlife you could possibly imagine. Club Novus. Here, I'll even give you a pass. It's a very exclusive and private club. Not just anyone gets invited. You won't be disappointed, but you can't say a word to anyone about what you've seen."

"I promise, I'm not out to ruin your marriage, but you might want to get a divorce as an outsider looking in," I said.

"Yeah, that sounds really practical and easy, doesn't it? Gee, I should have considered it earlier," he said sarcastically.

I found the whole exchange to be bizarre. But Mickey seemed like an odd person, to begin with. "I would love to go to Club Novus again."

"Again?" He scrunched his brow.

"Yes, I was there this evening. A friend had a pass, but she only had one. I'd really like to go back. Especially because I can't seem to remember the rest of my night there."

"You had that much fun, did you?" Mickey blurted and grinned, taking a deep breath.

I got the sense he was hiding something. "Do you have any idea why I can't remember anything?"

"Sounds like a you problem, pal." Mickey snickered, and his girlfriend playfully slapped his shoulder.

I glared at him, conjuring as much fury as my eyes and brow could muster.

"Sorry," Mickey uttered. "I didn't mean to make light of your situation. That sounds frightening. But I have no idea. How well do you trust the person that came with you to the club tonight?"

I held my hand out. "Just give me the pass to get in again, and I won't say a word to anyone about this exchange."

"That works for me. Here, darling, why don't you go in the room." Mickey fished the key from his pocket and unlocked the door, and his girlfriend went inside and smiled at me as she exited. Mickey reached inside his suit and pulled out a pen and a Club Novus slip. "All right, give me the name that's on your ID."

"Edward Wright."

Mickey scribbled my name on the back against the wall. He handed the pass back to me. "There you go, pal. Thanks for keeping this between us."

"Sure thing."

"Oh, and by the way, if anyone asks you how you got a pass to get in, tell them you became friends with me. We were eating lunch at the same time at Main Street Subs, we got to talking, and we became acquaintances. That's the story of how I gave you the pass, got it?"

"Got it. Can I ask you a question, do you work for Club Novus or something?"

"Yeah, I work with the operations. Now look, excuse me, but I don't want to keep my lady friend waiting."

"By all means."

Mickey went inside his room and slammed the door in front of me. I went down the hallway and took the elevator to the ground floor. That's when I saw Elizabeth typing away at the keyboard as her father was placing coffee mugs on the counter.

"Eddie, are you feeling any better?" Elizabeth asked and smiled at me.

My stomach dropped. I approached the counter and took a deep breath; I couldn't control my shaky hands. "Elizabeth, I have to ask you something strange when —wait— did you just ask me if I was feeling better?"

"Yeah? Earlier, you didn't look so well, and you said you weren't feeling that great."

"When you say earlier, what do you mean by that?"

"Uh, you came here around 1:00 a.m., so I guessed several hours ago? Are you all right? You look like you've just seen a ghost. Or do you need to go to the hospital? Are you feeling worse?"

I waved my hand at her. "No, no, it's not like that, or at least I don't think... I don't really know. Elizabeth, I'm a little scared. Tonight I went to Club Novus."

"You did? What was that like?" Elizabeth's eyes widened.

"I don't know. It's a nightclub, but something bizarre happened. I have no memory of leaving the place. I remember walking up to the dance floor, and then my mind went blank, or at least, that's what I have in my memory bank. I have no recollection of coming in here and seeing you. Did I say hello to you when I walked in?"

"No, I don't think so. You came in, walking at a slow pace, and you were reserved. Like the lights weren't totally on, you know? So I said hello to you, and that's when you turned around and said hello back. I asked if you were okay, and you said you weren't feeling well and that you needed some sleep. I said I was really sorry to hear that you were under the weather, and if there was anything you needed, just let me know, and then you got in the elevator. And that was that. It seemed out of character for you, almost like you were zombified."

"Do you know anyone else that has gone to Club Novus? That I can talk to?"

"No, I'm afraid I don't; I'm really sorry about that."

"That's okay, I'm not sure what happened, but something happened to me tonight that made me go on autopilot, I guess. And I have no memory. I need to investigate more."

Elizabeth nodded at me. "Yeah, that's so weird. I'm so sorry that happened. Do you think you were drugged or something?"

"I don't know, I think so. I was with Vicky, we had gone out together at Lorenzo's, and then we went to Club Novus because she had an invitation that had been sitting in her purse for a while."

"Oh yeah, we talked about going one time, but since we usually hang out with a group of friends, it would be weird for two of us to go without the others. You know what I mean?"

"Yes. I actually got another invitation a moment ago. There was a man up in the hallway, he's staying across from me. Do you know much about him?"

"I'm afraid I don't. But are you really going to go back there?"

"I have to. I have to understand or investigate what happened."

"Did you have anything to drink?"

"Yeah, I had the house cocktail."

Elizabeth contemplated for a moment. "You know, I have a pack of special straws that change colors if someone has slipped anything in your drink. I mean, you probably have fancy equipment with the FBI you could use, but if you're planning on going back there and trying to recreate what happened, perhaps you could use one of my straws?"

I mulled the idea in my head for a moment. "Yes, I think that will work for now. By the time I were to get anything from the FBI offices, it might not get here until tomorrow."

"Let me run home and grab it then. I can come right back here if you want."

"That sounds good. Sorry, I know you're just getting off work, and I hate to make you go out and come back here but, I really appreciate it. I owe you one. A meal or something, on me."

"You're too kind but don't worry about that. I just want to help out."

"Great, thank you, Elizabeth. I can't tell you how much I appreciate it."

Elizabeth nodded and walked around the counter. "Dad, I'm going to be right back; I have to grab something for Agent Wright."

"Okay," he replied.

Elizabeth left the lobby.

Her father went behind the counter and greeted me. "You doing okay, Agent Wright?"

"I'm hanging in there, I guess." I explained to him everything that had just happened and why Elizabeth would be coming right back.

"Wow. That's some pretty strange stuff going on. You know, I eat a lot of strawberries. I hear that helps with improving your memory."

I know that he didn't consider that as a serious remedy to my situation. Still, I said, "I could eat all the strawberries in the world, and I don't think I'd remember anything that happened tonight. Thanks, though."

He frowned. "Sorry, I didn't mean to... Never mind."

I waited in the lobby for a moment and then went into the bathroom and pulled out my phone, calling someone from the FBI Chicago office.

"Hey, Foster, how are you?" I asked.

"Agent Wright, what do I owe the honor at this early hour?"

"I want to get some blood work done at the local hospital I'm working near."

"You want them to send a sample to our lab?"

"That, and I need you to set up the appointment for me at St. Mary's hospital in Hickory, Indiana. I wanna see what they find right away."

"What's the blood test for?"

"I think I was drugged by someone."

"Oh, shit. Are you kidding? Do you know who did it?"

"I'm not sure how, nor do I know what drug. I was checking out this suspicious nightclub in the town of my investigation, and I have no memory of ever leaving or how the night ended. I fell asleep at some point and woke up with no memory."

"I'm not going to tell you what to do with your case or how to do it, but I think you might need to start issuing some warrants. At least a search warrant to this place."

"No, I want to do this fast. I want to see what I can gather from this place on my own. I feel like I'm getting close to something. I just want to know what was put in my body."

"If you say so. I'll get that appointment set up for you. The hospital will do some blood work and lab testing with a quick turnaround, but then we'll also get a sample size to do some of our own work for anything they might miss."

"Great. Thank you, Foster."

"Sure thing. I'll text you with your appointment details." Foster sighed into the receiver. "And really carefully think about what you're doing. You might be risking your life here waiting on a warrant. You understand that, right?"

"Yeah. I hear ya loud and clear."

"Take care now, Eddie. Heavy emphasis on the take care."

I quietly chuckled, but Foster was as serious as a heart attack. "I'll take care of myself, I promise. Thank you."

I hung up the phone, went out into the lobby, and sat waiting in the cozy chair. I wanted to fix myself a cup of coffee, but I also wanted to go back to my room as soon as I received the straw to try to salvage as much sleep as possible. *Perhaps if I fell back asleep, I might even remember a little bit more of what happened last night?*

I also had to text Vicky, but I wasn't entirely sure what to say. There was a lot that transpired in such a short time frame. Part of me wanted to wait to talk with her as if we were in the early phase of dating, but I had to know if her memory had been fuzzy at all. And I was also curious how her grandfather was doing.

The concerns outweighed the fantasies of dating someone I felt a connection to.

Pulling out my phone, I messaged her.

Hey, sorry about your grandfather being admitted to the hospital. I hope he's doing better. If you're able to call me soon, I'd appreciate it. Something happened last night to me, and I have no memory. I'm concerned, and I wanted to talk to you. No rush. Hope you're doing okay.

I sent the message after rereading the text a thousand times over.

17

A few minutes later, the front doors to the lobby opened, and Elizabeth came up to me with a plastic bag in her hand.

"Here you go. I have a whole pack of them." She handed me a fresh box of straws that changed color if any foreign chemicals or substances were added to a drink.

"Elizabeth, thank you so much for this."

"No problem."

"What can I bring you that would make you smile on your shift? Please, anything, I must repay this favor."

"You can just get me a grilled veggie wrap from Buckwheat's if you really insist."

"You bet, thanks again. You have no idea."

Elizabeth nodded and headed out of the lobby while I returned to my room.

I tried falling back asleep, but I couldn't. I lay down in bed, my mind racing with what could have happened or what drug could have done that to me. I mentally went through the possibilities, but nothing was making sense. A few hours passed by as I was sprawled over the mattress. Checking my phone, Foster texted me saying that my blood work could be done at any time today at St. Mary's. Still no word from Vicky, but I didn't expect her to answer me right away.

As soon as I saw the text, I threw some clothes on and rushed out of the inn. I went to Buckwheat's for a quick breakfast, and I didn't see the server I had hoped to see. It was a staff I wasn't familiar with.

Perhaps this is the weekday crew; I might have to wait another weekend before seeing the familiar faces at Buckwheat's.

I scarfed down an omelet and raced out of the restaurant, and hopped into my car. Driving to St. Mary's hospital, I called Martha.

"Yellow, g-man. What can I do for you?" She answered.

"Have you ever heard of anyone going to Club Novus and not remembering the rest of the evening?"

"No?"

"Well, I went there last night, and I can't remember a damn thing that happened to me after a certain point. I don't think anyone put anything in my drink because I had my drink next to me the entire time. It's possible someone slipped something in at the bar, but I have no idea, and to be honest, I'm pretty freaked out about it."

"Yeah, I can imagine. That's horrifying. We should get together and talk about it more and investigate."

"Yeah, sure, at the moment, though, I'm going to the hospital to get some blood work done to try to figure out what the hell happened."

"You should. Let me know when you're done. Come by my office, and we can talk about it more."

"Sounds good. I'll talk to you later. Thanks, Martha."

The call ended, and I continued my quiet traffic-less commute to St. Mary's hospital. When I arrived, I went through the main lobby and went to a counter that seemed to point people in the necessary directions. There was one person in front of me, and while I waited, I checked my phone, and I saw that I had a missed call from Vicky. I contemplated calling her back, but the person in front of me was receiving help. They were already walking in the direction they needed to go.

"I can help whoever is next," the woman at the counter said.

I approached. "Yes, I have some special testing that needs to be done. An appointment was made this morning, Edward Wright."

"Sounds good. Just let me look you up here." She fixed her attention on the computer monitor and typed in my name. "All right, so what you're going to do is walk straight down the center here, and you'll see a special area for lab testing on the left. Talk to the desk clerk there, and they will get you started."

"Thanks." I strolled through the massive atrium of the hospital lobby down the center path until I saw a collection of chairs and uncomfortable couches in the area to the left.

"Lab work," was the sign out front.

I approached the counter and was immediately taken in to receive a hypodermic needle to the arm, where they extracted vials upon vials of blood.

"Are you okay?" the nurse asked me.

"I'm hanging in there. Just picturing myself on a beach somewhere." I laughed to myself.

"You're looking a little weak. I'm going to give you some apple juice and a cookie after this."

I did feel light-headed. My vision grew darker.

"Stay with me now, young man."

For whatever reason, the only thing I could think of to keep me conscious was the investigation. "Any idea what happened with the blood stealing that happened the other night?"

"Yeah, that was on the news, but that's all I know about it. Don't worry though, your blood's not going to go missing. We have to work on this right away."

"Thank you, just curious."

I was clinging on to consciousness, and she finally removed the pinching needle after what felt like a lifetime.

"You're all done, sir. You can lay down if you'd like, but I'm going to get you a cookie and apple juice. Getting your blood sugar going will help."

"Thank you," I uttered.

After I snacked on the cookie and drank the apple juice, my arm felt a little tender, but I was back to normal for the most part. I stepped outside and looked at the front of the building from the sidewalk, and called Vicky.

"Hello," she answered.

"Hey, how are you?"

Vicky took a deep breath. "I'm doing okay, I guess. How about you? I got your text, and I'm pretty worried. To be honest, I remember everything pretty clearly from last night. No glitches in the matrix on my end. Do you have any idea what happened to you after I left?"

"Uh, yeah, the server actually sat down where you were sitting, and we talked for a little bit. But then she left the table, and I approached the dance floor, and that's all I can remember. I went back to my room, though, and typed in some notes around 1:30 a.m., before they even closed, but it's freaky because I have no memory of that."

"Yeah, I can imagine, that's so scary. I'm really sorry to hear about that."

"It's okay. Fortunately, I seem to be fine. What about you? What's going on with your grandpa? I've been thinking about him this morning."

"He's... I don't know. It's hard to tell. Still unconscious and has a variety of machines hooked up to him. I just got here a few minutes ago. My mom said he was stable."

"You're at the hospital right now?"

"Yeah."

"What room number, I'm actually here at the moment, and I'd like to say hello."

"Oh, uh, sure. Uh, he's in room 517. Are you really here right now?"

"Yeah, I can explain. I'll see you in a moment," I said as I went back inside and found the gift shop to buy some flowers.

141

Going up the elevator, I made it to the 5th floor and found room 517. There was no one there, except an unconscious old man attached to various cables with Vicky sitting by his side, reading a book.

"Hey," she said, her face lit up. "You didn't have to bring flowers."

I placed them on a little table across from the hospital bed. "It was the least I could do. How's my friend doing? Good to see you again." I held her grandpa's hand for a moment.

The only reply was the beep from his heart monitor.

"Thank you very much for coming. It means a lot."

"I figured if I was already here, I'd pay a visit. That's pretty nice that your grandpa has a room to himself."

"Yeah, I guess my mom hooked that up. The perks of having your mom as a doctor. Apparently, they're not too crowded, so it wasn't an issue finding an empty room for him which I'm thankful for," Vicky said.

"Has your mom talked at all about what happened with the missing blood incident?"

"She hasn't mentioned it at all."

"Huh. That's a little strange."

"I know, but then again, I haven't really seen her a whole lot lately. I do my own thing, and we work at different times, kind of. I'm sure she's probably a little freaked out about it."

"Is it strange to you that she hasn't brought that incident up at all?"

Vicky's head bobbled from side to side. "Yes and no. She talks about work so much that I've actually told her to stop. Like, I call her out on it whenever she brings up any drama or any issues. We've had a whole conversation about how she needs to separate work from her home life and keep those two starkly separate. She agrees so, whenever she starts with 'you wouldn't believe the day I had,' I just say, 'nor do I care to hear about it. You're home now,' and that's where it ends."

I rubbed my chin. "I don't mean to bother her at work, but do you think she might remember if she saw a limousine out in front of the hospital?"

"A limousine at the hospital? Was it some bougie dude who couldn't be bothered to go in an emergency truck?" Vicky chortled.

"The blood that went missing at the hospital. Someone gave the blood to someone in a limousine."

"That's wild. Uh, you could certainly try to ask her."

"If you were to rent a limo, where would you go?"

Vicky contemplated. "I might ask my neighbor."

I paused. "What makes you say that?"

"One of my neighbors who lives down the street has a limo in his garage."

"Really? Does he loan it out to people or something?"

"He might. I have no idea. I rarely see him take that thing out, to begin with. He's a really nice guy, though."

"Why does your neighbor have a limo?"

Vicky shrugged. "I don't know. He's like a retired mechanic, I think, and loves to collect cars. His garage barn is massive. I've talked to him before at a neighborhood party, and he seemed like a really nice guy. I feel like he'd loan me a limo if I wanted one."

"Interesting. I might ask him a few questions. Leave no stone unturned. Do you know his name by chance?"

"Yeah, Rudy. Don't know his last name, though. He's a few houses down from me."

"Thank you for this information. I'm glad I said something." I smiled. Inquiring further, I was able to get his address from Vicky. "Could I take you out to lunch? I'm incredibly grateful for the information you gave me. I think I'm going to stop by Rudy's house and ask him a few questions."

"That's okay. I'd like to stay here with my grandpa. My mom will be bringing me lunch from the cafeteria."

"I understand. I'll let you know if anything develops out of this. Thank you for everything."

I left the hospital and went back to downtown Wilton to get a submarine sandwich from the shop that Mickey mentioned to me. After devouring a cheesesteak inside, I went to the police station to meet Martha.

"I'm hoping I have a break in the case here. When I met with Vicky a few hours ago, she gave me some intriguing information about Rudy, who owns a limousine. Do you know him?"

"Yeah, I think I know who Vicky is talking about."

"I was going to stop by his house and knock on his door. Ask him a few questions. Would you want to come with me?"

"Boy, howdy, do I ever," Martha said and smiled. "I love your intuition, g-man. You might be onto something."

143

18

Martha and I got in my car and drove to Vicky's neighborhood, which had large plots of land between each house, and each brick home was two stories.

"Wow, these houses are beautiful," I said as the car crawled up in front of Rudy's house. To the right was a massive white barn garage with a roll-up door. Closed and clean. Putting the car in park, Martha and I got out and approached.

I was about to knock on the door, but Martha stepped in front of me and pressed the doorbell. A muffled ring went through the house. "Have you seen these new inventions? They're great. You don't have to worry about hurting your knuckles."

I smirked at Martha. "It's been a long day. I'm sorry if I'm feeling a little out of it."

"I'm only teasing ya, g-man. I know, you've been through a lot."

We waited there briefly. It was a lovely day out. I didn't take the time earlier to appreciate the sun beaming and the sparse clouds. A gentle wind breezed by. If I had closed my eyes, I probably could have taken a nap.

The door creaked open. An older gentleman in his late sixties smiled at us, standing in the doorway.

"Sheriff Martha, what can I do for you?" He asked.

"Hi Rudy, I know we haven't chatted too much, but I have my friend here, Eddie from the FBI. Now, there's nothing to worry about. He just wants to ask you some questions that might help with the case of the stolen blood at the hospital."

I studied Rudy's face, his eyes widened, and his brow arched. "Well, uh, wow. I mean, I don't think I'll have a lot of information about that." He chuckled. "But if you have questions, feel free to ask them."

Based on his reaction, I believed it was a dead end. There was no way he had any information based on the surprise and confusion. "Thank you, Rudy. This will be quick. When was the last time you took out your limousine for a drive?"

"Wow, I have no idea."

"It's been a while?"

He found the question silly. "It has."

"Any estimation at all?"

"Probably a year ago for my oldest son's wedding."

"I see. Congratulations, though, to your son."

"Thank you."

"What about someone else taking it out for a drive? Would you let a friend or a family member take the limousine out?"

"Sure, absolutely. As long as they can prove to me they can drive it okay, I'd loan it out to anyone I knew personally."

"So, is there a chance someone else has taken out your limousine recently?"

"I don't think so."

"Do you loan it out frequently?"

"Not really. I used to, but not so much anymore."

"When was the last time you gave someone permission to take out the limo?"

"I can't remember. A while ago."

"This year? Last year? The year before?"

Rudy laughed, but it seemed like it came from a place of nervousness. "I'm really sorry, I couldn't tell you."

"What about a name? Can you tell me someone who has driven it?"

"I guess my son Kevin has taken it out before, but I don't really keep track of when or where he takes it. That was also a year ago, most likely. I'm not really sure."

"That's fine. Thank you so far for all the information. This has been helpful if you can believe it."

"I can't believe it. I've given you nothing."

"Leave no stone unturned. That's just one less stone for me to flip over. But, Rudy, I'd like to tell you a little bit more about why I'm asking these questions. You see, the limousine company that's popular in this area is a bit of a drive away. Lennox Limousine. Are you familiar with them?"

"Oh, sure. I'm aware of them. I've never used their services personally for limousines since I got my own, but I know they loan out their hearses which I've used."

"I'm sorry to hear you had to use their services for that reason, but I went over there the other day to see if they had rented out any limousines recently, and they hadn't. The intriguing thing is that someone in a limousine pulled up to the hospital and received some blood from a pressured employee. Now, I'd appreciate it if you kept this information close to you and didn't share it, but I'm not going to swear you to secrecy. I haven't told you anything the media hasn't covered. I'm just trying to find out who might be behind it. So now, you can imagine why I'm here today?"

"Uh-huh, I understand." He smiled. "I wish I could be more help."

"Perhaps you could. Would it be okay if Martha and I took a look at your limousine in your garage?"

Rudy's smile turned into an apologetic grimace. "I really wish I could do that for you, but I'm a man that cherishes his rights. So if you have a warrant, I'll happily abide, but I don't want this meeting to further take up my afternoon. I'd like to go back to the Reds game, and then I have to take the dog out for a walk."

I nodded after a brief pause. "Of course, I didn't mean to interrupt your afternoon plans. It would have been just a quick check, but I understand. We might come back with a warrant if no other limousine owner comes out of the woods, just as a heads up."

Rudy nodded. "That's fine. Gives me some time to tidy up." He smirked.

I smiled back out of courtesy, but I was irritated. "I understand. Thank you, Rudy."

"We'll get out of your hair now. Thanks for your time," Martha said.

We walked off his porch and got back into my car. I started it up and began driving.

"Sorry, the trip didn't amount to much. But, what'd you think back there?" Martha asked.

"I'm annoyed he couldn't just show us his garage, so I could make note of his limousine. But I understand where he's coming from. I will say, something didn't sit well with me back there."

"Like what? He seemed pretty innocent unless you wanna give him an academy freakin' award for acting."

"Which he just might win. Do you know if he was ever an actor?"

"G-man, I know most people here, but I don't *know* them. You catch my drift?"

"Sure."

"I have no idea if he ever acted in stuff. I just know he collects vehicles in his big dumb garage."

"He seemed surprised and normal at first, but then he came off as mixed up and nervous the more I started asking specifics."

"Well, to be frank, Eddie, talking to an FBI agent, even if you did nothing wrong, is pretty goddamn nerve-wracking."

I rolled my eyes, but I laughed as I continued driving.

"Hey, where are you planning on going? We've driven in a circle," Martha said.

"I just want to see something real quick." I parked the car two houses away from Rudy's. There was enough space where Rudy couldn't easily see us from his living room window if he tried. I pulled out my binoculars from the backseat and held them up to my eyes.

"Whatcha see?" Martha asked.

My jaw dropped. "Maybe it's nothing, but I don't know. Rudy is peering through his living room window, and he looks like he's on the phone with someone. And he looks stressed."

"Jesus, Eddie, who knows? He could be really freaked out about just getting questioned, and he's calling his son, asking if he knows anything. I don't know! I'm just speculating."

I lowered my binoculars. "Yeah, you're probably right." I sighed. "I'm just hoping for a break or something in this case. I feel like I'm close, you know?"

"Set your focus on your return to Club Novus."

"Yeah. You're right. I am really curious what will happen if I go again."

"You have a pass, right?"

I nodded.

"From my understanding, you can bring a guest. I don't mean to invite myself, but do you want me to come with you? I think it might be good for you to have some backup."

"That's a great idea. And I'd love for you to come with me," I said.

Martha and I made plans to try to recreate the night as much as possible. We would go to Lorenzo's for dinner before going to Club Novus. We drove separately, and I met her there at around 7:00 PM.

I got to the table first, and I requested to be in the same booth. I only waited a minute before Martha came in looking stunning. A red dress, with makeup and her hair curly.

I beamed at her. "Martha, you look beautiful."

"Aw shucks, Eddie. You get to see a different side of me tonight."

"And what side is that?"

"Date night Martha." She winked. "Don't worry though, this is strictly professional. We are on a mission tonight to find out more about what-in-the-devil is going on at Club Novus."

"Good point. So let me ask you something. You said you went through Club Novus in the afternoon one day, right?"

"Yeah, I called up the place to give them a heads up I was coming in that morning. Since I was investigating the disappearances of those kids, I told them I could get a warrant. Still, it would take a long time and wouldn't look good if they were the only business not to comply just for a simple look around. I wasn't combing through the place, mind you. I was just hoping to take a stroll on short notice in case something was being hidden."

"So the owner obliged without even asking for a warrant?"

"That's correct, or at least I think so. I don't know. I didn't really talk to the owner, just his assistant."

"Do you remember his assistant's name?"

"I want to say it was Mikey? Maybe Micky? A squirrely fellow. Nice, but he's a little out there, I think." Martha chuckled.

I described to Martha the physical features of the man who was my neighbor at the inn.

"Yep, that sounds like him, all right."

"Holy hell. That would make sense. That's how I got this pass tonight—from my neighbor."

"Small world, eh?"

I nodded. "So, what did the inside look like when you checked it out?"

"Well, you know, it used to be an old train depot."

"I did not know that."

"Yeah, way back in the day. So, inside, it's got some high ceilings. Walking through though, you'd never guess it used to be an old train station for Wilton."

"So what else did you see?"

"He gave me a tour of every room. I saw the dance floor, the bar area, but all the party lights were off, and it just felt like a warehouse almost. We walked through the rooms behind the dance floor because you go into this hallway up the second floor, think there's like two rooms, and then on the third floor, there are another two rooms. I guess all the way up at the top is where the owner lives. But in all the rooms, nothing was incriminating. Just couches, minibars, and a storage room that the owner used, which was pretty large. He kept many things like tripods, cameras, rolls of film, tools for taking them apart, and a workbench. Nothing too crazy."

"Everything was all clean?"

"No. All the tools were covered in blood, and I just ignored it," Martha said sarcastically. "Of course, they were all clean. The place was as clean as a whistle. Hell, Mickey even took me up to the owner's room, and we walked around there. He's a total minimalist. Even though he uses a room for storage, his living room hardly had any aesthetic except for modern minimalism. It doesn't look lived in at all."

"How interesting. Have you met the owner?"

"I must have, once or twice, very briefly in passing. Seems like a nice fellow. He goes a little too hard with his style, the white suit, and blue circular glasses, but whatever. Who am I to judge?"

"What's his name?"

"He told me to call him Percy, but I think it's short for Perseus."

"Huh. What a name."

"Yeah, it's a real power name, wouldn't you say?" Martha snickered.

The server came over and took our order; neither of us chose any alcohol. We both just ordered food.

19

After we finished our delicious meal, Martha and I walked to Club Novus. It was around the same time I arrived the previous night. The same bouncer stood out front, underneath the glowing blue neon sign. I thought he might chit-chat with me or say something like, "back again, huh?"

But nothing like that happened. I don't even think he recognized me.

"Do you have a pass?" the bouncer asked Martha.

Martha pointed at me.

"Yes, and this is my guest I brought with me." I pulled out my wallet and handed him the blue slip.

We went through the ID exchange as he studied everything meticulously with his flashlight.

"Come on in." The bouncer let us through, and we went inside.

Entering the club, everything was nearly identical to the previous night. The droning industrial music blaring, the rainbow panels on the dance floor shining, people mindlessly dancing with each other, servers walking around with giant masks hardly wearing anything, and tons of fog.

"Wow, no wonder this place draws a good crowd every night. If I was younger, I'd be coming here every night." Martha cracked up.

There was a different server that approached us; he was tall and muscular, 6-pack abs. "Would you two like a booth?"

"Yes, that would be great," I said.

The server beckoned and escorted us to a booth near the table I sat at the previous night.

"Can I get you two anything to drink?" He asked.

"The house cocktail, please. For both of us," I said.

"Of course."

He strode off, and Martha turned around to check him out as he walked away.

"Good grief, this place is wild, huh?" Martha said. "I need to come here more often. Was he your server last night?"

My lip curled up. "No, it was someone else. But I haven't seen her around, but then again, I can't really see any faces here."

"Yeah, what's with the whole mask thing? They look amazing, but it's definitely creepy."

"Did you notice something else about him?"

"His buns of steel?" Martha smirked.

I laughed. "No, his tattoo on his arm. It looked like it was a minotaur."

"What's your analysis there?"

"Well, it looks like almost all the servers have a tattoo on their arm. It's hard to tell what it is with the fog and what little their outfit is covering, but the server last night had a Cerberus tattoo. Both of which are Greek mythological creatures."

"Huh. That's a little bizarre."

The server came back with two drinks and dropped them off at our table. "Enjoy."

"Excuse me, but I have a quick question I wanted to ask you," I said.

He stopped and stared at me. "Please make it quick. I have other tables to tend to."

"Is that a tattoo of a Minotaur?"

"It is."

"That's nice; I think it looks great. May I ask where you got your tattoo from?"

"A friend of mine gave it to me. Is there anything else you need?"

"Uh, yes. I suppose there's one other thing on my mind. I was here last night with a friend, she left early, but I stayed back, yet I don't have any memory of what happened when I went on the dance floor. Have you heard of anyone going through any memory loss as they're here?"

"No, I haven't. Now excuse me." The server walked away from our table.

"Wow, you laid it all out there," Martha said.

"I was just curious to see what he might say. That was hardly a reaction."

"The man seems pretty busy." Martha shrugged. "Let's try our drinks, shall we?"

"Good idea. The moment of truth." I reached into my coat pocket and pulled out two straws. Reading the instructions, if the straw turns purple, the drink was tainted with a substance. I opened up both straws and gave one to Martha.

We plopped the straws in our drinks and left them in for a minute before pulling them out.

"Looks like they didn't turn any different color. Dammit." I sighed.

"You're upset that your drink wasn't tampered with?"

151

"I was hoping to be one step closer. Proof of the tainted drink would have blown this case wide open."

"Since neither of those are tainted, I'll be a team player and drink 'em both. That way, even if there is something sneaky in here, you'll at least remember the night."

"Or we don't have to drink either of them. How about that?" I said.

"Eh, don't want them to go to waste though." Martha winked. "I guess I shouldn't though."

"I'm still going to take this drink with me and send it for some testing. It's not a bad idea to see if there might be something that the straw can't detect."

I pulled out a small plastic container and scooped it up full of the cocktail.

"Say g-man, where do you think those people are going?" Martha pointed with her head at the dance floor. I turned and looked to see a few people get approached by servers, who held the hands of someone and ushered them to the back of the club.

"I'm not sure. Last night I can only remember going up to the dance floor, and that's where things started to get fuzzy."

"Everyone on the dance floor seems to be having a good time. I notice that everyone seems to be in their own zone, almost hypnotized."

"Perhaps they're just really enjoying the music." I shrugged. It was hard to tell if something abnormal was going on with the twenty people dancing with each other in a pit, especially with all of the fog.

Our server came back to our table after we were watching the dance floor for a little while.

"Was there a problem with your drinks?" He asked.

"No, we're just taking our time with these. Thank you, though," Martha said. "While you're here, I have another question of my own."

"I have other tables to tend to."

"I'll make it quick!" Martha snapped. "Where are you taking those people?" She pointed at another server taking a couple to the back of the club.

"I have no idea." He replied and stormed off, but Martha grabbed his arm, and my jaw dropped.

"You must have an inkling of what's happening, correct?"

"Get your hands off of me, or your ass is getting bounced," the server muttered.

Martha let go of his arm, and he marched into the thick of the fog.

"I'm sorry about that, g-man, he was just being a brat, and it was driving me up a wall." Martha frowned.

"It's okay. I think we'll be all right. They seem to be doing something bizarre here anyway. Perhaps we should ask another server where they're taking them."

"Good idea."

The two of us slid out of the booth and approached another roaming server close to the dance floor. The music was louder, so I had to raise my voice so the waitress could hear me. "Excuse me, I'm not really familiar with this place, but I was just curious where the staff is taking some of the people on the dance floor?"

"We have some private suites in the back for people to enjoy a drink with some of the club's VIPs," she responded.

"Thank you, do you know how it's decided who is picked to go?"

"Those people are just regulars. They receive a special invite and show their pass to their server."

"Got it, thank you." I turned to Martha. "Did you get all that?"

Martha nodded and—

—Opening my eyes, I found myself in a dark room. It took me a moment to realize I was just sleeping.

I'm in my bed in the inn, tucked in by the sheet and comforter, wearing pajamas.

I turned on the bedside lamp and scrambled up, checking my phone, plugged into the charger. There were no messages nor any missed calls; it was 5:00 a.m. My heart pounded in my chest as my hands shook.

No, no, no! It happened again! What was the last thing I remembered?

I sealed my eyes shut and forced myself to recall everything that led up to that point, but the only thing I could think of was talking with Martha in the club.

That's the last memory I have.

Jumping out of bed, I checked my tablet and looked at my daily notes page, and it appeared I had filled in everything coherently. I also noticed I had an email from St .Mary's hospital.

Nothing in my blood suggested any foreign substances were added to my drink on Sunday night.

Good, but, damn. Another dead end. I looked through the notes I had written a handful of hours ago.

Martha and I went to the club, just the two of us. Neither of us drank the cocktail nor any alcohol, for that matter. We found out why people go in the back rooms, and then we left shortly after walking around a little bit more. The next objective will be to get an invite to the back rooms, but getting an invitation into Club Novus is hard enough. Martha and I each got in our respective cars and drove home.

I tried calling Martha, the phone rang a few times and went to voicemail.

"Hi, you've reached Sheriff Martha. Leave a voicemail."

"Hey, it's Eddie. Call me back as soon as possible. It happened again, and I want to know if it happened to you too?"

I ended the call and paced back and forth in front of the bed. I gazed out the window, hoping that looking at the street while still dark would jog any memories.

The sun was poking its way from the horizon. I couldn't think of anything. As I walked to the bathroom, I noticed there was an envelope on the floor. Someone must've slid it underneath my door, or perhaps I brought it in with me and dropped it on the ground. I picked it up; it was sealed. Opening it, there was a letter inside.

I THINK IT'S TIME WE MEET. I CAN HELP YOU. I'VE WANTED TO HELP YOU, BUT IT CAN BE DIFFICULT FOR ME. MY SINCEREST APOLOGIES. THE BEST WAY I COULD BE OF ASSISTANCE IS IF YOU MET WITH ME AT MY HOUSE.

1179 QUARRY RD WILTON, INDIANA.

I CANNOT STRESS THIS ENOUGH, DO NOT PARK IN FRONT OF MY HOUSE. IT WOULD BE IDEAL IF YOU WERE DROPPED OFF. IF YOU MUST DRIVE, PARK BEHIND MY GARAGE. SORRY FOR THE MESS. BUT COME IMMEDIATELY INTO THE BACKYARD AND HOP THE FENCE. DO NOT APPROACH THE PORCH.

SOMEONE MIGHT BE WATCHING.

COME SEE ME THIS AFTERNOON WHEN YOU'RE FEELING BETTER, 1:00 PM WOULD BE IDEAL. COME ALONE. THERE'S A LOT I CAN EXPLAIN.

-C.R.G.

I put the letter back in the envelope. Getting dressed, I rushed down to the lobby and saw Elizabeth getting ready to head out the door.

"Oh, hey, Eddie! I'm glad you're here. I just finished writing a note to leave for my dad for when he saw you next," Elizabeth said.

"Elizabeth, hey, thank you so much. Uh, what can you tell me that happened tonight when I came in?"

"Oh no, you forgot what happened again, didn't you? I kinda thought so. You came in with eyes glazed over and were very quiet and just wanted to go back to your room, so I didn't want to bother you, but something weird happened about five minutes after you came in. Another person came in an older man with gray hair and beard. He wasn't the most charming person to talk to, but this is how the conversation went: 'Hi, I have a letter I must give him,' he said.

'Okay, sure. I can give him the letter when I see him next,' I replied.

'No. I need you to go up to his room and slide this letter under his door immediately.'

'But I can't leave the desk.'

'You must do so immediately. It must get to him. Thank you. His safety relies on it. I'll watch the desk for you if you'd like.'

"I said I'd slide the letter under your door, and he agreed to leave. He didn't leave a name with me, though. I locked the door after he left and ran up to your room. Sorry I don't have more for you, Eddie."

"That's fine; you did wonderfully. Thank you very much. I got everything I need." I ran back to the elevator, went back into my room, and reread the note from C.R.G.

20

My phone vibrated. I checked it, and it was Foster.

"Hello?" I answered desperately.

"Eddie. Sorry for the delay. The hospital got me the information for your blood work as soon as they could. Are you ready for it?"

"I'm guessing it came up nothing?"

"Well, we still have to test your blood in our lab, but the hospital had nothing that suggested any drug was in your body that would've affected your memory. Only a small bit of alcohol."

"Thanks, Foster."

"Don't sound too defeated; I thought you might be relieved."

"It's a double-edged sword, I guess. But something happened, and I want to know what the hell it was."

Foster paused for a moment. "I'm sorry I don't have more for you, but when we do some more lab work on your blood at the office, I'll let you know what we find. We'll check it out... under the microscope if you will."

"Thanks. Anything else for me?"

"No laugh?"

"Not in the mood I guess."

"Sorry, I didn't mean to make light of what's going on with you. It's definitely concerning. Well, just be careful with your mission and hang in there. You holding up okay?"

"Yeah," I lied. I felt like I was on the brink of insanity, but the letter from C.R.G. gave me some hope. "I'll talk to you later, Foster."

"Sounds good. Take care now."

We ended the call, and then I looked up the address to C.R.G.'s house and saw it online. The grass was overgrown, the house was two stories but dilapidated to all hell. Chipped paint, patches of exposed wood, and dirty windows. My first thought was that the home must be abandoned, but I could see a car in the driveway in front of the garage.

Could it be a trap?

I tried to get some sleep through the rest of the morning, and I managed to get another hour of shut-eye. I had a missed call from Martha, so I called her back.

"Hey, Eddie," she said with no humor in her voice. "I got your message. Look, I don't really know what happened last night. My memory is faded. Like, it's horrifying. I have no idea how I got home. I guess I drove because my car is in my driveway, but it doesn't make sense."

"Yeah, the same happened to me, too."

"So, what the fuck Eddie?" Her voice broke. "I-I think of myself as a strong person, but I cried this morning. What is h-happening? Were we drugged?"

"I think we were. But I have no idea with what. What's the last thing you remember?"

"Talking to some practically naked shot-girl. She told us about the back rooms, and then everything just blanks out from there."

"Same for me. Look, I know this is distressing and horrible, but I think there might be some hope for us. I received a letter when I woke up. It was slipped underneath my door, and it says it's someone who might be able to help us. They even say to come see them at 1:00 p.m. when I'm feeling better, leading me to believe they know about the drugging."

"...I don't know what to say. You got some letter? I think we should kick in doors and start arresting people left and right!"

"Wait, I know that makes sense, but we both seem to be unharmed. Let's see what this guy knows before we throw handcuffs wildly. We might be able to capitalize on something here."

"Eddie, it's been a pleasure working with you, but I have to disagree with your approach on this."

"I know, I know it's crazy and a little unorthodox, but I want to know what this person knows. Now, I'm going to go there at 1:00 p.m., and as soon as I'm done, I will contact you. The person wants to meet one on one. I'll give you the address. Could you let me know who lives there?"

Martha gave out a deep sigh. "Yeah, I'll let you know as soon as I get in the office. What's the address?"

I gave it to her and then went to Buckwheat's for breakfast. As I mentally prepared myself for 1:00 p.m., I received a call from Martha.

"Hey, so I didn't go into work today because I'm not feeling like myself, but I did check the address for you from one of the guys down at the station."

"Yeah? Do you have a name?"

"Charles Robert Green."

"Great, thank you so much. I'm glad you took the day off; you deserve some rest. Take the day to relax and try to focus on other things. Just so you're aware, I'll be at that location at 1:00 p.m. in case anything happens to me or in case it's a trap."

"You got it, g-man. Best of luck to ya."

The call ended, and I stared out the window and couldn't help but smile. It finally felt like I had a promising lead. When I saw the initials at the bottom of the letter, I had thought it was Charles Green. He must've been watching me at all times, it seemed. Goosebumps popped up all over my skin.

I finished my breakfast at Buckwheat's, an omelet with a side of pancakes. I ate a large meal, so I didn't have to worry about food later on. After paying my bill, I went to the park. It was cloudy out, and not many people were enjoying the gray day, but a weird part of me was.

After walking around the park, I went to my car, put the address in my phone, and drove to C.R.G.'s house. It was a 10-minute ride, and hardly anyone was on the road, a clear route with flatland in the background. I was in a part of Wilton that barely had any houses, but I came up to a property with a half-acre of land out front and probably an acre in the back. The grass was tall, reaching my knee, but the gravel driveway was empty.

I turned right, and my phone GPS told me I had arrived. Idling through the driveway, I debated parking in front of the garage since the grass was overgrown in the back. Still, I figured it would be best to listen to every word on the note. As I passed by the house, I looked at the front door, riddled with scratches. There was a tiny window at the top, slid open, with two green eyes glaring at me. It was hard to tell if those were real eyes since they were completely still.

Chills crept up my spine.

Driving into the long grass, my car idled through just fine until I made it to the back of the white garage. The paint was dried out and chipping in other areas. It matched the house's personality.

It was 12:58 when I arrived. Stepping out of the car, I gently pressed the door shut, barely making a sound. Wading through the thick grass, I went up to the wooden fence that was too tall to see over, but there wasn't a door for me to get through. I took a deep breath and jumped, clinging onto the edge and pulling myself up and over. The backyard was no different than the side of the house. Overgrown, but there were some rusted metal rods peppered throughout. When I saw the door, my whole body jumped.

A man stood in the doorway, I didn't see him when I climbed over. He was an older gentleman with somewhat deep wrinkles and a fuzzy beard with thinning white hair. Narrowing his green eyes at me, I thought he would say something, but he only stared.

"My name is Edward Wright."

He put his finger up to his mouth, silencing me. He beckoned for me inside his house. I paused for a moment, tapping my side just to make sure I had my pistol ready to go.

The stone steps to get in the house were crumbling, but they were resilient enough to hold my weight. Inside, a sour stench hung in the air, like something may have been rotting. Nicotine was prominent too, but fortunately, it wasn't too overwhelming. The man stood inside the kitchen with the windows and curtains closed. He turned the center light on above, encased in a tainted yellow frosted glass with multiple dead flies at the bottom. Leaning up against the kitchen counter, he motioned for me to close the back door. I desperately wanted to keep it open to let out the stench of the house, but I didn't have a choice. I closed it.

"Hello, my name is Edward Wright. I work for the FBI. I'm investigating the murders that happened here at Wilton."

The man nodded. "Kind of thought so." His voice was deep and scratchy like he'd been smoking for a thousand years.

I was waiting for him to say something else, but there was nothing. An awkward silence. I felt a mental shove to keep the conversation going. "I got your letter. I'm here looking for more information."

"Meow," a gray-colored cat with knotty fur tiptoed into the kitchen.

"We have a guest, Bella. Go on, say hello," the man said, with a gentle voice I didn't think he was capable of.

I was repulsed by the man and his house, but the cat nudged my leg, and I petted its side. It began to purr immediately.

"She really likes you. That's a relief," the man said.

"It's nice to meet you, Bella." I kept petting her side while keeping an eye on the man in my periphery. "May I ask what your name is, sir?"

"Charles Green."

Bella brushed up my leg as I stood up straight. I couldn't help but smile. "It's nice to meet you. I've been looking for you."

"And I've been watching you. You haven't kept your eyes open. First two nights, you were keenly aware. But lately, not so much."

I scrunched my brow. "Why have you been watching me?"

"I get really annoyed, okay!" He snapped. "It's hard for me to talk to people. Because I want to help them, y'know? But when a man is working around in the shadows, ya can't just help people, y'know? No one wants to talk to a stranger in the middle of the night. I get that. I really do. So my approach is a little different. I figure I might be able to scare someone into staying all holed up if I think they're in danger."

"You thought I was in danger?"

"Yes, and at this very moment, without the proper equipment, you still are."

"But I have a gun. Is that not enough?"

"You can have all the firepower in the world. Chances are it's not. You don't know how to navigate these waters, y'know?" He pointed at his chest repeatedly. "I know what's going on. I know what's going on. Or at least, I have an inkling of what's going on. I know what's just below the surface level. Beyond that, who the hell knows. Only Vincent does."

"Vincent Nelson?"

"Very good. No wonder you work for the FBI. So you've been looking for me, but have you been looking for him too?"

"Yeah."

"I can't imagine you had any luck because you're not going to find him under that name."

"What name does he go by?"

"Perseus, I think. Maybe Percy for short. I don't really know. He and I don't talk."

"You two used to be close friends?"

Charles nodded. "He was practically my brother. We hung out so much and got along so well. And admittedly, deep down, I still love him as a friend, but he's too far gone now."

"Far gone? What do you mean by that?"

Charles' lip curled up. "You've got a lot to learn, Agent Edward." He reached into his shirt pocket and pulled out a cigarette. Lighting it up and exhaling a plume of smoke. The smell of burning tobacco was better than the rotten odor.

"I've got all day. Care to catch me up to speed?"

"Can I take you into my office? It's upstairs. It'll be a lot easier to explain."

"Sure. Lead the way."

21

Charles took a drag and stared at me. Something about his eyes made my skin crawl, but I wasn't afraid. He didn't strike me as evil, just misunderstood and depressed. He walked out of the kitchen, and I followed him into a living room with old furniture from the '70s. A plaid cushioned couch, chair, dark wood coffee table, and an ornate glass lamp, but hardly any light came in the living room, the curtains were closed. The rest of the house smelled like a rack of old clothes at a thrift store. We cut through the living room and went upstairs. The cat followed at my side and meowed. Going up the carpeted steps, I put my hand near my gun and kept a safe distance from Charles. Arriving on the second floor, he ushered me into a room that reminded me of the garage. There was a workbench, a drafting table, and a large desk with a lengthy adjustable lamp. Nuts and bolts weren't organized, but his tools and power tools all had their designated place, dangling from the wooden pegboard hanging on the wall. It smelled like fresh cut wood and metal.

He sat on a chair at the desk underneath a window with the curtain wide open. He pointed at the seat next to him, which I sat down at. Bella hopped up on my lap and purred as I pet her.

"Gee, she's a personable critter. I guess she's excited to see someone else other than me for once," Charles said.

"You don't get much company?"

Charles shook his head. "That's okay, though. I occupy enough of my time here now that I'm retired. I'm either in here or outside when I want to go out on my vigilante trips at night."

"What exactly are your 'vigilante trips' at night?"

"I'll get to it. So I guess it's good to start from my friendship with Vincent Nelson." Charles cleared his throat. "We'd been inseparable since elementary school, y'know, my best friend. He was always a really sharp kid. All the teachers in class knew that Vincent was going to go places. Standardized test scores, he aced. And every class, he aced. And to add to his intellectual prowess, he's charming as all hell. I think you'd be hard-pressed to find someone who didn't like him. But yet, he hung out with me. I guess it's because we went to a small elementary school, and he thought it was cool that I was one of the top learners. I don't know. Both of us did pretty well with our grades. I couldn't talk in front of people very well, though. Gave me too much anxiety. Still can't do it. On the other hand, Vincent was always a leader and a great communicator.

"So fast forward to high school. Classes get a little more challenging. We're able to expand our knowledge more with drafting and engineering, and that's where Vincent and I really made a name for ourselves. Always fixing issues on people's cars, cracking open an Atari system to figure out what kind of parts were inside, and both of us had a home computer. That's where we really got our hands dirty. We were excited to learn; we wanted to make our own inventions or improve things like cars, computers, hell, transistor radios. Making our own pirate radio station and pissing off the FCC." Charles chuckled, but then his laughter died down, and he took a deep breath. He frowned. "But then my parents died."

"I'm really sorry to hear that, Charles. It's not easy losing someone important to you at a young age. Especially in high school."

"You have no clue," he said like a bitter old man.

"You're right. I don't know what it's like to lose both parents in high school, but my best friend disappeared when I was in middle school, and it still affects me to this day. Our pains are different but still present."

Charles looked at me; his eyes brimmed with tears. "I'm sorry to hear about your friend," he said softly; it made my own eyes swell.

"I appreciate it," I said, suppressing the emotion in my voice.

We took a brief pause. Charles looked down at his desk while I kept petting the purring cat.

"Anyway. Vincent was my best friend. He looked after me, and I knew he got into an excellent school out of state, but when my parents passed away, he said he would stick around so we could keep hanging out. He said he was worried about me, and I told him he didn't have to do that, but I appreciated it. It helped soften the blow of high school graduation.

"Even though I was a wallflower, the routine of high school was pleasant. Everyone treated me much nicer, not that anyone was ever mean to me, to begin with, but even the attractive girls talked to me to make sure I was okay. It felt like I had a family, and I knew graduation would mean the end of that family. But if Vincent stuck around, I knew I would be in a decent place... And then I guess he changed his mind and ended up going to school out of Indiana without telling me right away. I was pissed. Vincent led me to believe that I could hang out with him all school year in the summertime and even in the fall. Then the rug got pulled out from under me."

"And that's when you started working with a limousine company?"

Charles stared at me and arched his brow. "Jesus. I didn't think you feds would know that off the top of your head. Have I been a subject of interest for a while?"

I laughed. "Don't worry. I am pretty thorough with investigating. A man in a limousine was actually used to intimidate a medical practitioner at a hospital. So I searched for the nearest limousine rental company and asked questions. I didn't think you'd have anything to do with them, but I had just been asking around if anyone knew you or Vincent Nelson. Sheriff Martha said she's had complaints about you following people, so I thought that was interesting and wanted to know more about it. So there, that's all I know. I looked through your high school yearbook as well."

"I see."

Part of me regretted saying anything. Charles looked like a deer in the headlights.

"Don't worry, I just wanted to be open and honest with you about everything I've known. I appreciate all that you've shared with me so far."

"Yeah, uh-huh. Anyway, you're right. I worked for Lennox Limousine for a little while. Cars became my specialty. I knew Purdue was a good engineering school, so I went there and focused on my own life. When I finished my degree, I knew that Detroit hired engineers to work for the big three automotive companies, so I moved out there. I figured since I didn't have anything here, I may as well move out and have a change of scenery. I kept this house, though, because I didn't want to sell it. A few people I told thought I was crazy not to turn a profit on it, but it held too much significance. When I worked in Michigan, I never really felt at home. I had a girlfriend for a little while but, once that ended, I came back here. And wouldn't ya know it, I had received contact from Vincent. He sent me a letter to my home address, and it was forwarded to me in Michigan as I was preparing to leave. Vincent told me we had to meet right away as soon as I returned to Indiana. But he had a name change and was now Perseus.

"So I came back to live in my house, and one of the first things I did was have Vincent come over to this very house. He had totally changed his look. He was bald, had blue sunglasses, and wore fancy clothes. But I definitely recognized him as the same old Vincent and talked to him as if hardly any time passed at all. It was surreal."

"What did you guys talk about?"

"First, Vincent said, 'Before we talk about anything else, my name is Perseus. You can call me Percy for short, but please, I need you to recognize me as such.' and I said it wouldn't be a problem. So I guess I should refer to him as Percy from here on out.

"Percy was all excited. He was telling me about how he wanted my help with designing inventions with him. 'There's no telling what we could accomplish with your brain and mine. I've found a way to come up with something truly amazing. A catalyst for inventions that you'd never think to use. Something more precious and incredible than oil.' And that's where all of this takes... a turn." Charles shook his head.

"What do you mean?"

"It might be better if I show you. Here's an invention he worked on. He told me never to show it to another person, but here we are. I think you need to see this." Charles pulled out a shelf on the left side of his desk and grabbed a cubed contraption with a light bulb at the top. He set it down on the desk in front of us, a cube encased in black metal, and he pressed the red button at the top. The bulb shined brightly. "This light bulb will never burn out, according to Percy."

"Why?"

"I don't know how it works. And I'm too afraid to understand."

"Why?" I asked again, feeling like a little kid annoying their parent.

"This cube was something he invented years ago, around the time of his doctorate. And he requested I work on a new project with him."

"So what? It's just a cube with a light bulb on top of it. It's impressive it appears to not run on any power but I'm guessing there's a battery inside that case?"

"Agent Wright, I'm not sure how else to explain this but, the light bulb on top of this cube is powered by blood."

"Blood?" I echoed.

Charles nodded. "Human blood."

"You've got to be kidding me."

"I know, it sounds like a joke or some elaborate prank, I'm sure, but this box is unbreakable. I can't see what's inside, but Vincent assured me that human blood is inside, circulating rapidly enough to keep this light fixture on 24/7."

I didn't believe him. Not because I didn't want to, but because it sounded too surreal and impossible. It didn't make any sense.

"Do you know anything about the project he requested your help on?"

Charles shook his head. "I didn't ask. He frightened me when he told me he was using his own blood for inventions. He had this hypnotized look in his eye, like he had discovered a new element and he was obsessed. The thought of it made me sick. I had no interest in exploring or experimenting with human blood for engineering anything."

"How did he react when you declined?"

"Percy was irritated, and he looked at me confused. He was upset that I wasn't curious to understand how or why, but it didn't feel right to learn that knowledge. How could he expect this to be a humane or a reliable method for technology? But he was upset. He swore me to secrecy and said he would know if I ever told anyone, and consequences would follow. I feel like he has eyes on my house, but I don't know how. That's why I let the grass grow, in case there's a camera in my yard somewhere. Maybe he bugged my house. It's hard to say."

"You really think he's spying on you like that?"

"He said he would know if I ever told anyone."

"It sounds like he's just threatening you. Making you live in fear."

"It's hard to say. If anyone could figure out a way to have me on surveillance, it's Percy. He's a man of his word too. But I had to tell you about it because I saw you going to his club twice."

Finally, we were getting to the root of something I wanted to know. I nodded. My knees bounced up and down rapidly. "What's going on in this club?"

"Right. So Percy was telling me to join with his invention adventures, or whatever you want to call it, but when I declined, he was saddened, but we were still talking. He asked me what I had been doing with my life, so I explained and asked him the same. Percy explained that he's been running Club Novus for a few years, and he really wanted me to attend. But I told him going to nightclubs wasn't really my type of thing, but he insisted that I go some night because it would really mean a lot to him. So I said, sure I might go some night, and that's when he pulled out a blue slip and said this would get me in the club."

Charles reached into the desk shelf again and pulled out the blue admission slip I had the previous two nights.

"This is what he gave me. As you can see, I never went."

"You were never curious enough to check it out?" I asked.

"Well, there's more to it than that. Percy had this devilish grin on his face when he gave me the slip. And I asked him what he was smiling about. Percy reached into his pocket and had these plastic tubes in his hand." Charles went inside the shelf for the third time and set six small plastic cylinders on the top of the desk.

"What is that?" They looked like the small pieces of plastic used to attach price tags to new clothes.

"Percy told me to put them in my nose, and there's a tiny button at the bottom of the container. When you put it in your nose, you press the button, and it expands into a specialized filter he developed. When I asked him why he would give me these weird nose filters, that's when he explained to me something that really creeped me out." Charles took a drag on his cigarette that had been slowly burning still. I forgot he had it

165

in his hand. "Before I go on any further, do you mind explaining to me what it's like on the inside of Club Novus?"

"Oh, sure. It's dark, lit with dim overhanging lights at tables. The dance floor has multi-colored square panels that light up. The servers are wearing these elaborate but beautiful art deco masks and next to no clothes. And there's also loud, obnoxious industrial music. Sometimes it's an overdriven drone of different notes. Sometimes it sounds like machines beating the hell out of each other."

"Can you think of any other detail that you might have left out?" Charles asked.

I was annoyed by his question, but I didn't want to show any frustration. I was grateful for everything he had given me so far. Thinking about what he said for a moment, I realized I had forgotten something. "The place is pretty foggy?"

"Exactly. Percy told me that if I were to attend his club, I would need to wear these nose filters."

My eyes widened. "Did he tell you what's in the fog?"

"He just said there's something in the fog that gets people loose and makes them enjoy themselves a little more. Mind you, Percy said all of this with this evil smirk on his face."

"How do those filters work?"

"Percy did a demonstration for me. So I will show you. You take one, put it in your nose, press the button, and watch." Charles took one of the plastic tubes, put it in his nose, and pressed the tiny button at the top. It expanded inside his nose, but I could barely tell.

"Whoa. That's pretty discreet. And you can breathe okay in it?" I asked.

Charles handed me two of the plastic tubes. "And when I press the button again, it contracts into its original state. I have to admit, it's nifty and impressive, but what exactly it's filtering out, I have no idea."

"But he told you it's needed if you go in the club? Did he tell you why?"

"That's correct, but no, he didn't explain what was inside the fog. Percy did tell me that I shouldn't be worried about seeing someone I would know at his club. He said he had a network of people give out invitations to others who were from out of town."

"Holy hell. Well, that just screams incriminating if that's true."

"I swear, Agent Wright, that is exactly what he told me. I asked him about it, why did he give invitations to out of towners? He had a bizarre answer. 'I just want to put Wilton on the map, create a unique club experience that's coveted by people around the world.' Apparently, Percy had been attending nightclubs in New York and Los Angeles. I guess to get his business going, he contacted friends out there. They came in, experienced it, loved it themselves, and then it started growing from there. People telling other people that they needed to make a special trip out to Club Novus. Apparently, it's quite the unique and euphoric experience."

"Well, I can't remember a single thing that happened to me."

"But you do want to go back there, yes?" Charles reached over the desk to grab an ashtray and squashed his cigarette butt in the center.

"Yeah, but it's for the investigation."

"You went there once, twice, and it looks like you're about to go back for a third time. Not that I'm keeping score, but it looks like Percy is winning against you at the moment." Charles puffed out a few exhaled laughs, but he noticed I wasn't entertained, and he stopped. "Sorry about that."

The realization of Charles' words shocked me. "You're not wrong, though," I said. "But I have no urgency to go back there because of what I felt. I just need to know what's happening in that club."

"I understand. I was giving you a hard time. Anyway, you want this admission slip to get in?"

I nodded.

Charles wrote down my name on the back and handed it to me. "There's another admission for you. And please, take these, let me know what you find." Charles gave me four of the plastic tubes. "In case you want to bring a guest with you."

"Thank you. Do you have any interest in coming with me?"

"Hell no."

I was relieved to hear that. I didn't want him to join, but I thought I'd be courteous and at least ask. "That's fine. Thank you for giving me all of the information that you have. Is there anything else you'd like to tell me before I leave?"

Charles leaned back in his chair and contemplated, staring at the wall behind me. I still had his cat on my lap, petting it the entire time. I almost forgot I had been petting his cat. Bella had been purring for so long it sounded like background noise.

"If I'm being 100% honest with you, I think the disappearances are because of whatever Percy is doing."

"It certainly seems like a lot of evidence is starting to point that way."

"Yeah. I think he's starting to lose control. And that's why, y'know, I started going on these nightly vigilante trips. I feel like I've seen so many out-of-towners go into his club. Y'know, I'll admit it, I'm a weird fella. And when I came back into town after Percy invited me, I parked my car a few blocks away from Club Novus, just watching people go in and out of the club for an entire night. I wanted to confirm that he was only inviting out-of-towners, and it certainly seemed that way. I checked license plates and noticed that they weren't from Indiana. A lot of Illinois, though, I think he attracted a Chicago crowd.

"As I saw all those people go in, I got it in my head that something weird was going on. I bumped into two people one night who got invited. They came in all the way from New York. I asked them if they were given anything for their noses. They looked at me like I had blood coming out of my eyes. It was a young couple, and they wanted nothing to do with me. I tried to warn them about going in, but they still went ahead. I don't know what came over me, but the whole conversation I had with Percy rubbed me the wrong way. The worst way. With all that blood inventions talk and having to wear a special nose filter inside the club, I had a feeling something corrupt was happening."

"You didn't tell the police about this?"

"I'm talking to you now, aren't I? Look, I messed up. I admit that I probably should have talked to Sheriff Martha sooner, but I also would have sounded like a lunatic. I feel like you actually listen. You believe me, even though everything I'm saying is bizarre. And so what was I supposed to do? I tried a traditional approach by telling people face to face not to go into the club. That didn't really work. In fact, I scared them into going into the club for refuge. That's when I realized that if I follow around an out-of-towner and freak them out, that's when they leave altogether. Sure, I've had the police called on me, but I feel like I may have saved some lives. Because I really think Percy and that damn club killed those six people. You saw they were drained of blood, right?"

"I did see that. Yes."

"But I couldn't tell Martha about my suspicions. I'm sure she already thought I was a lunatic because I was 'stalking' people at night. And I don't want to be an accessory to Percy's crimes if he is the one behind everything, which I think he is."

"That's all right. You told me a lot of valuable information. Better late than never."

Charles nodded. "I'm sorry."

"Everything will be all right. Thank you for telling me and inviting me to your house."

"You're welcome back anytime, especially with how much Bella appreciates your company." Charles smiled at his cat.

"Good to know. We might be seeing each other more if we find out that Percy is indeed the mastermind behind this all. I've got a feeling we'll be better acquainted."

"Whatever I can do to help."

"Thank you for your cooperation. Well, I have nothing else, so I'm going to head out now."

"I'll walk you out." Charles stood up and grabbed Bella off my lap. He whispered something to his cat I couldn't hear.

I followed him back downstairs to his kitchen, and just as I was about to exit the back door, another thought crossed my mind. "Do you know where people might go to get tattoos around here? I noticed the servers all at Club Novus have tattoos on them. Even through Wilton, I've seen people with them but no parlors anywhere."

"I have no clue."

"Right. I just thought I'd ask. And one last thing, is there anything else I should be on the lookout for with Percy?"

"Not that I can think of. Other than his affinity for engineering things, whatever he might have in his hand might be something else. You never know with him."

"All right, thank you. See you soon." I left the house. The breath of fresh air outside was relieving. I couldn't believe I grew accustomed to the tobacco and sour odor.

22

Getting inside my car, I gave Martha a call before driving off.

"What's going on, Eddie?" she answered, no humor in her voice.

"Hey, I followed my lead. I think we've been under the influence of some special gas inside Club Novus, and that's why we can't remember anything."

"Really? You think there's something in the air?"

"Yes, and it's in the fog, I believe. Charles Green gave me some filters to use and another pass to go to the club tonight."

"You didn't arrest him? It sounds like he works at the club."

"I don't think Charles does. He's a former friend of the owner."

"I still think we should keep our eyes on him. I don't trust what's going on here. Anything that has to do with that fucking club is corrupt. I'm convinced."

"I don't think Charles is going to flee. If we need him, he'll be there to testify against Percy. I really believe that. But first, we need to know for sure if Percy is the one behind the murders."

"And how are we going to do that?"

"I think everything is culminating tonight. They say third time's the charm, right? Well, I have another admission and some filter to weed out whatever is in that fog."

"It makes sense now why those servers are wearing those masks. They're probably used to keep them conscious. Dammit, what the hell is going on in that damn club at night?"

"Look, Martha, I know you probably want to come with me, but I ask that you let me go alone."

There was a brief pause. "You're not wrong g-man, I really want to go with you and not seem like a coward, but I'm still shook up about last night. I'm happy to sit in a patrol car, though just outside of Club Novus with some other officers if you think you might need some backup."

"That could work. I'll also let the FBI know where I'll be, so there's no confusion about tonight."

"What time are you planning on getting there?"

"Same time as the last two nights. Around 9:00."

"Copy that. I'll be watching from afar. Call or text me if you need me to bust in."

"Thanks, Martha."

"You bet. Talk to you later."

The call ended.

Turning on the car, I drove through the backyard and out of the driveway, heading back to the inn. I went up into my room, logged in notes on my tablet, and then called Foster at the FBI. I told him where I would be in the evening in case anything were to happen, the FBI would know that I had disappeared at Club Novus. That thought made my skin tingle. But that couldn't happen; I was well protected. Whoever ran the operations at Club Novus, they're smarter than that if they were the killer.

I practiced putting in the nose filters and taking them out. I was amazed at how resilient of an invention they were for it was nothing but a tube of plastic that could expand.

Pulling out my phone, I texted Vicky.

Hey, I hope you're doing okay today. Let me know if you need someone to talk to.

I pressed the send button and then sat in my chair in silence, staring out at the window at downtown Wilton. Imagining myself living in Wilton gave a certain amount of excitement in my chest. It was relaxing to have a break from all of the noise coming from downtown Chicago. I forget the tranquility that exists outside the city sometimes. Only when I'm working on missing person cases can I find an area with solitude and plenty of open space. It filled me with sadness sometimes.

Searching online for anything regarding Club Novus came up with no results. I found it strange that not even the Wilton Observer had an article about the club's opening. Nor was there an op-ed by an irritated old-timer renouncing the existence of a nightclub in the quaint Wilton. Of course, there wasn't even a website for Club Novus.

As dinner time loomed around, I went to Buckwheat's for a burger. It was crowded, but I didn't notice anything out of the ordinary as I scanned the restaurant. Before I left, I ordered a grilled veggie wrap and delivered it to Elizabeth. Then I spent the rest of my time walking around Wilton as the sun started its descent. The park was an excellent spot to burn some time. I sat at a bench along the water, watching the river flow. So much of it reminded me of my childhood in Michigan.

Did I really want to go back to a place like that?

Dusk settled in. The sun had set, but the sky was still orange and purple, and fireflies were glowing around me. People were walking out of the park; 9:00 p.m. was just around the corner.

I went straight to Club Novus, and by the time I got there, the sky was mostly dark. The bouncer stood out front, and I handed him my blue slip.

"May I see your ID?"

I pulled it out of my wallet and showed him my driver's license. "Third night in a row. I can't get enough of this place. Is that embarrassing?" I said.

The bouncer looked at me with his head tucked down under his brow. "You may proceed." He unclipped the stanchion and let me go inside.

In the vestibule with the sole blue light up above, I put in the plastic nose filter. I gazed at the bulb, wondering if it was powered by human blood like the device that Charles showed me.

The bulb seemed ordinary, but then again, it stuck out of the ceiling. I couldn't see what it was attached to.

Opening the door to the club, I strolled inside and saw a different woman as the host. I couldn't tell faces apart because they all had the same mask, but I could differentiate by the height and body.

"Would you like a table?" she asked.

I nodded.

The host took me to a booth next to one that I had sat at previously.

"Would you like something to drink?"

"Yes, sparkling water would be great, thank you," I said.

"You're no fun," she responded monotonically. But there was a slight playfulness to her voice.

"Perhaps I'll have something later. I just want to ease into the night," I said.

"I don't actually care what you drink. Just don't forget to tip."

I smiled. "Don't worry, I take care of all of my servers."

She smirked and stared at me.

"Can I ask you something? Doesn't that mask bother you? It looks like it weighs a lot."

She leaned closer to me, the closest I'd been to any of the staff. Her face was inches away from me and whispered in a sultry way, "It's actually light as a feather."

"How did you get that mask?"

"They make them here in house."

"That's impressive. Do you know who makes them?"

"I imagine a crafty individual."

"You're probably right. Is it part of the requirement to wear it at all times?"

The server nodded.

"What happens if you take off the mask?"

"You certainly ask a lot of questions," she said, her voice was seductive and hypnotizing.

"I guess I'm just a curious individual."

"Or you're a cop."

I didn't say anything. Internally I felt like a deer in the headlights, but I just grinned and laughed. She chuckled as well.

"I'll be right back unless you have any more questions?"

"No, I'm satisfied." I smiled politely.

The server left and gazed at me for a few seconds longer than she should've. My heart skipped a beat; even though I could barely see her eyes from under the mask, I felt hypnotized by her. I forgot to check if she had a tattoo. She'd been conversing with me far longer than any other server; she also seemed notably nicer. I was relaxed in her company.

I observed the dance floor, more wailing sounds of a distorted crunch guitar with too much reverb. Heavy drums hammering through speakers every so often. People moved along with the sounds, though. I could hardly consider it music. Maybe those young people were on drugs, perhaps an effect of whatever molecule was in the fog.

Did I dance like that the previous two nights? It's entirely possible.

The server came back with my drink and placed it in front of me.

"Thank you," I said and looked at her arm as she walked away. She indeed had a tattoo, but I couldn't make out what it was. "Excuse me!"

She stopped and turned around. "Yes?"

I dug through my pocket and pulled out a ten-dollar bill. "This is for you."

"You're too kind. Thank you."

"Of course. I know I've asked some other people here, and they seemed sensitive to the question. So if you don't feel comfortable answering, that's fine, but I was curious about your tattoo. What is it, and where did you get it?"

"Thinking about getting one for yourself?"

"I guess the thought has always been there." My lip curled up.

"We can talk more about tattoos when you've made up your mind." She grinned and walked away.

I couldn't help but laugh to myself. It seemed so absurd that tattoos were such a taboo topic. As I sipped my sparkling water like a potent scotch, time dragged on. The hours melted by, I saw a few servers take some of the dancing people by the hand and lead them to the back. Martha texted me asking how everything was going, and I said: *The usual unusualness.*

I stood up and went to the bathroom. Inside was a dark singular room; it was also foggy with only a blue light bulb on up above. I was only in there for 2 minutes before walking back out. I surveyed the club, and in the booth next to me, someone had fallen asleep. A server approached them and whispered something in their ear. The person nodded, stood up, and wandered out of the club. Then I looked at another table all the way to the right. Through the fog, someone was slouching over, again, a server talked to them, and they nodded, heading towards the exit. It was close to midnight.

I returned to my table. On my way, I noticed other people were leaving, but they were drifting out like zombies. No one was on the dance floor, but the music still droned on. Sitting down, I surveyed the rest of the nightclub, and a chill rattled my spine.

From left to right, every server in the club stared at me with their mask on.

Silence.

I reached for my gun in my shirt pocket, I didn't pull it out, but I kept my hand on the grip.

The music stopped. The fog still thick in the air.

Within my line of sight, 10 people stood like statues. The clacking rhythm of heels echoed through the club. A figure emerged from the fog, another woman whose body I didn't recognize, but then again, a lot of them looked the same. I pulled my hand back as she approached my table. She put her arms on top, leaning forward.

"How are you doing tonight, sir?" she asked in a breathy voice and smiled.

"I'm doing pretty well, thank you. How are you?"

The server who waited on me earlier approached us, standing next to the taller woman.

"Would you like to go to the backroom for some after-hours fun?" the new woman asked me.

"That would be wonderful. Do I need anything special? Like a pass, or—"

"Just come as you are." She reached out with her hand open.

I held her hand and slid out of the booth.

"Allow me to take your other hand," my original server said.

"That's quite all right, thank you, though."

"Please, I insist. I'd love to hold your hand," she said.

"Please, hold her hand, won't you?" the other woman asked.

Much to my chagrin, I obliged. I was being guided by both women. Their hands were warm while mine were slightly cold. Walking through the fog, The rest of the staff in the club stared at me with their masks on. I could see their silhouettes from the periphery.

They took me to the back of the club, an exposed brick wall with a door guarded by a man wearing next to nothing but a mask.

"We have an extraordinary guest with us," my server said.

"Right this way, you three. Have fun." The man grinned as he opened the door.

Both ladies giggled.

23

We walked into a foggy hallway with a metal staircase going all the way up to the third floor. It was chilly. My skin tingled, and the ladies next to me both had goosebumps. Blood rushed to my head as my heart hammered away in my chest. I couldn't tell if it was fear in me or the two attractive women holding my hands that made my heart bounce around wildly.

"Where should we take him?" my server asked the other woman.

"He seems to be a VIP guest. Probably a good friend of Dr. Percy's," she said. "I think it's best we let the two friends catch up."

The women walked past a door to our left, I heard giggling and a consistent loud buzz coming from the other side.

"What's in there?" I asked.

"We're not going in there. No need to concern yourself with that."

"It sounds interesting. I'd like to take a peek if possible."

"You can go with Dr. Percy later if you're still curious. We're supposed to take you to him right now."

They continued to guide me until we went up the metal steps. We stopped at the second level, and they took me to a dark wooden door. It had a brass knob with a diamond-shaped plate behind it; I couldn't believe the detail. Art deco lines symmetrically running along the edges, something from the 1920's.

The woman to my left pulled out a black skeleton key and inserted it into the lock. It clicked open, and both women ushered me in. There was a circular plush couch, with three people seated. Two of them were sitting close together, a man with his arm around a woman. The other guy was large, buff, but wore a tight-fitted suit. To my right was a bar, liquor bottles lit up by bright blue and red light on glass shelves. A man stood behind the counter, mixing together a variety of liquids. He wore blue glasses and a white suit.

We stepped to the couch, where the ladies let go of my hands. They took off their masks and set them by the bar. They were stunningly beautiful. My server joined the bulkier man, and the other woman sat next to me, her leg entirely up against mine. She whispered in my ear, "My name is Sheila."

The hairs on the back of my neck rose.

I looked at the couple and recognized them as my neighbors from across the hall at the inn. Mickey and his girlfriend.

"We brought you your friend, Dr. Percy," the woman to my left said.

The man behind the bar slowly grinned at me. "Splendid. Yes, my good friend. How are you this evening, Edward? Is everything to your satisfaction?" Percy asked.

As I breathed in to talk, Mickey whipped his head in my direction. "Hey, I know you. You're the fella that has been staying across from me." He turned to his girlfriend. "You remember him, sweetie, don't you?"

His girlfriend scanned be up and down and smirked. "Yeah, how could I forget? Such a handsome man."

"Lori, could you have a little respect for yourself?" Mickey snapped.

Lori didn't seem fazed. "I don't get mad at you ogling the other girls here at the club."

"Edward. How are you?" Percy raised his voice.

"I'm doing all right. This is some nightclub you have here," I said.

"Can I fix you something to drink? Although as someone who's a government agent, it's probably unwise to be drinking while on the job."

"You're right. It would be unwise to have any alcohol."

"I thought as much. Sorry you can't properly indulge with us, but your company is tremendously appreciated. However, it's getting late, and I know you have an affinity for coffee. Would you like me to fix you a cup?"

"That won't be necessary. I'm wide awake."

Percy nodded and poured numerous drinks for everyone from the mixer. He brought over the tray and served everyone a cocktail. Percy gave nothing to me but smiled warmly. He sat across from me.

"I think some introductions are in order. This is my associate Leonard and his partner Amber, and you've already met Mickey and Lori. And you should've met Sheila by now." Percy snickered. "It'd be awkward if you hadn't."

"Can I ask you a question, *Vincent*?" I said.

I took all the air out of the room. Dead silence.

Percy's lips fell into a flat line.

"You must think you're pretty cute," Percy said.

"I'm sure it's similar to how you're feeling." I was referring to him openly telling me I was a government agent when he knew damn well this was the first time we'd ever met. I wondered how he knew that, but the instinct I had about Percy was that his intelligence was nothing to dismiss.

He's been doing his research, and I wonder how long he knew I was in town. Perhaps his cohort Mickey informed him about me.

Percy smiled again. "Do you know why I've chosen the name Perseus?"

"No."

"You sure you don't know?"

I shook my head.

"You're not as sharp as I thought you might be, Agent Wright."

"That's a little rude," I said.

Percy's upper body bounced as he laughed silently. "Aren't you curious why my name is now Perseus?"

"I'm dying to know," I said monotonically.

"As you may have gathered by now, I have an affinity for Greek mythology."

"Makes sense."

Percy paused. "Why does that make sense?"

"I've noticed the tattoos around here."

"At least you've kept your eyes open. Did you want one?"

"A tattoo?"

"Yes. But it has to be a Greek mythological creature." Percy pointed his finger in the air.

"Where would I even receive the tattoo?"

Percy's lips curled up as he pointed at the ground. "Did you want one?"

"No, thank you." *It made sense why I heard the buzzing earlier. Must've been a tattoo gun.*

"Should you reconsider, let me know. I'll give you one free of charge. Not by me, of course. I have an artist here that can help you with that." Percy snickered. "I can barely keep in the lines for a coloring book. Could you imagine the disappointment if I was inking your skin?"

"I'm still waiting on why you changed your name."

"We have all night to chat, don't we? It's still early yet. Only midnight. Although I'm sure, it's past your bedtime."

I cracked a smile at Percy. If I kept a cold hard stare and my responses short, I'd be giving him what he wanted, and it wouldn't get me far. This was a mental game of chess. Every word had to be calculated. "You're right. It is past my bedtime, and I guess I'm a little tired."

"I can fix you up a coffee," Sheila said next to me.

"Sure, why the hell not," I said.

"Attaboy. Cut loose, you're among friends," Percy said.

Shelia slowly stood up from the couch and sauntered behind the bar. She pressed a button on a chrome pitcher and turned back to me. "I think you're going to love this coffee."

"I order it from the same supplier as the cafe in town. Only the best for my guests," Percy said.

"I appreciate that, thank you." I felt the slightest tinge of energy smelling the freshly brewed coffee in the room. She poured it from an oblong carafe, unlike anything I had ever seen.

Sheila came back around and set the specialized mug on a saucer at the table in front of us. She sat down next to me, again our legs touched, and she put her arm around me.

"Don't you want to have some?" Percy asked.

"It's hot. I wanna wait for it to cool down."

"You've never had coffee from my invention. Please, take a sip. You'll find that it's the perfect temperature already. I know the struggle; I'm a busy man. I don't have time to wait around for my coffee to cool down."

I feigned a smile and picked up the saucer, and held the mug just beneath my lip. There was water vapor pluming out, but It didn't feel overwhelmingly hot. I took a sip. It was delicious and at a perfect temperature.

"This is very good. Thank you," I said.

"Ah yes, you were curious about my name change. Allow me to explain. In Greek mythology, arguably one of the greatest heroes and monster killers was Perseus. There's one story in particular that resonated with me. You see, I'm a bit of an inventor. I studied anatomy, physiology, biology, but along with that, I always had a fascination for mechanical engineering as well. Technological advancements never ceased to amaze me." Percy shook his head. "I'm sorry, I'm digressing a bit too much. Like I was saying, there is a story of Perseus killing Medusa, chopping off the monster's head. Later, it became affixed to a shield that would be wielded by Athena. The Aegis. The combination of such different objects, both living and inanimate, was fascinating to me. Do you follow me so far?"

"Yeah," I said, taking another sip of coffee. "You invent things like... Special light bulbs." I wondered how Percy would react, but he didn't flinch. Just a nod.

179

"Sure. That's one of them. But I'm sure my old friend wasn't able to tell you what I'm currently working on."

"What are your current projects?"

Percy's lips curved up wider. "Why don't we go upstairs? Unless you like the room to yourself with Sheila here. You two seem to really hit it off."

"That's okay. I'm curious to see what you've been working on."

"I bet you are, Agent Wright. I bet you are," Percy said.

The hollowness in my voice made my skin crawl.

"Let's go upstairs then, to the red room." Percy grinned and stood up.

Sheila held my left hand as I had the coffee mug in my right. Mickey and Leonard gestured for me to walk in front of them. Pulling my hand forward, Sheila guided me behind Percy.

"Why is it called the red room?" I asked.

"You'll see why in just a moment," Percy said.

He walked past more doors and went up to the third floor using the metal staircase. All I heard was *clang clang clang clang* going up the steps.

Making it to the top, Percy opened the first door in front of us. He ushered us inside, and Sheila took me to a couch on the right. The room was painted dark red, and the carpet was dark red as well. Three brown couches were on each side of the small room. A standing brass lamp in the corner gave more light than I had seen in the club, but it was just an ordinary bulb plugged into the wall.

Leonard and Amber sat on the couch directly across from the entrance. Mickey and Lori whispered to each other as they sat across from Sheila and me. Percy closed the door and waltzed in.

"Do you see why it's called the red room now?" Percy asked.

I nodded.

"You probably thought it had something to do with blood, I'm guessing?"

"Why would I think that?" I asked.

Percy smirked. "I'm going to be right back. Sit tight." He stepped out of the room and closed the door. Mickey and Lori were only focused on their conversation while Amber and Leonard stared forward like a pair of drones.

24

I sat there in the red room, wondering where Percy had gone.

"Sheila, do you have any idea what's happening?" I whispered to her.

Her mouth hovered over my ear. "I think Dr. Perseus wants to show off his latest invention. It's awe-inspiring. I think you'll love it."

The door swung open, and Percy propped it still. He pulled in a massive tripod and set it at the center of the room in front of a black leather chair. The tripod looked solid and durable, capable of balancing an anvil.

"Is this it?" I asked.

"It's coming, Agent Wright. Please, I ask for some patience. Mickey, could you give me a hand?"

"Sure thing," Mickey said, and he followed Percy out of the room.

I heard a door shut from the hallway, and then there was silence for a few minutes. A cart wheeled closer and closer until Percy and Mickey showed up. They had a mahogany trunk on a flatbed. Guiding it towards the tripod, they stopped, and Percy reached in and hauled out a black object that was smaller than what I was imagining.

"Thank you, Mickey," Percy said. When Mickey went back to the couch with Lori, I saw the device on the tripod.

My blood ran cold.

I stiffened up.

I became frozen.

I couldn't take my eyes off what I was looking at.

It was a large, black human heart with a lens in the upper right corner.

Percy sat behind the device, turning knobs, clicking with each minor adjustment.

"Wh-what is th-that?" I asked.

"It's a camera I've been working on, and this is a successful prototype. It's my pride and joy. I can't tell you how long I've been building this. And it works, it really works."

"What does it do?"

"It takes pictures, of course." Percy grinned.

"I see."

"You must think I'm a real pile of shit, huh?"

"I never said that."

"Correct, but I know you think it."

"I don't even think that either. You're different, but we all are. Everyone has their eccentricities. You've done nothing to suggest that you're a 'pile of shit,' yet. You've been a very gracious host, actually," I said.

"Well, I'm sure you have your deep-rooted suspicions, and your instincts might be telling you that I'm guilty of something or another. Otherwise, why would you be here?"

I opened my mouth to respond, but Percy held his finger up.

"You don't have to answer that question. But you know something, I truly do want to help you. And with your power alone, you can make all of this go away."

"All of what?"

"Don't be coy. I get what you're trying to do, Agent Wright. You come here two nights in a row, you probably don't remember much about the evening, and now you're here a third time with the help of something I regretfully gave to my old friend. No matter what, you will pursue legal action against me, but it doesn't have to be that way. I'm sure you want to arrest me, but you really don't have to."

"Are you trying to bribe me?"

"No. Not at all. I'm trying to help you like I said just a moment ago. *Help* is the keyword."

"What could you possibly help me with?"

Percy smiled and took a deep breath. "Why don't I show you, my friend. It's so exciting because My colleagues here know everything I'm doing and what my ideas are. But you haven't seen my work. I honestly think you'll appreciate it." Percy cleared his throat. "Leonard, Amber, say cheese."

Amber and Leonard stood utterly still. Percy pressed a button on the top of the heart camera, sounding like a syringe sucking up a liquid. I couldn't believe my eyes, nor my ears, but the camera began to beat like a heart. Percy pressed a second button, and a red flash beamed out of the camera. Paper slid through a print roller. The black heart device stopped beating, and Percy held a photograph in his hand. He beckoned me with his finger.

Sheila moved over, and I stood up from the couch. I looked at the deadpan Leonard and Amber and then at the grinning Mickey and Lori. I stepped up to Percy, and he got out of his chair and showed me the photo that the camera had taken.

It was a 5x5 photograph. Even though it was aimed directly at Leonard and Amber, the image was something very different.

It was a man sitting on a chair, reading a book underneath the open window in the middle of the day. This person in the photograph seemed to have no idea that a picture was being taken. His clothes looked like something out of the early 1900s. The picture quality was exceptional, like it was taken by a professional photographer. I could see that the man in the photo was reading Joseph Conrad's *Heart of Darkness*.

"What is this? Why does this look so different? Where are Leonard and Amber?" I asked.

"Take a look at some of the settings I have on the camera. It might make a little more sense." Percy pointed to the massive dial on the back of the camera with six rings.

Every year from 1900 to 2010 had a mark on the outer ring. Then the next ring had 1 through 60, and the following was 1 through 60 again. The next circle had the numbers 1 through 31, and another 1 through 24, and inside the tiniest dial was 1 through 12. There was a red hash mark at the top where all of the numbers could be lined up.

I read the markings at 1908 30:30:15 - 13 - 11.

"This is some kind of joke," I uttered. I said it without thinking; had I been thinking, I probably wouldn't have said anything. It felt like a prank, but at the same time, I didn't imagine Percy being one to pull an elaborate joke like this.

"Believe it, Agent Wright. The camera took a picture of this room at that exact point in time."

"And what exact point in time is that?"

"Let's see. 1908, the year. The first 30 is 30 minutes. The second 30 is 30 seconds. The 15 is the day of the month. The 13 is the hour, so 1 p.m. And finally the 11, is the month, November. It's laid out like this because I had to fit all the dials together into one cohesive ring. I didn't want a bunch of separate ones. You understand?"

"I don't believe it. This photo is a reprint or something."

"Look at the ceiling tiles. Don't they look quite similar?"

I focused on the ceiling tiles in the room and the ceiling tiles in the photo.

My body was covered in goosebumps.

They were the exact same, except the current ceiling tiles were cracked in some spots but more worn out in comparison.

183

"Take another photo," I said.

Percy snickered to himself.

"What's so funny about that?" I asked.

"Taking a photo. It uses precious and valuable resources."

"I'll pay for you to take another, so I know you're not kidding."

"It's not a matter of dollars, Agent Wright. But if you insist, I can take another photo. I'll even let you adjust the dials as you see fit."

"Take the picture out in the hallway. This could just be a setup where you always take photos here. How would I know?"

"Are you familiar with the concept of Occam's razor?"

"Yes, and at the moment, the simplest solution is the fact that this is a prank. You're pulling my leg."

Percy paused. "Let's take it out in the hallway then." Leonard and Mickey both stood up and picked up a leg from the tripod. Percy helped them as well.

Walking into the dimly lit hallway, they set the tripod down, and Percy aimed the camera below the ground floor.

"Go ahead. I'll let you adjust the dials this time," Percy said. "This used to be a train station back in the day with an inn and a restaurant up above. The train station was active from 1900 to 1930, so go ahead. Take a photo down below. Make the adjustments you'd like. The train stopped here every hour, top of the hour."

I adjusted the dial from 1908 to 1915 and to 7:00 PM (labeled 19). I also changed the month to March.

"Go ahead, take another photo," I said.

"This one is on your hands, Agent Wright," Percy said as he pressed the first button. The black heart device began thumping like a heart. The sound reminded me of my own existence and my own heart beating away in my chest. It made me lightheaded for a brief moment, but I was quick to regain my balance. That syringe-sucking sound happened again, and Percy pressed the other button on the camera. A red flash illuminated the entire space.

The sound of print rollers pushing out a document returned. Percy held a photo in his hand. "Come with me. Let's look at it." Percy guided me back into the red room, and he showed me the photo underneath the light.

In full color, there was a train station illuminated with standing lights, people walking around in hats, and old clothing styles from 1915. The train was an all-black locomotive, shining with pride.

I stepped away from the photo. I thought I was about to pass out. "This is a dream. This is a dream."

"It's not, Agent Wright. This camera is the closest thing we have to time travel. I don't have to tell you this, but can you imagine what we can accomplish with this camera?" Percy asked.

I couldn't tell who was in the room. I had a rush of blood in the head. The only thing I could focus on was Percy and the photograph. Sheila, Lori, and Amber were probably still in the room, thinking I'd gone crazy, but it didn't matter to me.

"I want you to take another photograph," I said.

"Do you remember how I told you it uses valuable resources? Very precious indeed," Percy said.

I nodded.

"I don't care to take photos up and down my nightclub just to prove to you it works. I've already taken enough to show you how real it is."

"It's just hard to believe. It's science fiction," I said

"Yes, I know, it's unsettling. But it's quite the miracle, is it not?"

"What does it use to take a photograph?"

"I think you already know the answer to that question. You're a smart man, Agent Wright."

My breathing grew louder, my inhalations and exhalations were erratic. I tried gaining control of my usual rhythm, but I couldn't.

"You seem so terrified, but there's nothing to be afraid of. I wanted to use this camera to help you. We can forget about everything else, and we can use this to find Michael."

How did he know?

I fell into a mental bear trap. Tears surged their way forward until they covered my eyes.

Percy put his hand on my back and rubbed my shoulder. "We are all friends here. We want to help you find your friend. Truthfully. With this tool, we can find Michael."

The thoughts began racing through my mind of what could happen.

I would get in a limousine with Percy and his cronies. We could go back to my hometown in Michigan. Go to the abandoned building, turn the dials where they needed to be, and get to work in the middle of the night. Find out everything, narrow it down to the second, what happened and where. Get a perfect look and picture of the perpetrator, something we never got a hold of.

"Think about Michael's family, and the closure they deserve," Percy said to me.

You son of a bitch. You know precisely what you're doing.

As an FBI agent, I have to be mature. There's a level of mental toughness needed, and I always prided myself with that tenacity.

But it felt like it had been flushed down the drain.

I became a child again.

My emotions were raw and hollow in a way I had not felt in a long time.

Helpless.

"This all goes away with you, Agent Wright. I respect your work and what you do. Stick around town, keep investigating if you must, but in the meantime, we can slip out and help find Michael for you."

"How do you know about Michael?"

"It's not really important, is it? You did your research on me. I did my research on you. All is fair in love and war, and I love you as a friend. Please, Eddie, let's find Michael together."

It weighed on my mind like a thousand boulders. It was soul-crushing. I had to make a decision. I finally had a key. I finally had a break in my lifelong case. This was it. Just a little bit of corruption, hell, that happens from time to time in every occupation, but how corrupt is it if it would be saving a life, perhaps even more lives?

But is it the right thing to do?

I've never had the urge to throw out my badge until that moment.

I thought about the families of the victims.

John and Barry.

Mitchell and Carol.

Ray and Cole.

They were gone, and those six families deserved closure. Right?

"Let me think about it overnight. I'll come back tomorrow," I said.

"Fat chance," Mickey said, walking into the room with a gun pointed at me.

"Mickey, what the hell are you doing? Eddie here is our friend," Percy said.

"We either do this tonight, or we don't do it at all. I need his commitment, and I need him to give me his gun and his phone. And any other equipment he might have on him," Mickey said.

I stood there, debating my options in the few seconds I felt like I had.

"I'm not feeling very patient today. Give me the gun and the phone. We're finding your friend."

"Mickey! You're starting to get on my nerves!" Percy snapped, the room became silent. "Don't listen to him, Eddie. We want to help you find Michael. Let's just keep it at that, hold onto your gun and your phone. Mickey, lower the pistol, please."

"Sorry, boss, I need to make sure He's not lying to us. Eddie is a smart guy. He'll understand."

"Yes, of course. I'm with you, Percy. I think we should go find Michael. Out of a show of good faith, you can have my gun and my phone," I said. Reaching into my pocket and my holster, I grabbed what I needed.

"Set it on the floor. Don't look behind you. If you try anything funny, Leonard has a gun pointed at you too," Mickey directed.

"Sure thing." I set the gun and phone on the floor.

"If one of you ladies could be so helpful and take away Eddie's items, that would be tremendously appreciated."

Percy sighed. "Eddie, I'm sorry about Mickey's sensitivity here."

Sheila came up from the side and grabbed the phone and gun. "I'm sorry about this, honey."

"I get it. We haven't known each other that long, so we need to establish some trust. I just wish I had some collateral," I said.

"You're insane if you think you deserve collateral from us. We are trying to help find your friend," Mickey said.

"Yeah, trying to help find my friend while you took my belongings with a gun pointed at me."

"And I'll keep on pointing it at you until we leave!" Mickey shouted.

"Enough! I don't want any arguing, nor do I want our guest here to feel uncomfortable. I think we should move out now. Amber, could you please bring the Escalade to the back of the building. We'll load in the camera, and only some of us will go. Mickey, sorry, buddy, but with the way you're acting, you're not coming along for this trip," Percy said.

"You've got to be kidding me?"

"Go ahead. You and Lori have the night off. Go back to your room."

Mickey grumbled something to himself and put his gun away. He looked at Lori and shrugged. "Come on, let's get out of here, Lor."

Mickey and Lori walked out of the red room, and it felt like a lot of stress went with them. Although I didn't trust Percy, he did a lot more to make me feel welcome and comfortable than anyone else I was near, including Sheila.

"Do you mind if we change back into our normal clothes?" Amber asked.

"Please do, ladies. Thank you for working this evening. I appreciate everything you two do. Let's help our friend, and I promise to pay you some overtime for tonight," Percy said.

Sheila and Amber left the room. On their way out, Amber said, "I'll pull the car out back."

"Excellent, thank you. And with that, Eddie, Leonard, let's take the camera downstairs."

The three of us put the camera back into the container that was wheeled inside. Before we put the lid on, I gave one last look at the horrifying invention.

So many questions.

They wheeled the cart into the hallway and went down an elevator. Making it to the ground floor, we went to the back of the building, where there was one exit door but not even an exit sign for fire code purposes. I wondered if the fire marshal had inspected the place.

Going through the back door, a Cadillac Escalade was waiting for us with Amber at the wheel. Sheila opened the trunk, brought the cart over, hauled the camera into the empty compartment, and placed the tripod next to it.

My heart was racing, I still wasn't sure if I could trust any of these people, but I didn't have a choice. I wished I had texted Martha to come storm inside and start putting handcuffs on people, but alas.

25

I stared at the black box inside the trunk of the Escalade, weighing my options for everything that I could do.

"Come on, let's get inside the car," Percy said as he stood with the door open, waiting for me.

My pause probably wasn't the best look for me. I couldn't let him know I was second-guessing the whole process.

I got inside the car in the backseat, and Percy sat next to me.

Sheila sat to my right, Amber was behind the wheel, and Leonard was the passenger.

"We're all good to go, Amber," Percy said.

"Where am I heading?" She asked.

"We are going to Lockweed, Michigan."

"Shit, that's like a four-hour drive from here," Amber said.

"Yes, if you're feeling tired, we can swap drivers. We can get some sleep on the way," Percy said.

"It's not that I'm complaining about it -it's just- that's a long drive to spontaneously do in the middle of the night."

"Let's face it, we have nothing else happening. This is important. We can help unlock the truth for our friend. How would you feel if your best friend disappeared and you had no idea who took him? And then finally after all those long years of searching you finally have a tool that can—"

"All right, I'm sorry. I get it." Amber put the car in drive and sped out of the parking lot.

"Relax, it's not a race," Percy said. "We've got plenty of time, right, Eddie?"

I hesitated, still wrapped up in a mental chokehold. "Sure. I've got all the time in the world."

189

"See? There's nothing to worry about. Whatever it takes to help our friend." Percy put his arm around me and patted my shoulder.

The car hit the road, and there wasn't any conversation. Leonard had put on slow-moving jazz music that made me tired. Lazy drums swept across the snare, a piano played lonely notes, and occasionally a muted trumpet would hum. I closed my eyes, trying to imagine what another date would be like with Vicky. I also wondered what Vicky was up to.

She was probably asleep right about now.

Sleep. That sounds delightful.

But I couldn't close my eyes with my heart still racing. I felt lingering adrenaline. I still had no idea what their intentions were. Was I going to get murdered like those other young folks?

"Hey, Percy, I don't mean to alarm you, but there's this car that's been following us. I'm wondering what I should do?" Amber asked.

"It's probably just another person out on the road," Percy said.

"I don't know. It looks like one of those cop cars, to be honest."

"Maybe you're just being paranoid," Leonard said.

"Could one of you give me my phone? Someone knew I was in the club this evening. She has probably been trying to contact me," I said.

"You had the police waiting for you?" Percy asked.

"I'm afraid I did, but that's before any of you showed me hospitality and willingness to help find my friend. So I didn't have a chance to tell her I was okay," I said. "Here, if I could have my phone back, I can call her and let her know that—"

"Aw dammit!" Amber yelled.

The rapid flickering of red and blue lights filled the interior of the Escalade.

"What should I do?" Amber asked.

"Pullover," I said.

"Why? So you can just trap us?"

Percy held his hand up. "That's enough, Amber. Just pull over. I trust that Eddie will diffuse the situation properly."

Amber took a deep breath. "Fine."

Sheila reached into her bag. "Should I give his phone back?"

"I think that would be wise, yes," I said. "It would have been better for everyone involved if I had my phone, say, 20 minutes ago to tell them everything was all right. But we'll handle this now."

Amber stopped the car and rolled down the front two windows. A symphony of cricket chirps filled the cabin. The smell of grass hung in the humid air.

The police car behind us kept its lights on, and then I heard the prompt footsteps of the officer. They waved a flashlight into the backseat, but the windows were tinted.

I felt tired earlier but I didn't any more. My heart raced. I had no idea how this would play out.

What should I say?

What is Amber or Percy going to say?

What are the police going to do?

"Hello, I'm looking for someone that was in the club this car came from," Martha said, shining a light into the backseat. "And there he is. All right, everyone out of the car. How you doin', Eddie?"

"Actually, Martha, everything is under control. We're all good here. No need for everyone to get out of the car," I said.

"What? You can't be serious? Did these freaks brainwash you or something?"

Sheila discreetly put my gun against my leg.

I held the piece up. "Martha, seriously, we're all good here. See? I have my gun."

"Yeah, but you haven't been answering your texts or any of my calls."

"We've actually been talking all night. So much, I haven't even had a chance to really look at my phone."

"Bullshit. Something weird is happening here. You all need to exit the vehicle," Martha said.

"No, seriously, it's okay. I had my phone on silent, and I forgot that you were watching me for backup in case anything went down."

"I don't care. These creeps are under arrest for drugging people in their club through some laced fog shit. They got to you, Eddie. They're going to kill you, drain your blood for whatever sadistic, satanic reason, and then they're going to drop your body off somewhere."

"That wouldn't happen. They know that I'm an FBI agent. They're not going to hurt me. They're smarter than that."

"Then where are they taking you?"

"They're taking me back to my hometown. I know it sounds crazy, but I need to go with them. This could help save someone's life."

"What do they have to do with your hometown?"

"They have information on a missing person's case. Look, I can't explain the connection. It would take too long. But please, let us go."

"Sorry, g-man. I can't let that fly. I need to put some people in handcuffs."

"But please, I need to go to my hometown with them."

"How about this? I'm going to handcuff everyone that's not driving the car and take them to the holding cell in Wilton until you come right back with the driver," Martha said.

"What if you arrested all of us but Percy in the backseat? It's more important if Percy goes with Eddie," Amber said.

Leonard and Sheila both took a deep inhale, but neither of them said anything.

"Fine. I'll take all of them to the station and put them in a holding cell until you get back," Martha said. "I think that's a pretty fair deal."

"Yes, I agree," I said.

"Fine by me," Percy said.

"All right. Step out of the vehicle and don't try anything silly. There's more than just me here," Martha said.

Everyone got out of the car. Martha and her backup police officers put handcuffs on Sheila, Amber, and Leonard. They were escorted to a patrol vehicle while Martha stared at Percy and me.

"Something still doesn't feel right to me about this. Are you sure I can't come with you?" Martha asked.

"Yes, I'm sure," I said as I got in the passenger seat, and Percy sat in the driver's seat.

"You have your phone on you, right? You should see how many times I called you." Martha said.

I checked my phone, Martha had called me five times, but I had a new message from her.

Blink a bunch of times if you need help.

"How many times did I call you?" Martha asked.

"You called me five times," I said to her with my eyes open, feeling dry and wanting to blink. I kept the staring contest going.

"All right. Don't try anything funny now, Percy. I got your license, your car, and the fact you're going to Lockweed, Michigan. If anything funny happens, expect a manhunt, Percy."

"All right, thank you, Sheriff Martha. I'll bring the boy back in time for supper." Percy smirked.

Martha glared at him. "I really don't care for that joke, Percy."

Percy's lips fell. "Sorry, you're right. This isn't the place or time for humor. Thank you, though, for caring for our friend here."

Martha shook her head. "I don't care what you say. You still give me the creeps. Good luck, Eddie."

Martha walked back to her patrol car as Percy started up the Escalade and drove off. We still had a lot of ground to cover, and it was already 1:30 a.m.

I checked my phone. I had a message from Vicky.

Hey, give me a call when you have a chance. No rush.

I didn't respond. I slid my phone back in my pocket and focused on the road.

Don't worry Michael, I never forgot about you. We are closer to the truth now than we will ever be. I'm not going to give up on you.

Our car ride was silent most of the way, except for the slow-moving jazz music coming out of the car stereo. Percy didn't look tired in the slightest. I wanted to ask him questions, but I felt like they would go nowhere, and it would distract me from the mission. There was nothing more for me to say to him.

Driving through the empty lands between Indiana and Michigan, the stars glittered in the sky, and the moon shined as bright as I'd ever seen it. It was entirely full. I hadn't been paying attention to the moon cycles since I was in Wilton, but it sure looked mesmerizing floating up in the sky.

Arriving in Lockweed, goosebumps coated my body, and memories came rushing back to me like a raging river. Both the pleasant and not so pleasant.

I sniffled. I could feel my eyes brim with tears.

It's okay, Michael, everything is going to be all right. We're going to find you.

"If you don't mind, I'm going to need a little guidance on this," Percy said. "We're here in the downtown strip of Lockweed, but where's the train depot?"

"Keep going straight. You're going to reach a path with woods on the left and right sides. Once you reach a bump, it's an old train track. Can't miss it. Drive with your brights on, and turn right as soon as we reach the area," I said.

Traveling along the dark road, we drove over a railroad bump.

"Was that the one?" Percy asked.

"Yep. Pull off the road. You should be able to drive through the path."

Percy steered to the right until we were on the bumpy grass. The car was going at a snail's pace, and we were immediately stopped by a chain-linked fence with a NO TRESPASSING sign hanging in front of it.

"Damn. It's about time they put up that fence. Can't believe it took this long. Do you think there's a way we can get the camera over the fence?"

"No, but I have an idea," Percy said as he slammed on the gas pedal. The engine roared, the tires reached thousands of rotations per second, and we launched into the fence like a raging bull. We obliterated past the chain-linked barrier, a horrible scraping sound probably traveled for miles, but Percy slowed down and turned off his car lights.

"You can't be serious! Are you trying to get us caught?" I yelled.

"I don't think there was going to be another way," Percy said.

"Well, if you wanted to do this discreetly, you threw that option out the window."

"Even you have to admit it, the town right now is as dead as a doornail. Everyone is sleeping. Lockweed isn't a lot different from Wilton."

"Believe me, I've noticed." I scoffed.

"Sorry, but let's regroup. Where am I going now?"

"Keep going slow for a little while. We'll be coming up to the depot shortly," I said.

Percy kept the car at a crawl until a shadowy structure became prominent.

"Turn your lights on," I said.

Percy turned a knob, and then there was light over the old train depot in Melville.

26

I hadn't been to the Melville abandoned train depot in years. The memories came flooding back, and I shuddered. A sign on the front now said "NO TRESPASSING," and every opening had been boarded up. Getting inside didn't look possible unless we had a sledgehammer.

Percy and I sat there in silence. I studied the building.

"Michael got lost in there, right? It might be tricky getting inside. I'm not willing to ram my car through the front," Percy said with a chuckle.

I shook my head. "Michael and I made it out of there okay, but we split up. Michael went in the opposite direction with his bike. The perpetrator followed him."

"Do you ever wonder what would have happened if the criminal had followed you instead?"

"I used to have nightmares about it all the time. I had to go to therapy for a little while."

"I'm sorry to hear that. That can't be easy."

"Let's just take the photo," I said.

Percy put his hand on the car door handle, but he observed me as I sat there like a statue.

"Well? Are we going?"

"So those six people, Ray, Cole, John, Barry, Mitchell, and Carol. were sacrificed for your invention?" I asked, turning my head to him.

"I'm not sure I follow?" Percy said, deadpan.

"The six people found dead in Wilton. The blood stolen from the hospital. Is that your doing?"

"Let's just go outside and take a picture of Michael and his perpetrator," Percy said.

"You're not answering my question, though," I said. My heart rate steadily increased.

"I can't tell you much about them."

"Why can't you?"

"Because I don't know anything. Now, let's get out of the car and uncover the past." Percy turned off the vehicle, and pulled the door handle, but he didn't open it all the way. "No need to keep stalling."

"You're right. We should finish this up before the sun rises," I said. I checked the time, and it was 4:30 in the morning.

Outside the car, the crickets chirped. It was muggy out, and I could see a few mosquitoes flying around.

"I'm going to need your help here, Eddie. Where should we put the camera, do you think?" Percy asked as he opened the trunk.

"Here, I'll guide it."

I joined Percy at the trunk, and we both grabbed the box and lifted it together. It was heavy and awkward to hold, but we managed to waddle our way out in front of the abandoned building. We set the box on the ground. Percy went to the car and grabbed the tripod, he carried it back, and we proceeded to put the human heart replica on top of the tripod. Percy made a few adjustments and aimed the camera at an angle that was probably best for capturing both Michael and the perpetrator.

"You know the exact time Michael would have encountered this person?"

"For the most part, yes," I answered.

"Well, you need to be pretty precise with this."

"Yes, I'm aware."

"All right, I'll let you turn the dials then."

Percy stepped back, and I approached the camera and held a flashlight up to the dials. They clicked as I adjusted them to the exact date and time I thought the man made his appearance.

Based on what I knew, he was approximately sprinting out of the depot around 2:05 based on all the reports and estimations from the investigation all those years ago.

The dials were set, and I backed away. "It's all yours, Percy."

"Now, before I perform the final fine-tunings, we need to have a gentleman's agreement sealed by a handshake. You're a man of your word, aren't you?"

"I try, to the best of my ability," I said.

"Well, then, here's what we're going to do. I'm going to take the photo, even if we have the timing off, I'm going to take another one. We have enough supplies for five more photos, and that's it. But the thing I want you to swear on, Eddie, is: in exchange for these photos of the man who abducted your friend, you're going to let me walk away."

"Let you walk away?"

Percy nodded. "I don't think we really have time to go over all of this, but you will say that I ran away in your reports. You did everything in your power to arrest me, but you couldn't. You will have the photos though, you can tell people that I had them the entire time, but the fact of the matter is, I get to put all this behind me. I'll pack up, take my camera, and leave you with the photos, do you understand me?"

"Yes, I understand you. Loud and clear. You give me those photos, and I'll let you take the camera back and you can hit the road. You have my word."

Percy shook my hand; tight and firm.

"Marvelous. Now let me grab the materials." Percy went back to the car and pulled out a duffel bag. Approaching the camera, he pulled out some tubes and a specialized wrench, connecting things to the camera and tightening small valves.

I reached into my holster, clutched the grip of my pistol, and I unsheathed it from my shirt, aiming it directly at Percy. My arms twitched and I took a quiet deep breath, but I still had him in my line of fire.

"Perseus, put your hands up. Let go of all of the materials in your hands," I ordered.

Percy continued working on the camera without looking back at me.

"So I guess you're not a man of your word." Percy tightened a screw on the camera then stopped and glared at me. "I'm disappointed in you, Eddie. This is the closest you'll ever come to finding the monster that captured Michael, and you're throwing it all away."

"Put your hands in the air," I said.

"Eddie, did you notice that your gun is a lot lighter than usual?"

I didn't notice how much lighter it was in the situation's intensity and everything that led up to that point, but he was right.

The ammo clip was empty.

"I don't know what you're talking about," I said.

"You can't fool me, Eddie. I know Sheila emptied your gun. You may as well be holding a children's toy. Now, there's still time to go back on that egregious decision. I haven't taken the picture yet, but it's close to being ready. I know what you want to do. You want to find Michael, and I can help you find your best friend. His family deserves to know. This community deserves to know. You have the power to make it all happen." Percy took a step closer to me, but I stood my ground as my lip trembled. "What's the matter? Let's talk it through."

"This gun is loaded. I had a secret magazine in my pocket. There's no talking we can do. I've made up my mind. Now stop and put your hands up. You're under arrest."

I kept a close eye on Percy's tool he used on the tubes connecting to the camera. He rubbed the tool with his thumb before pressing a button. A blade slid out.

"I said freeze!" I yelled.

Percy leaped at me with the blade out and stabbed my arm as he aimed for my heart. With my rush of adrenaline, it only felt like a needle for a shot.

In my other hand, I still had the gun. I struck him on the forehead with the barrel of the pistol. Resilient metal colliding with his skull. Percy stammered back, holding his forehead.

I sprinted up to him, and he swung his blade at me wildly, cutting my same wounded arm. I shouted in pain, but I knew I had to stop him. He couldn't win. Gripping his forearm as he almost stabbed me again, I knocked the blade out of his hand. And although he had a larger frame than me, I managed to take his arm, bend it around, take his other arm, and snap a pair of handcuffs on him. I threw him to the ground on his stomach.

"Eddie, you made a poor judgment call." Percy took a deep breath. "We can still reverse this. You need those pictures. It's your life's mission to find Michael. You're so damn close, closer than you've ever been and you're throwing it away."

I didn't respond. I stood there, gripping my bleeding arm.

Rather than shoving him back in the car and driving all the way back to Wilton, I called the police department in Lockweed.

After telling them where I was, their response time was five minutes to arrive at the scene. I held Percy at the spot, and not another word was exchanged between us, but as he was put into the back of the police car, Percy stared at me completely stoic and hollow, like the eyes of a dead man.

"You've let down your friends Michael tonight. Never forget that," Percy said.

I ignored him as he was driven away to the police station. I conducted the other officers to put the camera inside the Escalade and take it to the evidence room. Meanwhile, I was driven to the hospital to get my arm sewn up, which at that point, the adrenaline wore off, and I needed medical treatment. I felt dizzy, and close to passing out.

At my outpatient surgery, I was given some painkillers, and I was released from the hospital.

Sitting in the hospital lobby, I had a lot on my mind, but regret wasn't among my thoughts.

I'm sorry, Michael, I didn't help you like I could've, but I know you would understand.

I cried silently to myself. Only a few tears crawled down my cheek before I wiped them away and took a deep breath.

Looking at my phone, I reread the message that Vicky sent me earlier. Just a simple text to call her back, but it still made my heart swell with warmth seeing her name on my phone. I felt like she wouldn't believe the night I had. I thought about texting back, but I decided to call her later.

I had to call Martha right away.

"What's the word, g-man?" Martha asked.

"Martha, I arrested Percy," I said, almost out of breath. "It's been a long night. Keep those people in the holding cell, and we'll work on it all tomorrow. I need some sleep."

"Okay, Eddie, I'll talk to you soon. Take care of yourself, buddy."

The call ended.

It was 6 a.m. when I left the hospital. I was picked up by a patrol car from the police department. They dropped me off at the Lockwood Inn, where I booked a room. It was a small room with a queen sized bed and wooden floors and wooden cabinets. It felt like a cozy cottage. I fell asleep as soon as I lay on the mattress.

Seven hours passed.

I woke up without any nightmares. I was relieved. In fact, I couldn't remember my dreams.

Even better.

Checking my phone, I saw that it was almost two in the afternoon.

I finally called Vicky back.

"Hello?" she answered.

"Hey. I'm really sorry it took me so long to get back to you. You wouldn't believe the insane night I had or, hell, the past 48 hours, really."

"I'm sorry to hear it's been crazy for you. It's been tough for me too. But, uh, I wanted to call you and let you know that my grandpa passed away last night." Vicky's voice broke towards the end of her sentence.

"Oh no, I'm so sorry to hear that, Vicky."

She sniffled and said, "It's okay, he'd been really struggling, and he can finally rest now. He had a great life."

"I'm sure he did," I said.

"Well, I have to get going now, I'm meeting with some family, but I'd like to see you soon."

"Of course. I'm in Michigan right now, but I'll be back in Wilton as soon as I'm able. Thank you for telling me, Vicky, and I'm really sorry for your loss."

"Okay, I'll talk to you soon. Bye Eddie."

I sat on the edge of my bed, taking a minute to think about her grandfather. I whispered a prayer to her family, and then I sighed.

Time to get back to work.

Calling Martha, I told her to expect me later in the evening.

27

In the following days, justice took its course.

Percy was relocated to Wilton, and Mickey was also arrested as he walked out of the Wilton Inn's lobby.

Percy had confessed that Leonard was the one who stole the blood from the hospital, and Mickey was the one responsible for the murders. It was maddening to me that he had others do his bidding, but although it lessened his years in jail, he would still be sentenced for a long time.

The camera was taken back to the FBI for further analysis, but no one could figure out how to get it to function in any of the labs. It was marked as my responsibility, and I could choose what would happen next with the cursed device. I didn't tell anyone a word about what it could do. The magic of the camera was kept a secret, but I still had a lingering curiosity about it. There was an idea still brewing in my head about the camera, but for the moment, I wanted it to be tucked safely away in storage.

The FBI gave me some time off, but before I took a break, I informed the six families what happened to their children, and I confirmed with them that the killer had been captured.

It was heartbreaking to deliver the news to so many families. While they all cried, at least they were relieved and felt a sense of closure. No, it wouldn't bring back their loved one, but no longer would anyone else suffer the same fate as they did.

The monster had been caught.

I had done my job.

And while I wished I could do more for those families, I did the most I possibly could. At least that's what my colleagues told me.

I stayed in Wilton at the inn as everything transpired. It was beginning to feel like a home for me. Even though it was just a temporary home, I grew to enjoy the small interactions I shared with the staff at the inn and working alongside Martha.

But there was another reason that I stuck around.

Vicky gave me the information about her grandfather's funeral. I attended the viewing and the mass before his internment. I didn't get to talk to Vicky very much as everything was happening. Still, I went to the burial at the cemetery, and I stood the farthest back from her family and friends there. Everyone cleared out once they had lowered the casket in the ground after exchanging hugs. I stuck around thinking about leaving until Vicky approached me. Her eyes were a little red, and she had bags underneath them.

"Hey. I just wanted to say thank you for coming. It's really nice to see you," she said.

"Of course, I'm terribly sorry for your loss."

Vickey tightened her lip and nodded. "Would you like to get dinner later this evening?"

"Absolutely. I'm happy to treat as well."

Vicky nodded. "Well, I have to get going back to my family. I think we're going to visit for a little while, but I should be free around 6:00."

"See you around then."

I was excited to spend another evening with her after everything that happened, but I wished the circumstances were different. Why did we have to go through such tragedy? Why couldn't we just be two locals in Wilton enjoying a simple life?

We went out to dinner in a lovely country restaurant serving classics like meatloaf, steak, mashed potatoes, fish, and a variety of other dishes. It was a quiet restaurant, with a simple design, low hanging lamps, and dark green curtains and on top of the wooden booths in between tables.

We had a seat by the window. Vicky smiled at me as if relieved for the first time in what seemed like a while.

"I feel like there's so much to tell you," Vicky started. "But you already know everything. It's hard losing my grandpa. Some people have been telling me that they thought I'd feel relieved that I no longer have to worry about him or take care of him, but he did a lot of help with raising me, especially with my mom working at the hospital all the time. There's a lot of memories there, and it's just tough to lose someone in general. He was a great guy."

I nodded.

"And as it was all happening, I just kept thinking about how much I wanted to talk to you and see you again." Vicky grinned. "This is some much-needed relief for me, being here with you now."

"I couldn't agree more," I said.

"But that's the thing that scares me. I like you a lot, and I'm feeling emotionally vulnerable, and it sounds like your case is already done."

"Yeah, and?"

"I'm just worried we might spend more time together, and you might leave. That would be really difficult to handle, especially after everything that's been happening with me."

"I see." I took a deep breath, my heart sped up, and my chest tightened. The conversation took me by surprise. "So, I'm thinking about staying here for a little while longer. I'm finding Wilton to be a cozy town, and I'm still involved with the police department here for a little while."

"Yeah, but what's going to happen after that? How long do you think you'll stay here for?"

I took a moment to think about it. I hadn't thought too far ahead in the future.

"Won't you have to go back to the FBI offices in Chicago? Won't you be assigned to something else, and then you'll be gone to another city or state?"

"Yeah, I guess that's how the job typically looks."

Vicky didn't say anything, she only stared at me with her warm eyes, but her lips were on the verge of frowning. I was getting lost in my own thoughts.

"Perhaps we can still keep seeing each other and keep doing things until I get word on what might happen next?"

"But aren't we kinda prolonging the inevitable? I'm not sure if I'd want to be with someone who's gone so much." Vicky took a drink of beer. "I know, I know. I'm probably getting ahead of myself talking about all this stuff, but I feel like I'm already developing some feelings, and I wanted to know where we might stand."

"It's okay Vicky, I think we can relax. We haven't even kissed yet. Let's take things slow and hang out. Who knows, I might be around here for a while."

Vicky giggled dryly. "You're right. We can just take things slow."

"I still have to tell you about what happened to me that wrapped up this whole case. But I'll tell you about it after dinner," I said, scanning the restaurant. There were other people around, sitting at tables. I didn't want anyone else to potentially overhear the conversation. The waiter arrived, delivering our food.

After we finished eating, we decided to take a walk in the park a few blocks away. The sun was setting, but there was still plenty of light outside. Fireflies hadn't made an appearance yet. The park was wide open, sprinkled with trees and other people meandering further away. There was a boardwalk along the river that we strolled on together. A small ice cream shop was in the center of everything where a line of people had gathered, ranging in all ages. We considered waiting in line for ice cream, but it didn't sound too appetizing since we had a couple of drinks each.

As we moseyed along the boardwalk, I told her about everything that happened the night I arrested Percy. I even included all the information about Charles Green and how Percy had someone steal blood for him. Then I told her about the camera that Percy had invented.

Vicky stopped, we sat down at a bench together. "Sorry, Eddie, I'm just having such a hard time understanding. The camera could take pictures of the past?"

"I know it sounds insane, but it's true. The camera is currently in evidence storage at the FBI offices," I said.

"Wow. This is just so surreal."

"You're the only person I've told so far about what this camera can do."

"You didn't tell Sheriff Martha or anyone else?"

"I don't think anyone else would believe me."

"Honestly, I'd have to see it for myself. I don't think you'd lie to me though about this, but you do understand how insane it sounds, right?"

I chuckled. "Yes. I'm keenly aware of how ridiculous it sounds. In fact, part of me thinks what I saw was an illusion. It all certainly seemed like a dream, but it wasn't. I've questioned my own sanity over it, but I can't figure out how to operate the damn thing."

"Do you want to?"

"Yes, more than anything in the world, I need to learn. But it uses a resource I don't really feel comfortable with expending unless it's my own."

"Just try not to get too obsessed over what that camera can do. I feel like it could lead to a dark path." Vicky reached out and held my hand.

My heart was whole, and I felt like I was on cloud nine. My lips curved up. It was the first time we had held hands. "I promise, I won't let this get the better of me."

We stared at each other, our faces hurt from smiling, but even then, we continued through the discomfort.

"Let's talk about something a little happier, eh?" Vicky said.

"Sounds good. I think we owe it to ourselves."

We talked about some of our favorite music, films, and television shows we grew up watching.

As the lights in the park turned on and the sun fell below the horizon, I walked Vicky home.

When we made it to her doorstep, we stopped and gazed into each other's eyes.

"Goodnight," Vicky said. "I had a wonderful time with you this evening. You were a nice change of pace from all the other emotional—for lack of a better word—bullshitery I've been going through."

"You've been a breath of fresh air for me as well," I said.

We continued our playful staring contest. She leaned in, and I leaned in as well, and we kissed for a brief moment.

She pulled away. "Perhaps we can get together this weekend?"

"Yes, of course," I said.

Vicky beamed. "I'll see you later then. Goodnight, Eddie."

"Good night, Vicky."

Back in my room at the inn, I couldn't stop grinning. I kept thinking about how Vicky held my hand and how we finally kissed. After many complicated years, this felt long overdue. Always focusing on finding missing persons and criminals linked to disappearances, finally something to smile about.

But my life's work and mission were still not over. Even though I felt quite accomplished, there was still much to be figured out.

The following day after my blissful date with Vicky, I received a phone call from my friend Foster at the FBI offices early in the morning.

"Hey, Eddie, sorry it's taken me some time to get back with you, we've just been trying to understand the camera you brought in."

"Did you figure out how to operate it? It runs on a liquid. I know that for sure," I said.

"No, we haven't discovered its operations, and we're confused on how we'd get any liquid inside this thing. Eddie, we're not sure how to get the camera to accept any sort of input. Do you have any other information that might be able to give us a clue?"

"Not really."

"What's the deal with this camera anyway? I mean, it's certainly bizarre-looking and freaky, but was there anything special about it? Does it just take regular pictures or really high-def pictures?"

"I don't know. Percy said he wanted to show me what it could do."

"Yeah, but don't you think it's weird he wanted to show you how to use it in a random city in Michigan?"

"Yeah, I don't know what's up with that. Percy knew where I grew up, and something happened to me there a long time ago, and I guess he wanted to trigger some sort of emotional response. He claimed that the camera could take pictures of the past. He was trying to emotionally bargain with me."

"Ah. That's pretty weird. Do you think this thing can really take photos of the past?" Foster snickered.

"I don't know. It sounds like science fiction to me, but Percy was confident. He also dispersed that fog in a nightclub with a makeup that we've never seen before, right?"

"Psh, yeah, you're not wrong about that. The lab people are still dumbfounded about what drug was in that fog."

"See? This guy Percy is a genius. He worked on things and made his own inventions without publishing any of his work."

"Yeah, I feel like we have a big ball of yarn that we have to unwind with this guy. Well, I just wanted to let you know at the moment, the camera is in storage. We're not going to spend much more time on it unless you tell us to do so or get any new information about it."

"I understand. Thanks for doing what you could."

"You bet. Until then, I'll talk to you soon. Congrats again on catching this guy and his cronies."

We ended the call. I stood in my room a little longer, contemplating my next move. My next adventure seemed to be coming along the horizon faster than I anticipated. Knowledge about this camera gnawed at my brain. Perhaps I was on the verge of obsession. Vicky's warning echoed in my head.

I had a chance to go to Perseus' holding cell because a question burned in my mind. Walking down the hallway of locked doors and gray walls, a guard walked me to Percy's cell. Inside was a glass partition protecting me from Percy. He sat in a chair staring at the ceiling with his legs resting on his bed.

"I'll be right outside if you need anything," the guard said.

It was just Percy and me. He looked at me as soon as the guard left, a crooked grin, but it seemed sincere and not diabolical.

"It's nice to have a visitor. Time certainly drags on in this place," Percy said.

"I can imagine. That's why I do my best to follow the law."

"We can't all be upstanding citizens like you, Agent Wright. Some people need to steal food to feed their families. But many people would consider that illegal, and those trying to serve their families to keep them from starvation are arrested. Are they criminals?"

"In my eyes, no. But, you weren't stealing bread to feed a family."

"I invented the camera that can help find your best friend. Did my miracle tool really cross the line?"

"It uses human blood. So yes, it crosses the line."

"I think we can get into a morality debate here. I'm sure some people think we are both right and righteous. Much like the highly contested debate of capital punishment or the legalization of recreational drugs."

I paused.

What could I say that would catch him off guard? "Would you tell me how to operate the camera?"

Percy exhaled one laugh. "I do like you, Agent Wright. But unless I can leave this cell, I'm not telling anyone how to use my invention."

"Understood. You might be surprised to know that it's not the only reason I'm here."

"Surprised? Have you seen my inventions? I don't get surprised much these days."

I smirked. "So I did have a question for you though that I wanted to ask. I noticed quite a few people in Wilton had tattoos of a Greek mythological character or monster. You were giving tattoos from your club like lollipops. I couldn't figure it out."

"Yes, I see your curiosity. But if you must know, it was part of my brand." Percy shrugged. "They were my employees, and I liked the idea of having my employees marked eternally. We were all part of the same band of misfits. And I've always had an affinity with Greek mythology, and I thought it would be a perfect way to tell who's on what team. They looked to me as their leader, and I paid them handsomely for any occasion they could find someone from out of town passing by. They would give those people passes to the club. And I always told them to never tell locals about it, but some slip through the cracks.

"And of course, I offered the club to my helpers whenever they wanted to come in or work a serving shift. There is good money to be made there. Some of the servers were locals, but many weren't. None of them knew why I wanted out-of-towners stopping in, but I always ensured they knew little about what happened behind the curtain. Travelers were the perfect specimen to work with. No one knew where they stopped on their road trips because it's a minor detail in the grand scheme, and so it made it much harder to find anyone. Especially if they were paying cash? All the better.

"Often, I told the servers to pay for tabs even if the out-of-towner did have a credit card, and of course, I reimbursed my employees.

207

"Unfortunately for me, my close associates grew lazy and made some idiotic mistakes, which had me switch to trying to acquire blood from hospital banks. My partner in crime—" Percy chuckled. "It's funny because The expression actually works. But yes, Leonard reached out to his old buddy who had a limousine in his garage, and he borrowed it for a little bit. We always wanted to make it as insulated as possible. Don't use any companies, rely on word of mouth, meet with people face to face, you know, typical criminal behavior, I guess." Percy sighed. "Still wasn't enough. Is that all you had questions for?"

"Yeah. You had quite the system all worked out."

"Everything good must come to an end."

"I don't know how much good you were doing experimenting with human blood."

"Again, we could debate ethics all day. One thing that cannot be argued is I made inventions beyond my imagination."

"You murdered six people. You forever ruined the lives of their families and friends. You cannot argue that what you did was virtuous."

"The technology, though. You can't deny the miraculous ability of my device."

I shook my head. "I could ask a million questions about how it worked and its science, but I figure it would go over my head."

"Probably. I quickly learned not everyone is as intelligent as I am."

"I appreciate your modesty."

Percy and I analyzed each other through the glass for a few silent seconds. I took a deep breath. His focused, widened eyes made my skin crawl.

"I'm afraid I have to get going, but I'm sure I'll see you again soon," I said.

"Come back and visit anytime. Always a pleasure to see you." Percy waved, and his devilish grin reappeared.

I left Percy in his cell, and an idea crossed my mind.

I decided I'd go to Charles Green's house. I hadn't contacted him beforehand. I just pulled up on his driveway and once again drove through the thick tall grass until I was behind his garage. Getting out of the car, there were no signs of life from his house, but that wasn't anything different from the last time I paid him a visit. Climbing over the wooden fence, I made it to his backyard. Everything looked the same.

I knocked on the back door, and Charles Green answered it but didn't say anything. He was stone-faced.

"First, I just want to say thank you for all the help you gave me. If it wasn't for you, we probably would not have arrested Percy for a while or even discovered all of the information we've uncovered about him," I said.

Charles nodded but still didn't look happy in the slightest.

"Anyway, I was wondering if I could ask you something?"

Charles walked away from the doorway into his kitchen. "Feel free to come inside if you'd like," he said.

I stepped into the kitchen, and again the pungent odor in his house of tobacco and something rotten hung in the air. His cat Bella came up to me, meowing.

Charles smiled. "Someone is happy to see you again."

"I'm happy to see her again, too. It's a pleasure being back here."

"What can I do for you, Agent Wright?"

"You can call me Eddie or Ed if you'd like."

"Calling you Agent Wright is a little more fun. I feel like I'm in a movie or something." Charles smirked.

"I have a question I wanted to ask you. I think I need your help with something."

"And what's that?"

"I want to figure out how to operate Percy's inventions."

Charles drew in a deep breath and stared at me, expressionless.

Afterword

This book was inspired by my love of Twin Peaks and X-Files. I'm thinking of making a sequel at some point. I know the ending kind of leaves off on a cliffhanger but I felt it was the best spot to end. Will Charles say yes or no?

If you'd like to chat, feel free to reach out to me at randallfcooper12@gmail.com. Also, I'd love to hear your thoughts on the story. If you want to see a picture of my dog, I'll happily email you one too.

About The Author

I work in the educational sector in Southeast Michigan. When I'm not writing, I'm watching a movie or studying.

Please join my website's mailing list at www.randallfloydcooper.com, and I'll let you know whenever there's a new release.

Acknowledgements

I've said this before and I'm happy to say it again, if it wasn't for my fans on Reddit, I don't know if I'd have the confidence to publish something. Thank you all!

www.ingramcontent.com/pod-product-compliance
Lightning Source LLC
Chambersburg PA
CBHW051951220626
47052CB00004B/900